THE BLUECOATS ATTACK!

Long Rider had almost reached his mother's lodge when the main body of soldiers poured in among the tepees. Long Rider emptied two saddles with one of his revolvers, but then he couldn't see anything clearly in the smoke from all the shooting. He saw that the force of the charge had carried the soldiers through the thin line of warriors who'd been ready to meet them. The bluecoats ran deep into the village before they could turn their horses to face the Arapaho again.

But now there were women and children caught between the two lines, overtaken by the soldiers in their headlong rush. Cut off from their escape, some of the women took lances and clubs from fallen warriors and ran through the smoke and bullets to stand with their defenders.

LONG RIDER

CLAY DAWSON

CHARTER BOOKS, NEW YORK

LONG RIDER

A Charter Book/published by arrangement with
the author

PRINTING HISTORY
Charter edition/November 1988

ISBN: 1-55773-121-7

PRINTED IN THE UNITED STATES OF AMERICA

10 9 8 7 6 5 4 3 2 1

WHAT WENT BEFORE
Fort Laramie, 1862

Gabe Conrad was pitching hay into a corral when he heard a whisper of movement in the dry grass behind him. He recognized immediately the steady sweep of human steps and knew it was a tall man by the length of the stride. But Gabe's ears told him more than that. He had been taught from childhood to listen to all sounds at the same time at which he observed what made them, carefully remembering how and why they were different. Now he was aware of a sharp snap as the grass was brushed aside. It meant that the man coming up behind him wore hard-soled boots instead of moccasins.

A dark look came over Gabe's face as he took a tighter grip on the handle of his pitchfork. He also shifted his balance a little, in case the footsteps started coming too fast or too close. Nor did he relax when he recognized the voice of Captain Stanley Price.

"I know you hear me," said Price. "So quit playing possum and get my horse."

Gabe clenched his jaw and separated another flake from the bale, not trusting himself to turn around. He had been living with the whites for three years now and trying to learn their ways, but the soldiers made him ashamed of the sandy hair and gray eyes that marked him as a white man by birth. He had refused to cut his hair, wearing it straight and long over his shoulders in the style of an Oglala warrior, but he could not hide the pale eyes or the light color of his skin.

Gabe glanced at the captain's pony as he tossed the flake of hay over the rails of the corral. It was a spirited sorrel gelding, and Gabe liked the animal a lot more than he did the captain. Gabe also knew without looking that Price had been tapping a whiskey bottle at least since supper.

"I want that horse *now*," said Price, coming a step closer. "I came to teach the son of a bitch some manners, boy, and I can sure as hell do the same for you."

Gabe finally turned toward the captain, straightening slowly to his full height and squinting slightly against the sun that was sinking toward the rim of the prairie. Gabe was only seventeen that summer, but already he was bigger and stronger than most of the soldiers on the post. He met the captain's stare without flinching.

"What the hell's your problem?" said Price. Gabe didn't say anything, and the captain shifted from one foot to the other, looking a little uneasy but taunting Gabe with a nasty smile. "Are you worried about your momma, boy? Is that it? Are you thinking about her being all alone up there, getting fucked by all those redskins?"

There was no change in Gabe's expression, no change in the emptiness of his pale gray eyes. "It's almost dark," he said.

The captain's head snapped back an inch and his eyes turned hard. "I can *see* that, boy. Now get me the horse."

"Might be safer to wait till tomorrow."

"Jesus Christ!" the captain said, exploding. "Safer for who? You're worried about the horse, not about me."

Gabe knew he should deny it, but the words didn't come to his tongue. He wasn't used to the idea of telling lies just to avoid trouble. He watched the captain come toward him with fists clenched at his sides.

"Dammit," said Price, "get a rope on that gelding before I take one to you."

Instead of retreating, Gabe dropped his shoulders a little and planted his feet in the dirt. It was nothing more than a reflex—another result of his boyhood training among the Oglala Sioux—but he was still holding the pitchfork, and now his eyes were glowing a dusky red in the dying light of the sun. Price halted in mid-stride, wary and uncertain.

Gabe had been ready to retrieve the horse from the corral. He knew that any serious defiance would not be tolerated by a man like Price, who had behind him all the power of the U.S. Army. But the momentary, almost accidental flash of defiance turned to contempt the instant he saw Price's hesitation. Among the Oglala there was nothing worse than a warrior who showed his fear, and those who did were sure to receive severe and instant punishment. The captain was a big, rangy man with glossy black hair and the kind of rugged features that were pleasing to women, but now he proved to be no better than a woman himself. Gabe lifted his chin a little and made no more effort to hide his scorn.

Price may have noticed the change in Gabe's expression, or he may have had a sudden vision of the scene as it would look to a spectator: a cavalry captain unnerved by a stable boy. His windburned face turned even darker with rage.

"Son of a bitch," he breathed, coming toward Gabe again, "I believe you *are* the one who needs bringin' down to size."

Price cocked his fist while he was still three feet away and came in fast with a high, overhand blow. Gabe lifted the handle of his pitchfork and easily blocked the captain's arm, then slammed the wooden shaft against the side of his head. Price yelped and staggered back, clutching his right ear. Blood poured between his fingers. Gabe almost thought he could taste the blood; it was the first taste of battle, and it fired his own blood with fierce exhilaration.

But Gabe wanted nothing more than to be left alone. He couldn't allow the captain to strike him—it would be too much for his pride to bear—but his common sense prevented him from pursuing the fight with a cavalry captain. Rather than press his advantage, Gabe merely waited to see what would happen next, hoping Price would quit and go away. He stood there calmly and watched while the captain took his hand from his ear and stared at the blood that covered his fingers.

"Son of a bitch," he said again.

Price looked up at the boy and then rushed him a second time, grabbing for the pitchfork with both hands. Man and boy wrestled each other in a contest of nearly equal strength, scuffling in the dirt until a cloud of dust rose up around them. The dust glowed red in the low-slanting sun. At its center was a strange silence, broken only by an occasional grunt or a harsh gasp for air as each contestant tried to twist the handle from the other's grasp. As they grappled, the tines of the pitchfork gleamed dully in the sunlight filtering through the dust.

Price swept out a leg and hooked it behind the boy's knee, grinning in triumph when Gabe lost his balance and fell. But Gabe held on to the pitchfork and pulled it toward his chest as he rolled back onto his shoulders. At the same time he bunched his legs and planted his feet in the captain's belly, kicking hard to flip him up and over. Price landed flat on his back, head to head with Gabe, a great whoosh of air escaping from his lungs. When he let go of the handle, Gabe jumped to his feet, watching the captain's eyes fill with fear once again as he struggled desperately to breathe. The fear turned to panic when Price saw Gabe standing above him with the pitchfork still in his hands. The captain's hand went to the flap of the Army holster on his hip.

Gabe frowned at that. He didn't understand why Price thought it necessary to use a gun, and in his surprise he hesitated for the time it takes to blink an eye. He would never make the same mistake again. The captain had already grasped the butt of his revolver, and the only thing Gabe could do was lunge with the pitchfork as Price yanked the gun from its holster and raised his arm. He was hoping to pin the arm uselessly to the ground. But he was in a hurry and the light was poor, and he felt a grating resistance before the tines buried themselves in the dirt.

Price screamed and began to writhe in the grass, reaching for the prongs of the pitchfork with his other hand. He couldn't move them. Gabe was still leaning on the handle as he stared with terrified fascination at the long point of steel passing through the captain's wrist. Blood spurted up from the hole and covered the prongs, which made Price's fingers slip uselessly as he fought to free himself. Blood covered the captain's fingers, and the yellow grass where he lay, and went on spraying from the hole in his wrist. Gabe watched as if from a great distance, his eyes still glowing red while the captain writhed beneath him and screamed in fear at the sight of so much blood.

CHAPTER ONE

Fort Laramie, May 18, 1865

Through the guardhouse window Gabe Conrad could see white puffs of cloud blow freely across the sky. In his heart he could also see the golden grasses of the prairie bending beneath the same wind that moved the clouds, and since there was no limit to the vision of his heart, he let it fly far north toward the land he knew as a boy.

The People would be there now, still in winter camp along the waters of the Greasy Grass. Gabe knew that his visions were only the memories of a happy childhood among the Oglala Sioux, but sometimes they came with such power that they did not seem like memories at all. Then Gabe would feel that his spirit had truly been able to leave his imprisoned body and he was seeing his old friends at that very moment, as they went about their daily tasks.

Most of the time, however, Gabe could not escape the stale odors of damp earth and iron, the sour smell of his own excrement collecting in a tin pail in the corner. The joy of his memories would then become like a hot knife twisting in his belly—nothing more than the knowledge of everything that was denied him.

This was a curious thing that Gabe had thought about many times: that his only pleasure was also his greatest agony. He could not possess one without the other. He knew he could escape the heaviness in his heart by refusing to dream of the freedom that waited beyond the guardhouse walls, but it was not his nature to take the easy way. He had long ago accepted the price that he must pay for his memories, and he had learned not to dwell on this hard choice that had been forced upon him.

It had not always been so. During his first year in the guardhouse Gabe's nights had been haunted by visions of dust and spurting blood. His endless days of solitude had been filled with bitterness and hatred. Then the helper spirits assigned by his boyhood adviser had come to him in a dream, bringing the wisdom of the grandfathers. He was shown how to learn from the things that had happened to him, and how to put away his bitterness.

Gabe was trying to remember the sounds of children laughing and dogs barking when he slowly became aware that several men were coming toward the guardhouse, the scuffle of their boots barely audible at first above the steady murmur of the Laramie River. A moment later the door was thrown open and two Oglalas were pushed inside by a guard detail of three soldiers and a sergeant. The bluecoats stopped just inside the door, blinking their eyes against the gloom while the Indians waited impassively. Gabe Conrad felt a stir of excitement when he recognized the subchiefs Two Face and Black Foot, but two of the young men in uniform were cursing the Indians bitterly, pushing them along with more violence than necessary.

"If it was up to me," one of them said to the Indians, "you'd be hangin' from a trace chain right now."

"Pulled up slow," said another. "So's you could strangle for a while."

"A *long* while," said the first soldier.

"You'd be tryin' to breathe," said the second, as if the idea gave him pleasure. "You'd be thinkin' of how you'd give anything for one more taste of air. But all you'd feel would be that chain stretchin' your neck, cuttin' into the skin . . ."

"All right boys," said the sergeant.

Two Face had turned his big head to look at the second soldier, his eyes still as blank as if he were watching a spider crawl up a blade of grass. The soldier's eyes burned hotter.

"I saw what you done to her," he said, ignoring the sergeant. "As far as I'm concerned, your life ain't worth shit around here."

"All right," the sergeant said again, patient and weary. "Let's put the irons on 'em and get out of this hole." He was an older man whose face had become like leather in the wind and sun of the high plains.

The second soldier had not taken his eyes off Two Face. "I wish Mrs. Eubanks was here," he said. "You know what she'd probably do?"

Without warning the soldier swung the stock of his rifle up between the Indian's legs. Gabe Conrad winced, hearing the dull thump of hard wood on soft sacks of flesh. Two Face did not wince, or make any move to protect himself. His wrists were tied behind his back and he was helpless. Gabe noticed that the chief did bend forward a little—half an inch or so—because his blanket slipped off his shoulders and fell to the floor. Gabe also saw that his eyes were glittering sharply, as if they were filled with slivers of glass.

The soldier didn't notice the Indian's eyes. He had already turned toward the other headman, clearly hoping that the old man would offer some resistance. But Black Foot made no move.

"Yellow coward," the soldier said with contempt, turning to Two Face again. "And *this* bastard ain't got no feelins.'"

It was on Gabe's tongue to say that only a coward attacks a man who is already bound, but he had the example of the silent chiefs. And the memory that carelessness had put him where he was.

The sergeant was moving toward the soldier, looking a little uncomfortable. "Come on, Tuttle—"

"But look at him," the soldier protested. "He ain't got my point yet."

The soldier slashed with the barrel of his rifle this time, knocking the Indian's head to one side. When Two Face straightened up again, Gabe saw that the front sight of the rifle had left a jagged tear from ear to chin. Blood was pouring down over the Indian's neck and shoulders, but Two Face didn't try to wipe it away or stop the flow. His eyes filled with contempt as he watched the soldier raise his rifle again, nor did he show any relief when the sergeant gripped it from behind.

"Give it up," said the other man. "You ain't got a snowball's chance in hell of makin' 'em say ouch. These are Oglala braves you're fuckin' with."

"Braves," the second soldier said with a sneer. "Shit, they ain't no better'n animals. We oughta wipe 'em all out and get it done with."

The sergeant sighed and said, "Just like that, huh?"

"Christ, Sarge, you could do it with half a platoon on Sunday afternoon."

The sergeant shook his head. "Each one of you recruits talks dumber than the last," he said. "Ain't you heard about Julesburg?"

Gabe had heard of Julesburg, even in the guardhouse. First there had been the stories of Chivington's attack on the southern Cheyenne, who were camped under a white flag of peace at Sand Creek. The Cheyenne had begun taking their revenge a month later, in the deepest part of the winter, joined by some of the Sioux and Arapaho in two separate attacks on the army post at Julesburg.

"Well, sure," the second soldier was mumbling, "when all of 'em get together at once like that . . ."

The sergeant shook his head again. "Better send a letter to your mother, Private Tuttle. Tell her there ain't much hope of your comin' back alive."

Two Face laughed abruptly, a fine mist of blood spraying from his lips and cheek. "He speaks the truth," said the chief. "I have killed many foolish bluecoats like you. I will kill more if I can."

"Listen to him!" said the soldier named Tuttle. "He's *braggin'* about it. Let me kill the bastard right now."

"Yes," said Two Face, "let the little man show his bravery by killing a man who cannot fight back."

"God damn you! " cried Tuttle, struggling to tear his rifle out of the sergeant's hands.

"Forget it," said the sergeant. "Private Stone, you and Hobart secure the prisoners."

"Legs and arms both?" said Stone.

The sergeant thought a moment and then nodded reluctantly. "Let's make sure they're still here when the colonel gets back."

"He better hang 'em," Tuttle said.

"Prob'ly will, boy. And someday you'll wish he hadn't."

"You're crazy!"

"Maybe you didn't hear," the sergeant said in a deep drawl, "but Two Face bought Mrs. Eubanks from the Cheyennne. Why do you think he did that, *Private,* if you know so damn much about Indians?''

Tuttle shrugged and looked away, his gaze falling on the other two soldiers as they untied the ropes that bound the headmen and then snapped iron cuffs around their wrists and ankles. The Oglala settled to the ground with their legs folded in front of them. Gabe saw that Two Face was moving with difficulty, his jaws clamped tight, but he also noticed that the blood was flowing more slowly on the Indian's neck. It was already turning thick and dark along the open slash on his cheek.

"Two Face wanted to make friends," the sergeant was saying. "He brought Mrs. Eubanks in because he wanted peace. And your brilliant idea is for us to hang him. What are the other Oglala gonna think about trying to make peace if we do that?''

"Why should I care?''

The sergeant sighed and picked up Two Face's fallen blanket, tossing it across the old chief's legs. "Because they make bad enemies," he said, swinging the cell door closed and locking it with a heavy key. "If any more of 'em throw in with the Cheyenne and Arapaho, we got even worse trouble than we already got.''

"We can handle it.''

The sergeant opened his mouth, then closed it and shook his head once more. "All right," he finally said, "let's get the hell out of here.''

The four soldiers filed out through the door and closed it behind them, throwing the small guardhouse into darkness and silence. Once more there was only the soft rush of the river that curved around the post, and the song of early-returning birds. The features of Two Face and Black Foot slowly became distinct again as Gabe's eyes adjusted to the gloom. He waited for a sign that they had recognized him, fighting the desire to ask them a dozen questions. Finally he spoke as if he had just joined the headmen in camp. His tongue remembered the dialect of the people who called themselves Lakota—known to the whites as the Teton Sioux—of which the Oglala were but one band.

"Does the spring hunt go well, grandfathers?''

Two Face and Black Foot turned their attention on him, their dark eyes intent. "Who are you?" said Black Foot.

"I am an Oglala," said Gabe. "A nephew of Red Cloud.''

The headmen frowned, looking from Gabe's face to the arms

and hands that had grown pale in three years of imprisonment. Then Black Foot grinned, and Two Face laughed aloud, his laugh ending abruptly in a groan. Gabe felt ashamed not only for the whiteness of his skin but also for his anger at the injured chief.

"I tell you the truth," he said quietly. "Do you not remember the one who came with news of the soldier chief, Raynolds?"

The Oglala peered at him thorugh the shadows.

"It was six years ago," Gabe said. "I came during the Moon of Popping Trees," he told them, meaning December, "in the Winter When the Babies Died Off. I brought word that One Horn was going to tell the soldier chief he could not cross our country. But we had to let him pass, anyway."

"I remember the one we called Long Rider—" Two Face said slowly.

"Yes!" said Gabe. "That is the name my people gave me, to honor my journey through the heavy snows."

"—but Long Rider is dead."

A shiver ran through Gabe's body. "Who says such a thing?"

"The one who bore him," said Black Foot. "She says he must be dead, for he has not returned to be by her side. She still mourns the memory of her son."

Gabe felt an even greater coldness come into his heart. "I have no mother," he said. "And she would not mourn me, for it was she who sent me away."

Two Face looked more closely at Gabe, puzzled by his outburst. "They say she was in great sorrow," he said. "Keening for four days and four nights. She chopped her hair, they say, and she still bears the mark of the knife on her arms."

There was a stinging in Gabe's eyes that added to the confusion in his heart. "Her hair is gone?" he said.

"It came back," Black Foot said, "but it is not the same. Nothing is the same since Long Rider went away. Yellow Hair laughs very little."

The mention of his mother's name made the memory of her long, golden hair even stronger. It had been a source of awe and wonder among the Oglala, not only for its honey color—like the sun on prairie grass in the fall—but also for the way it fell in soft waves and curls. Gabe thought of his mother's hair as it had once looked, the memory becoming so strong that she might have been standing there before him in the guardhouse. Gabe thought of her crying out in despair, slashing her arms with a knife in the Lakota way of mourning. Then he saw the headmen watching him, their eyes slightly averted, and with a great effort he pushed the picture from his mind.

"I have no mother," he said again. "She threw away the son she bore and left him without a place among his people. So he has thrown away her memory."

The subchiefs listened in the Indian manner, without expression or comment, sitting so quietly that they might have been asleep with their eyes open. But when Gabe had finished, they looked at each other with the natural bewilderment of children who are confronted by something they do not understand. "I can hear that your heart is bad," said Two Face, "and it makes me think that you believe what you say. But I have also seen her with these eyes. I have seen the old wounds on her arm."

Gabe looked through the high window and said nothing. The first mention of his mother had found a place in his heart that still held hope, but the hope had brought pain and he had closed his heart again. He held it closed against the thought of his mother cutting her own flesh, and against the confusion caused by the chief's story.

"You say she sent you away," said Black Foot, "but she tells everyone that you left in the night without speaking to her."

"She lies! I could not dishonor myself that way. I was taken against my will, by a white man who knew my mother. He told me that I had become a burden to her. He said she wished never to see me again."

The headmen looked at each other again. "Who was this white man?" asked Black Foot.

"The one called Blanket Chief by the Crow. The whites call him Jim Bridger."

"Bridger!" said Two Face. "But he is here at the fort."

Gabe leaned forward, excited in spite of himself that the answers to his confusion might be found only a short distance away. "Do you know why is he here?"

"I do not know," said Black Foot. "Perhaps he will scout for the bluecoats." The chief looked thoughtful for a moment. "Was he not scouting for the soldier chief, Raynolds?"

"That is how he came to be in our camp," said Gabe. "But I believe he already knew my mother."

"Did he bring you to this place?" asked Two Face, looking around at the walls of the guardhouse.

"Only to the fort. He spoke to the bluecoats, and they put me to work with the horses."

The old Indian's eyes gleamed with wicked amusement. "Did you try to steal them, Long Rider?"

Gabe looked at the floor, knowing that a positive answer would have brought him honor with the Oglala. "There was a fight," he said reluctantly. "A soldier chief attacked me and I had to defend myself."

"Did you rub him out?"

"I should have," Gabe said. Then the fire went out of him. "No, that is foolish talk. The fight should not have happened at all. It was the act of a child to fight with a soldier chief in a soldier fort."

Two Face nodded approvingly. "You speak with wisdom. Perhaps the name of Long Rider is not falsely remembered. But the whites—" Two Face broke off and shook his head in exasperation. "You have just now heard what happened to us. One never knows the right thing to do when it comes to the white man. In that you are not alone."

"Thank you, Grandfather." Gabe hesitated, then spoke almost shyly. "It is true, then, that you bought the white woman from the Cheyenne?"

"I gave them three good horses! And now the soldiers will kill me as a payment for my gift."

"You are blamed for her treatment at the hands of the Cheyenne?"

Two Face looked at Black Foot, who looked at Gabe. "I thought she would be grateful to us for getting her free," said the other headman, "so I gave her the chance to thank us. I wanted only to mount her, not to beat her as the Cheyenne had done. But she cried out and fought me off." His forehead creased in a deeply puzzled frown. "You have lived among the whites, Long Rider. Can you explain to me why they brought us here?"

"I am not sure, Grandfather, but from the talk I hear, I believe that white women do not enjoy being mounted."

"That is the way she acted," Black Foot admitted, still frowning, "but I could not believe it."

"I think it is true," Long Rider assured him, feeling more

confident. "They do not enjoy the act, and yet they place great importance on it. Much persuasion is required before they will even permit it."

"And that is why the soldiers want to kill us?"

Gabe saw the absurdity of that and shrugged helplessly. "The soldiers believe all Indians are alike, so perhaps you are being punished for what the others have done. You say the Cheyenne beat this woman?"

"She was taken by a cousin of White Antelope," said Black Foot.

Gabe waited for more, until Two Face saw that the name was not enough for an explanation.

"White Antelope was rubbed out at Sand Creek," Two Face continued. "They say he folded his arms and stood in front of his lodge, to show the soldiers he was peaceful. But the whites shot him down and took his hair. They say the soldiers shot down a six-year-old girl who was carrying a white flag and butchered the women who sent her to beg for peace. The soldiers cut out their private parts and stretched them over their saddle horns. It made the warriors' hearts very bad."

Black Foot waited a moment, until it was clear that Two Face had finished. "It is not only the Cheyenne," he said then. "They sent the war pipe to the Lakota and the Arapaho. I fear much blood will flow before the next snow falls."

"What of your own?" said Long Rider. "Is it true that they will hang you?"

"I believe they will," Two Face said. "The Lakota at the trading post say the new soldier chief has a bad heart for the Indian, and so do the soldiers. They warned me to stay away, but I said I had not been making war against the whites. I said I was bringing Mrs. Eubanks back to her people."

The chief looked at Long Rider for a moment with a small twist at the corners of his heavy mouth. Gabe thought it was the look of one who is enjoying a sour joke on himself.

"I am very sorry, Grandfather," said Gabe.

"Only the earth lives forever," said Two Face. "I am thankful to Wakan-tanka for the many good years I have had in this life, while the Oglala were still free. Now the soldiers invade our hunting grounds and drive away the game, and soon I believe the whites will be everywhere. It is not a good time to be a Lakota." The old man met Long Rider's gaze once more, his black eyes suddenly intense. "When you are free, you must go to your mother."

The unexpected words found the hopeful place in Gabe's heart again, as if he had taken a sharp blow to the breast. He felt a mask come across his face as he shook his head. "I have thrown her away," he said tonelessly, "just as she threw me away many years ago."

Two Face was silent for several minutes, staring sadly at a point on the wall to the right of Gabe's shoulder. "I said you had gained wisdom," he told the boy. "But I can see that in some ways you are still blinded by the small number of your years. I will pray to Wakan-tanka, that He might show you the way."

Another guard detail returned for Two Face and Black Foot at dawn. The soldiers were different but they were led by the same sergeant, and in his face Gabe could see the fate of the Oglala headmen. He knew that they saw it also, for they began to sing their death songs as the bluecoats removed the shackles from their wrists and ankles.

The songs were a terrible sound in Gabe's ears. He had talked through much of the night with the Oglala, learning news from his village and whatever they had heard of his childhood friends. He learned that an end had come to the war the whites were fighting among themselves, and that the Great Father in Washington, Abraham Lincoln, had been shot down.

The headmen told him that the whites continued to clean out the Lakota hunting grounds and cheat the People of the trade goods that were promised by treaty in return for the emigrant road along the Platte. It was not a happy picture they painted for Long Rider, and they said it was getting worse. Spotted Tail of the Brule still hoped for peace, but Red Cloud himself was talking strong for war. Two Face mentioned this more than once but refrained from pointing out that Long Rider's mother might be caught in the middle of the fighting.

Two Face was being helped to his feet by the soldiers when Long Rider suddenly heard his name on the old man's lips. It still sounded as if the chief was singing his death song, but the Lakota words were meant for the young man.

"Listen to what I say, Long Rider, and hear me well," said Two Face. "The spirits have spoken to me. They told me you will go to your people and save many lives."

Gabe looked quickly at the soldiers, but their faces showed no expression. Then he opened his mouth to protest the headman's vision, which he knew could not be right.

"Do not speak!" Two Face said harshly. "Sit still no matter what happens, and listen to my words while there is time. They are given to me by Wakan-tanka."

The old man had drawn his blanket over his shoulders, and now he was hobbling past Gabe's cell toward the door, a soldier holding each arm. They were ignoring the words that tumbled from his mouth.

"I know that the spirits have told me the truth," Two Face said. "I have the power to hear them, Long Rider, and they have told me that you also have power. You will use it to help your people, but first you must learn to communicate with the spirits yourself."

Two Face stumbled, falling to the ground in front of Gabe's cell. The soldiers gripped their rifles and watched the Oglala carefully. When nothing further happened, two of them reached down to help the old man up again. This time he shrugged off their help. He stood with great pride, letting the blanket fall from his shoulders as he continued his chant.

"Beneath the blanket is my final gift in this life," he said. "You must not let the soldiers see it, for they destroy things of the spirit whenever they can. But do not despair. I have seen that you will leave this place very soon. I have seen that you will gain great power, perhaps even greater than mine, and you will help all people who suffer in these hard times. Wakan-tanka has told me this, and it is so."

Two Face was outside the building now, trailing behind Black Foot. They began singing their death songs again as the soldiers led them away. Gabe watched the Oglala as long as he could, until the sergeant closed the door of the guardhouse, and then he listened to their songs until he could hear them no more. He did not move for a long time, and it was longer still before his gaze moved to the blanket that lay outside his cell, as if he feared that the object beneath it might come alive and spring up at him. Two Face had called the object a gift, but Long Rider understood that the gift would carry with it a great responsibility. He was not sure he wanted such a gift.

And yet he knew that this was selfish. He went over and

pulled the blanket through the bars of his cell. Inside was the chief's ceremonial pipe. Long Rider held it lightly in his hands, considering the meaning of the gift. He knew that it had been the chief's most treasured possession, the very source of his power. The bowl had been carved from the red stone of the sacred quarry to the east, and hanging from the bowl were four strips of colored cloth, along with an eagle feather. They represented the spirits of the four directions, and the Great Spirit above them all. Gabe was filled with a reverence that he had not experienced in many seasons. He prayed now with the pipe, holding it up to the west and then to the north, east, and south. Finally he held it down toward the mother earth and up toward the heavens, offering thanks to the spirits for bringing such a gift to him.

But he stopped short of offering his own powers for the protection of the Oglala. It was not the place or the time to make such a serious decision, for one thing. He knew he was full of impurities. He also remained unsure of the things Two Face had said, and afraid of them as well. He reminded himself that whatever powers the headman possessed, they had not been strong enough to keep the soldiers from hanging him. Gabe wondered what he should do, and then he realized that the decision was no longer in his hands.

I will wait to see if I am released as Two Face said, he thought. *That would be a sign. There will be plenty of time to decide after that.*

CHAPTER TWO

Gabe was not surprised when the sergeant returned alone the following day, or that he came toward the door of the cell with a key in his hand. Two Face was known among his people for the power of his vision, and it seemed only natural to Gabe that he was going to be taken from the guardhouse, just as the old man had forseen.

But the sergeant didn't use the key right away. He stopped outside the cell, his eyes going to the place where the chief had fallen the day before. The old brown blanket he had left behind was no longer there; it was now lying next to Gabe on the floor inside the cell. The sergeant's gaze drifted slowly up from the blanket, coming to rest on Gabe's face. The two men studied each other through the pitted iron bars.

"I figure the old man gave you something," the sergeant said.

Gabe continued to meet the sergeant's stare and avoided the temptation to glance at the blanket, which covered the sacred pipe.

"You don't think I was fooled by that stumbling act, do you?" said the sergeant, watching Gabe closely. "I know you lived with the Sioux, so I figure the old man was talkin' to you when he went out of here, tellin' you there was somethin' in that blanket."

"Did you hang him?" said Gabe.

The sergeant sighed and turned his head away, looking out through the open door. "Yeah, the colonel hung 'em all right. Look here, kid"—he turned back to Gabe—"that blanket didn't worry me none, 'cause I searched the chief myself before I brought him in here. I know he didn't leave no weapons behind."

Gabe still didn't say anything, remembering the headman's warning.

"Well, I sure didn't think so," said the sergeant, narrowing his eyes. "But the colonel says he wants to see you now, and that changes things a bit. It wouldn't go too well for me if you pulled a gun or a knife on the colonel. So I gotta search you before you go."

Gabe's eyes glittered with harsh amusement, because the sergeant's worst fear was his own strongest desire. More than anything else Gabe wanted to kill this colonel who would hang Indians when they were trying to make peace—wanted to watch the terror come into his eyes as he felt the knife sinking into his belly. But Gabe also knew that he had to start exercising the patience he had learned at such great cost. For now, at least, it would be enough to meet the colonel. He pulled the pipe from under the blanket and got to his feet, coming toward the bars so the sergeant could search him.

The sergeant looked relieved. "I figured it was something like that," he said, probing Gabe's clothing through the bars. "I know Injuns put a lot of store in such things. I bet you could get a good price for it in St. Louis." The sergeant finished his search and opened the cell door. "Put that thing away and come on out," he said. "The colonel's waiting."

Gabe moved cautiously toward the sun-splashed door of the guardhouse, tucking the pipe inside his shirt. The stone bowl felt cold against his flesh and Gabe thought the pipe might be trying to communicate with him, but he didn't have the chance to listen. He was already outside in the harsh glare, trying to shield his eyes at the same time that he tilted his face toward the warm glow of the sun.

The sergeant waited until Gabe could see well enough to walk before leading him silently past the mess hall and around the edge of the parade ground. The bachelor officers lived at this end of the post, and it appeared that most of them were clustered in front of one of the buildings. They laughed at something, then fell silent again as Gabe and the sergeant drew near. A moment later Gabe heard a familiar voice.

". . . ridin' fer my life, I can tell yuh that," the voice said. "All I had was my six-shooter, an' they was six o' *them*. On the fastest ponies I ever did see. Well, the fust Injun was closin' in on me, so I turned in my saddle an' picked him off."

The sergeant was slowing his pace, moving toward the crowd with a look of almost childish pleasure on his face. "Ol' man Bridger," he whispered to Gabe. "This is one I ain't heard yet."

". . . an' then the third," Bridger was saying. "An' the fourth and the fifth went down jes' as clean, one shot apiece. So it were jes' me and that last Injun, an' he wouldn't give it up. This chil' couldn't shake him off nohow."

Gabe and the sergeant reached the edge of the crowd, stopping behind two fresh-faced lieutenants who waited breathlessly for the story to continue. Bridger himself was squatting beside another officer on a stoop in front of the barracks, as if they'd started out in a friendly conversation and drawn a crowd. Gabe knew the scout had seen at least sixty winters, but his body was still lean and strong beneath the old buckskin shirt and fringed leggings. His blue-gray eyes were still clear and bright, and they turned sharp for a moment when they met Gabe's. If there was any meaning in the glance, Gabe could not understand it. Bridger shook his head over the memory of what he was telling, as if he were unaware of the excited faces around him. But when he was sure the suspense had risen as high as it would go, he went on with his story.

"Well, pretty soon we was nearin' the edge of a gorge. Deep an' wide, it was. No horse could leap over that awful chasm, an' a fall to the bottom meant sartin death. So I turned my horse sudden, an' that Injun was upon me! We both fired to once, an' both horses were killed. Then we went to fightin' hand to hand with butcher knives. He were a powerful Injun—the biggest I ever did see. It were a long, fierce struggle, I can tell yuh. One minute I had the best of it, and the next the odds were agin me."

Bridger shook his head again, his eyes far-off, as if lost in memory. None of the listeners dared breathe while the silence stretched on. The two young lieutenants in front of Gabe looked at each other finally, and then one of them called out, "So what the hell happened?"

Bridger looked up, a little surprised, and answered in a dead-serious tone, "Why, that Injun *killed* me, son."

There was another moment of silence, and then a roar of laughter from the men. Bridger watched them with a smile. Gabe smiled, too, until he saw that the scout's keen eyes had come to rest on him once again. He still could not tell the meaning of the glance, except that it made him wary. He was filled with a sudden sense of caution, a feeling that he should think very carefully about each thing he said or did.

The lieutenants in front of Gabe were wiping tears from their eyes. "What a liar," one of them whispered to the other. "I wonder if anything he says is ever true."

"Nothin' but hot air," his friend agreed. "I can't figure out why they hired the old coot in the first place."

The sergeant scowled at Gabe and jerked his head toward the parade ground, then tramped away with his boots digging hard into the sod. "Goddamn youngsters," he muttered. "Oughta keep their mouths shut when they don't know what they're talkin' about. Ol' Gabe's been in this country longer'n they been *alive*—longer'n both of 'em been alive *put together!* An', by God, you can take that to the goddamn bank."

The sergeant finally remembered to look around to make sure he still had his prisoner. A long note from a bugle drifted mournfully across the parade ground, and the sergeant's eyes seemed to lose their focus. "Old coot?" he said with a snarl. "That old coot could still whip a dozen of them goddamn lootenants. He's been fightin' Blackfeet and Crow and grizzlies all his life, and he's still here to talk about it. Old coot, my ass."

The sergeant shook his head for several paces, looking down at the dead winter grass that covered the parade ground.

"You was lucky today, boy. Someday you'll tell your kids about it. You'll say you actually laid eyes on Jim Bridger, one o' the toughest men that's come out o' this here country. Old coot. By God, I wish they wasn't lootenants!"

Gabe fought back the urge to laugh, letting a few seconds go by before he asked, "What was that other name you called him?"

"You mean Ol' Gabe? That's your name, too, ain't it? But it weren't Bridger's name to begin with. They say Jed Smith was the one that started in callin' him that."

"Jed Smith?"

"I keep forgettin' where you was brung up. Yeah, Jed and Jim used to trap together. They about had the mountains all to themselves once. Besides the Injuns, of course."

Gabe nodded and fell silent, thinking about the man whose name he bore, but they were already approaching a large house with a veranda running around three sides. Wooden chairs were scattered here and there in the deep shadow just behind the railing, and in one of them sat a uniformed officer who watched them approach.

The officer wore a dark blue frock coat with gold-braided epaulets, and once Gabe had climbed the stairs to the veranda, he could see the shoulder patches with the silver eagles that marked him as a colonel. Gabe looked more closely at the man's face and saw an expression that imitated shrewdness. The colonel studied Gabe with a piercing look, yet there was little intelligence behind his eyes. Gabe had expected to find an evil man, and he was a little disappointed to find him only stupid and arrogant. The colonel had dark, heavy brows that were furrowed above deep-set brown eyes, and he continued to make a great show of looking Gabe over while the sergeant introduced them.

"Colonel Thomas Moonlight," said the sergeant, "this is Gabe Conrad."

"I certainly know the name," Moonlight blustered. "At least I do now. I only wish I'd heard it sooner, boy."

The colonel took his eyes off Gabe long enough to glance at the sergeant, who had taken a position off to one side. A gust of wind blew across the parade ground and whipped around the house, chilling the flesh on Gabe's arms now that he was out of the sun.

"Has the prisoner ever given you any trouble?" Moonlight asked the sergeant.

"No, sir."

"Were you here when he was jailed?"

"No, sir. I was back at Leavenworth."

Moonlight turned abruptly back to Gabe. "Almost everyone

went back with Colonel Collins in March,'' he said. ''So I don't have too many people I can ask about your case. Nevertheless, there have been some developments.''

The colonel's frown had grown even deeper, reflecting profound puzzlement. Gabe watched him without expression, deciding to remain silent.

''I don't know quite what to make of them,'' Moonlight said, almost talking to himself. ''But I'll tell you what, let's start with your story.''

''My story?''

''Tell me how you wound up in the guardhouse.''

A few seconds passed, during which the colonel studied Gabe's blank eyes and wondered whether the boy had gone daft during his confinement.

''I want to hear the truth!'' Moonlight said impatiently. ''Don't you want to tell me?''

Gabe shrugged, unable to see any harm in telling at least certain parts of the truth. ''There was a fight,'' he said. ''Captain Price said I tried to kill him with a pitchfork, so they locked me up.''

''*Were* you trying to kill him?''

''No, sir.''

Moonlight waited a moment, then shifted impatiently in his chair. ''Well, then, what did happen?''

''I was only trying to pin the captain's arm to the ground. I was afraid he was going to shoot me.''

''Did he have reason to?''

Gabe frowned. ''Wouldn't you have to ask him?''

''I mean, were *you* threatening *him?*''

''No.''

''Had you struck him?''

Gabe thought back to that night almost three years before. ''I hit him with the handle.''

''Why?''

''He was trying to hit me.''

''He struck the first blow, then?''

''He tried to.''

The ghost of a smile came to the colonel's lips. He lowered his head, staring thoughtfully at the floorboards while his chin sank into the folds of a golden silk kerchief around his neck.

"Fascinating," he murmured, looking up at the sergeant after half a minute or so of contemplation. "This young man has had no visitors, as far as you know?"

The sergeant shook his head.

So did the colonel, meaning a different thing. "Well, his story matches the one I heard from Captain Price this morning. In every detail."

Moonlight had turned to watch Gabe for a reaction to the news, showing his disappointment when there was none.

"The captain elected to continue his frontier duty," he said to Gabe. "He's still here. And this morning he came to tell me he had made an error in accusing you of murderous intentions. He now believes he was wrong."

Gabe understood the perplexity he heard in the colonel's tone. He had similar feelings. It was a great surprise that a man of Price's nature would voluntarily confess such a serious mistake. It could embarrass him in front of other officers and hurt his career in the Army. Nor could Gabe think of anything he might gain by his confession. The whole thing was a mystery.

"Do you understand what I'm saying?" Moonlight asked. Gabe had still failed to show any emotion, and that made the colonel uneasy. He began to draw out his words, as if talking to a person of retarded intelligence.

"I believe so," said Gabe, surprised by the question.

"In other words, I have no reason to keep you locked up."

"That's right."

"So I can set you free, as far as the captain is concerned."

"That would make me very happy."

Moonlight gave the sergeant a quizzical look, then turned back to Gabe. "The captain said he was moved to talk to me by the arrival of Mrs. Eubanks, and the ghastly treatment she suffered at the hands of those savages."

Gabe didn't say anything to that.

"He tells me your own mother was abducted by the Oglala before you were born. Apparently you were forced to live among them during your childhood?"

Gabe nodded stiffly.

"Is your mother still alive, son?"

Gabe almost nodded again, until he remembered that he would have had no way of knowing except for the imprisoned chiefs. "I'm not sure," he said, wondering if the colonel had tried to trick him. "She was three years ago."

Moonlight gave him a thoughtful but sympathetic look, suddenly gripping the armrests of his chair and pushing himself to his feet. "Come let me show you something," he said. "Maybe it'll make you feel better to see what we intend to do with the stinking bastards."

CHAPTER THREE

Two Face and Black Foot were still hanging from a scaffold on a hill beside the Laramie River, more than a day after they'd been taken from the guardhouse. Their bodies swayed and twisted in a steady breeze, and when they turned, Gabe could see that their eyes had been eaten by birds. There were flies crawling in and out of the empty sockets.

Gabe looked away, down the slope toward the river and the waving yellow grass on the other side, but he could still hear the creaking of the ropes as the bodies swung slowly back and forth. He listened to the ropes and looked at the river, and for a moment it seemed that he was reliving the time just before his fight with Captain Price. At first he thought it was the low-hanging sun and the smoky red color of the sky that reminded him of that earlier night, until he realized that his memories had been caused not by anything he saw but by the way he felt inside. The sight of Two Face and Black Foot had fired him with the same lust for blood that he had felt nearly three years before.

"A fitting end," said Colonel Moonlight. He was standing between Gabe and the sergeant, staring up at the chiefs with a look of grim satisfaction. "And a fitting example to the rest of the scum."

"An example of what?" Gabe said evenly. He was looking at the bodies again and noticing the way a noose digs into a man's neck. It added to the heat in his blood that was making him a little careless.

"An example of what!" Moonlight said. "Jesus Christ, man, it shows them we won't be trifled with. That we have resolve."

Gabe kept his eyes fixed on the dead chiefs, aware that the colonel was watching him with a puzzled expression. "I see," he said. "So that's what it shows them."

"You're damn right it does."

Gabe nodded in a vague way, looking at Moonlight only after the colonel had turned back toward the scaffold. He found himself studying Moonlight's throat above the golden silk scarf.

"As far as I'm concerned," said the colonel, "hanging was too good for the bastards."

Gabe could imagine the way a well-honed knife would melt through the soft flesh, and the way it would feel as it sliced through muscle and tendon.

"I had to restrain myself when I heard Mrs. Eubanks telling her story," said Moonlight. "Sometimes I wish torture was a legitimate act of war." He stiffened suddenly and looked at Gabe, who lifted his eyes from Moonlight's throat and wondered if his thoughts had become transparent. "Please forgive me if I'm stirring up painful memories," said Moonlight. "I forgot for a moment that your own mother suffered the same fate."

"Not exactly," said Gabe.

"What do you mean, not exactly? She was taken by Indians; was she not?"

Gabe glanced at the sergeant, who stood a few feet away and met Gabe's eyes with a level, concentrated stare. If the colonel thought himself a shrewd judge of character, Gabe saw that it was the sergeant who might truly have the power to look into a man's heart. He knew he should be careful in the sergeant's presence, but there was still the fire in his blood and something in Moonlight's manner that provoked him.

"My mother was taken by the Bad Faces," Gabe said. "By Oglala, not Cheyenne. And the soldiers hadn't made them angry by attacking a peaceful camp."

"So you've heard about Chivington," Moonlight said with a somber shake of his head. "I suppose Mrs. Eubanks *was* paying a price for Sand Creek, and a terrible price it was. But as far as I'm concerned, it only means we didn't get the job done."

"What job is that, Colonel?"

"Wiping the vermin out, dammit! Pushing them back so hard that they don't ever dare to stick their necks out again. Hell, boy, you should know that better than anyone."

Gabe saw that the colonel and the sergeant were both looking at him, and he knew he was on dangerous ground. The mood had turned sour at the fort during the winter, with Collins gone and Moonlight in command. Now he had the feeling that any hint of sympathy for Indians would only get him tossed back in the guardhouse. If that happened, Colonel Moonlight and Private Tuttle would stay safely out of his reach. Gabe fought the recklessness that burned inside him, working to control his tongue.

"You were one of the lucky ones," Moonlight was saying. "You got away. Captain Price tells me it was Jim Bridger himself who rescued you from the Oglala."

Gabe only nodded, although he wanted to say *captured* instead of *rescued*.

"I know it must have seemed a hollow victory," Moonlight said with a heavy sigh. "It's a shame Bridger had to leave your mother behind.

Gabe nodded again, not knowing what to say. There was much he failed to understand about the things that had happened to him.

"How long were you forced to live among the heathens?"

"Until I was fourteen," said Gabe, remembering them as the happiest years of his life.

"Fourteen? But that would mean your mother was abducted in the mid-forties." Moonlight looked at the sergeant. "The Sioux were still behaving themselves, weren't they? I don't remember any white women being abducted on the trail to Oregon."

The sergeant shrugged and Gabe said, "It didn't happen on the trail. The Bad Faces weren't even living here. It happened in the Black Hills."

"That still doesn't make sense, Mr. Conrad. The Black Hills are off-limits to white people. White settlers have no business there."

Gabe nodded in bitter agreement, gazing off to the north as

the shadows grew longer on the prairie. "It was my father's idea," he said after a moment, trying to keep the bitterness out of his voice, "but he talked some other people into going along. There were twenty-two of them all together. They left the trail somewhere beyond the fort."

"My God," said the colonel, "twenty-one people beside your mother? And the Indians killed them all?"

"They were trying to enter the Black Hills," Gabe said. "It made the Lakota very angry."

The colonel frowned at Gabe. "Maybe I missed something," he said, "but I still don't understand why your father and the others went to the Black Hills in the first place."

Gabe wanted to say: Because they were white men. That should have been enough. Surely everyone knew about the greed of the white men. "It was my father's idea," he said again, trying to hide his hatred for the man who had put his mother in danger. "He convinced the others to go when they heard there might be gold in the Black Hills."

"Gold!" said Moonlight. "You mean there were rumors even then?"

"My mother told me they heard it from a trapper, a man named La Compte. He showed them some of the yellow metal and said it came from the hills."

"It's possible," said Moonlight. "We're still hearing the same rumors. Captain Raynolds even found some indications just before the war." The colonel turned suddenly to Gabe. "Well, sure," he said, "I'm forgetting you joined the expedition later on. Bridger was scouting for Raynolds when he found you."

"I remember."

"They skirted the Black Hills on their way out here, the summer before Bridger learned about your mother. Maybe you heard some of the troopers talking about gold?" Moonlight hesitated, but Gabe didn't say anything. "I also talked to Bridger, you know. He said your mother had been teaching you English right along, just on the chance she could find a way to get you free."

Gabe remembered that, too, the long and happy hours spent by his mother's side as he learned to interpret the strange markings in her black book. The memories brought a warmth into his heart that quickly turned to longing and sadness. He pushed the memories away, until it seemed that they belonged to someone else.

Moonlight had tilted his head a little, making a show of watching Gabe's eyes. "I can only imagine how much you miss her," he said. "She sounds like a wise and courageous woman."

Gabe remained silent, staring off to the north while he listened to the wind in the grass and the steady creaking of the ropes on the scaffold.

"Would you like a chance to go and find her, son?"

The sergeant stirred suddenly and cleared his throat. "Colonel . . ."

"It's obvious you know the country better than anyone," said Moonlight, "and you could be a tremendous help when—"

"Colonel!"

"What *is* it, Sergeant?"

"Well . . . is it a good idea to talk about the Army's plans, sir?"

"I can hardly offer him a job without revealing them."

The sergeant glanced at Gabe and shifted the weight on his feet. "Well, sir, I'm wonderin' about that too. Maybe we could talk about it later when—"

"Talk about *what*, Sergeant?"

"Well, sir"—another hooded glance at Gabe—"the point is, I ain't too sure about this boy's loyalties."

"Loyalties? For God's sake, Sergeant, just take a look at his skin!"

"Yeah, but he was *born* out there, Colonel. He was raised right from the start like any other redskin."

Gabe remained silent while Moonlight studied his face with a thoughtful frown. Gabe was remembering the old chief's vision and thinking that this might turn out to be one of the ways in which he could help his people. He sensed that he was about to learn something from Moonlight that could help prevent more suffering among the Oglala. He tried to think of words that would take away the colonel's doubts, and then his instincts told him that he should only stand quietly under the colonel's scrutiny and say nothing. Somehow he sensed that the colonel had already made up his mind and would convince himself.

"So he lived with them," the colonel finally said with a shrug of his shoulders. "Don't forget that they killed his father,

Sergeant. Don't forget that his mother was teaching him to read out of the Bible.''

"I heard all that, sir. But I still ain't too sure about him."

"Give me one good reason."

"Well, for starters, you might want to look under his shirt. Old Two Face gave him a peace pipe before we took him out of the guardhouse."

Moonlight frowned again and said, "Is that true, son?"

"He's got it with him," said the sergeant.

Gabe reached inside his shirt, moving more carefully when he saw the sergeant's hand go to the flap of his holster. "It's a ceremonial pipe," Gabe said as he passed it to the colonel, thinking about the best way to say his next sentence. He put a small emphasis on the first word. "They use it to pray to the spirits."

Moonlight hefted the pipe, running his fingers along the smooth stone stem. "Why did Two Face give it to you?"

"He wanted me to pass it on to his son," said Gabe, wondering if the chief had a son.

"How do you expect to manage that?"

"I don't," said Gabe, glancing at the sergeant. "I'm hoping to sell it in St. Louis. I figure somebody'll pay a lot of money for a real Indian peace pipe."

The colonel laughed and returned the pipe to Gabe, whose look of amusement had a sharp edge of contempt in it that the colonel didn't see. "See there?" Moonlight said to the sergeant, still chuckling. "I don't think we have anything to worry about from Mr. Conrad. He may have grown up with the heathens, but he still knows the only thing a peace pipe is good for."

The colonel laughed again at his own joke while the sergeant looked steadily at Gabe. It was a look that said: "Don't think you fooled me the way you fooled him." Gabe returned the stare without blinking, challenging him to do his best.

Moonlight didn't notice any of this. His laughter had died away, and now he was gazing out across the rolling prairie toward the northern horizon, his lips pressed together in a hard line. "It's a bad business," he said. "Have you heard that they're investigating Chivington? They're saying he might have let his troops get a little carried away at Sand Creek."

Gabe looked at the bodies of Two Face and Black Foot and remembered the stories they had told him, passed on from the

Cheyenne to the Oglala. He felt an even greater heat in his blood than before, but he spoke in a tone of curiosity.

"Could it be that they just thought it was wrong to kill the women and children?"

"What the hell do they know?" Moonlight demanded. "They're all safe in Washington. It's like Chivington said last winter, 'Nits make lice.' Maybe if they listened to a man with some *experience* for a change, we'd get this problem taken care of."

Gabe didn't say anything. He was looking up at the chiefs, trying to control his rage by remembering how they had behaved.

"It did get them riled up," Moonlight said with a sour laugh. "I'll admit that much. There was a time when the redskins were attacking everything that moved on the Overland Trail. Did you hear much about it in the guardhouse, Mr. Conrad?"

Gabe shook his head.

"Well, the savages weren't sparing many women and children themselves, son. That's when Mrs. Eubanks was captured, back in January. The whole damn bunch of 'em came right by here on their way north, but the Army was helpless. The war was still on, and most of our troop strength was committed in the East."

Moonlight stared into the distance while Gabe thought about the battles he had missed. The wind whistled through the timbers of the scaffold. The bodies of the chiefs swayed fitfully, and there was still the steady creaking of the ropes. Then the colonel raised his chin—as if to expose his neck, Gabe thought for an instant—and pointed with it toward the horizon.

"Now they're all up there," he said. "Most of the Arapaho and Cheyenne and the worst of the Sioux. They're up there in the Powder River country and feeling safe, and by God, we aim to get them once and for all."

The sergeant cleared his throat and looked uncomfortable. The colonel ignored him.

"They got off scot-free," he said to Gabe. "They raided the Overland Trail with impunity, and so far they haven't been punished. Now they're attacking John Bozeman's road, stopping all the traffic to the gold diggings at Virginia City. And what I want to know from you, young man, is this: Would you like to help us stop them?"

"Me, Colonel?"

"None other," Moonlight said with enthusiasm. "Bridger likes the idea as much as I do. He thinks you'd make an excellent scout."

"A scout," said Gabe, tasting the word on his tongue. He had been expecting this, but it still came as a surprise. The idea also made him want to laugh: out of the guardhouse and into the scouts. "Is that what Bridger's been hired for, then?"

"The plans are being made right now in Denver," said Moonlight, his eyes gleaming with childlike excitement. He raised his arms and spread them wide, slowly bringing them together until he could lock the fingers of his hands. "More than two thousand troops in three separate columns, Mr. Conrad, killing Indians wherever they find them. They'll be converging on the Rosebud River, where they plan to *build a fort*. Right in the heart of their stronghold!"

"The Sioux sure won't like that," Gabe said mildly.

"I hope not," Moonlight snapped. "I hope they fight. You know who's commanding the invasion? General Patrick Connor."

Gabe shook his head to show that the name meant nothing to him.

"From Utah," said the colonel. "The hero of Bear River. He killed more than three hundred Bannock and Snake a couple years back. You can bet they stopped bothering the Mormons after that!"

Gabe looked away, feeling sick with sadness for the People who would come under the general's guns—and hoping he could warn them in time.

"How long before we could see some action?" he asked.

The colonel grinned at that. "I had a feeling about you," he said. "I'm glad I was right. With you and Bridger along, I don't see how the general can fail."

Gabe nodded briefly to acknowledge the compliment, feeling disappointment when Moonlight suddenly turned his back on the scaffold and began to walk. "Come," he said, "let's get off this hill before we lose all our light."

Gabe followed the colonel down the hill, the sergeant immediately behind him. Their boots made a familiar scraping sound in the dry, brittle grass. Gabe ignored the new rush of memories, waiting until it became clear that Moonlight had either forgotten his question or was ignoring it. Gabe considered asking it again, but he could almost feel the sergeant's gaze on the back of his head as they walked. And since Connor hadn't arrived at the post yet, Gabe decided there was plenty of time for learning more details.

He didn't learn anything more from the colonel. Moonlight contented himself with aimless chatter during the long walk back to the fort, apparently happy with the evening's results. It seemed as if Moonlight were congratulating himself for coming up with the idea of hiring Gabe, and looking forward to the effect it would have on his prestige when Gabe found plenty of Indians for Connor to kill. The colonel parted company with Gabe and the sergeant in front of his quarters, offering his new scout a firm handshake and hearty congratulations.

"The sergeant will fix you up," he told Gabe. "He'll show you where to eat and where to bunk. Welcome to the cavalry, Mr. Conrad."

Gabe thanked him, looking a little bemused. He was wondering how a man like Moonlight could rise to such a high position in the Army. Among the Lakota, a chief kept his power only as long as he was successful and the people still believed in him. Gabe felt as if he were in the middle of a strange dream, until he turned to face the sergeant standing beside him.

A kind of understanding passed between the two men. Gabe thought they both held the same opinion of the colonel, and it united them. At the same time there was something else that kept them apart.

"Now you know," said the sergeant.

Gabe pretended to be puzzled by the remark.

The sergeant sighed after a moment. "Well, there ain't nothin' I can do about your knowin'. But I can damn well make sure the information don't get into the wrong hands."

"Do you want to make it easier for them to kill women and children?"

"That won't happen here."

"No?"

"It damn well better not. That ain't the way a soldier's taught to fight. But the point is, I got a duty to my men. And the things you just heard could get a lot of 'em killed if it's told to the wrong people."

"What makes you think it will?"

"All right," the sergeant said with a scowl, "you can pretend if you want. But I'm warnin' you right now. Don't plan on leavin' the post."

Gabe blinked. "Where do you think I'd go?"

"Downriver, maybe. To visit the Loafers."

"They seem harmless to me," Gabe said with a shrug, hiding his scorn for the "Laramie Loafer" Indians who camped nearby. They had given up the old ways, and now they lived on trade goods or handouts, or whatever menial work the women could find at the fort.

"Sure," said the sergeant. "So harmless that the northern tribes get most of their weapons and ammunition from them. I ain't stupid, boy. I know the pelts they trade for guns come from the hostiles, and then they give away the guns for more pelts. Not to mention the gossip they hear around the post."

Gabe studied the sergeant's angry expression. "Anyway, I didn't hear the colonel say anything about restricting my movements."

"Yeah?" the sergeant said sarcastically. "Are you really surprised?"

"But you don't have the authority to—"

"Fuck authority!" The sergeant leaned closer to Gabe, his face flushed with anger. "I didn't want that idiot talkin' to you in the first place, but he did. So you and I gotta live with it. That's why I'm warnin' you—I'm *askin'* you—don't do anything stupid."

The sergeant closed his eyes for a moment and leaned back and started breathing a little easier, but when he opened his eyes again, they were hard and serious.

"I don't want you leaving the post," he said. "I don't want you talkin' to any friendlies. If I catch you, I'm gonna have to kill you."

Gabe liked the idea of being a free man, but he didn't think life in the U.S. Army would be much of an improvement over life in the guardhouse. It was a good thing he didn't plan to stay. What he most wanted to do after his talk with the colonel, for one thing, was take a walk down by the Laramie River. He wanted to listen to the water and the meadowlarks while he thought about the sudden changes in his life. Instead the sergeant took Gabe to the quartermaster's store for a regulation uniform.

Gabe was also glad he didn't plan to wear the uniform very long. The quartermaster's clerk issued him a dark blue flannel forage cap that sat too high on his head and looked as if it wouldn't serve any useful purpose, while the chin strap and leather sweatband felt stiff and uncomfortable on his head.

"We'll get a scout's patch for that tomorrow," said the sergeant, eyeing Gabe closely. "If you're still here."

Gabe didn't say anything. He was hefting the rest of the uniform in his hands and frowning over its weight. The dark blue uniform jacket and sky-blue trousers were made of heavy wool fabric, as were the gray stockings and gray pullover shirt meant to go under the jacket. All of them were rough and scratchy, and Gabe tried to imagine how they'd feel on a hot day in August.

The sergeant noticed his frown. "Don't worry," he said, "nobody wears a shirt when it gets hot. Half the time they don't even button the jacket. And they sure as *hell* don't wear the stock, at least in the field."

"You mean this thing?" said Gabe, fingering a black leather band.

"Yeah, it's supposed to go around your neck under the jacket collar." The sergeant showed a sour grin. "You heard of raw recruits, ain't ya? How do you think they got the name?"

"What about weapons? Don't I get a carbine and a revolver?"

The sergeant lost his humor and fixed Gabe with a cold eye. "Tomorrow," he said. "Come with me."

Gabe stacked everything in his arms, then picked up a pair of high black leather boots from the counter and followed the sergeant outside. The sky had turned a deep shade of violet, except for a lingering band of silver-gray light near the horizon that silhouetted the main buildings clustered around the post's parade ground. The sergeant angled north, however, leading Gabe toward the bathhouses on the other side of the sutler's home. The sergeant began digging in his pockets as he went through one of the dark doorways, and a moment later there was the flare of a match inside, followed by the dimly flickering glow of candlelight. The sergeant came back out and stood for a moment on the stoop, his body filling the lighted doorway. Gabe couldn't see his face against the light, but he knew the sergeant was giving him another close look.

"You know where the mess hall is," the sergeant said. "I

wanna see you there in a half hour, lookin' like a soldier.''

"Yes, sir.''

"An' I ain't no officer, thank God. Call me Sergeant.''

"Yes, Sergeant.''

The big man came down off the stoop, his leathery face catching some of the dim light from the bathhouse. "You might as well bury those rags you're wearin','' he said. "But remember, boy, half an hour. I'll come lookin' for you if it's one minute longer. An' if I have to do that, you better hope I don't find you.''

Gabe didn't say anything to that. The two men stared at each other, the sergeant wishing Gabe would look at least a little nervous or intimidated. But Gabe only dipped his chin by way of acknowledgment before he went past the sergeant and disappeared inside the bathhouse. He thought the older man should have known enough not to worry. Gabe would want more preparation—a waiting horse and a good weapon would be helpful, not to mention a better head start than half an hour. Gabe also wanted to learn more about the Army's invasion plans before he went to warn the people who had raised him. So he had no intention of disappearing just yet. His only plan was to wash off the smell of the guardhouse as well as he could, then change into his new uniform and go to the mess hall to have supper with the sergeant.

But Gabe had also intended to go and get the sorrel pony that Captain Price had asked for three years earlier. Things just seemed to turn out differently sometimes, no matter what he planned. This time there were four men waiting for him when he finished his bath, and he didn't see the sergeant again for a long time.

CHAPTER FOUR

The men swarmed over Gabe as soon as he came through the door of the bathhouse. He had just blown out the candles inside and he was blinking against the smoke, vaguely aware of being vulnerable in his blindness, but he had no enemies he knew of, and no sense that he might be in danger. At first he was only confused when the four black shapes closed in on him. He dropped the bundle of guardhouse clothes he was carrying, to free his hands, but before he could do anything more, his arms were caught in a tight grip and the barrel of a revolver was jammed against his ribs. Even then he tried to struggle, until he heard the hammer being eared back on the revolver.

"We'll kill you," one of the men warned him in a harsh whisper. "We can always say you were trying to escape."

"Escape what?" said Gabe. "What are you after?"

"We got what we're after," said the man. "Just shut up and come with us."

Gabe let himself be dragged along by the four men who surrounded him, alert for any slackening of pressure in the grip on his arms and the revolver against his belly. It never came.

He was also trying to figure out the meaning of his abduction, and with that he had better luck. It was so obvious, in fact, that Gabe was ashamed of his carelessness. If he had given more thought to Colonel Moonlight's explanation for his release, and to the character of Captain Stanley Price, he would have been prepared for these four men. Gabe had never seen anything to make him think of the captain as a forgiving man, or the kind who would have a change of heart. It had to be something besides mercy, then, that had moved him to tell a different story about the fight. Gabe had a feeling that he knew what it was now: Price wanted a more satisfying form of revenge than watching someone sit in a guardhouse.

So Gabe was no longer surprised when the four men circled the bathhouses and started moving toward a dim glow of light coming from the stables, not far from the corrals where he'd been shoveling hay on his last night of freedom. Surprise had been replaced with anger at himself, for his failure to be more careful. He could blame no one else for whatever was about to happen. It was another important lesson: From then on he would always think about all the possible consequences of anything that happened to him, and all the possible reasons for *why* it happened.

If he survived the night.

One of the men whistled softly when they got close to the first stable building, and a moment later the big sliding door was opened a few feet, its iron wheels squealing on their tracks. The men holding Gabe's arms pushed him inside and threw him to the ground. He was expecting something like that, and instead of resisting them, he used the force of the shove to keep tumbling, rolling over onto his feet. He felt a little better about his instincts when the prongs of a pitchfork buried themselves harmlessly in the dirt where he'd just fallen.

Captain Price himself was at the other end of the handle. He yanked the pitchfork out of the ground and came toward Gabe with a tentative jab, his lips twisting into a grin of anticipation as the two men began to circle each other.

They were at the center of a dim pool of light formed by candles and lanterns mounted on the stalls. The other men had stepped back to the edges of the circle. Gabe glanced at them just long enough to see that the one holding the revolver had put it back in his holster, but he also saw that all four of them had holsters, and that all four of them had loosened the black leather flaps that covered their six-shooters.

Gabe had the fleeting impression that he'd seen a couple of the men earlier that day, in the crowd listening to Jim Bridger's story, and they all looked like officers. They watched him with coldly curious expressions as flickering shadows played across their faces. One of them was smiling faintly. Beyond them, the rest of the stable was lost in blackness, almost as if that part of the building didn't even exist. But Gabe could hear the movement and occasional snorting of horses in some of the stalls at the far end.

Price lunged with the pitchfork again, and Gabe moved easily out of the way, warned by the captain's right foot as it came out just ahead of the thrust. Gabe tried to grab the pitchfork and move in around it while the captain was leaning off-balance, but Price stepped back in time to keep the iron prongs between them, forcing Gabe to stay at a distance. The captain's black eyes glittered in the candlelight, and he was still grinning, the muscles of his face set in harshly rigid lines. Gabe thought the face looked like death, and it made him shudder.

"Well, well," Price said in a raspy voice, "you don't like it so much when you're on the other end, do you?"

"I did not attack you like this."

"No? Then how did I get this hole in my wrist?"

"I only tried to keep you from shooting me."

"You were trying to *kill* me!" Price shouted. "I saw it in your eyes!"

"If that was true, you wouldn't be here."

"Goddamn arrogant son of a bitch!"

Price lashed out again, but this time when Gabe moved to avoid the pitchfork, he ran into one of the other officers and didn't get far enough out of the way. The prongs tore into the sleeve of his new uniform jacket, grazing his arm. He made another grab for them, but his arm was jostled and the pitchfork slipped through his fingers. Price pulled it back, grinning again when he saw the blood.

Gabe continued to circle, watching the captain's foot for a warning of the next lunge. But he sensed that someone else had closed in behind him. That would mean there was a man on either side now, trying to limit his moves and make him an easier target. He realized how useless it was to stay on the defensive. They would only make it harder and harder for him. Then he saw the grin fading from the captain's face, leaving a pure black hatred in the eyes that measured Gabe's body. Gabe fixed his attention on the head of the pitchfork, settling himself while he studied the prongs. There were only four of them, with plenty of room between each one. When Price feinted suddenly to the right and thrust to the left, Gabe stayed rooted where he was and calmly put his hands out to block the weapon.

The captain grunted in surprise when his momentum was stopped short. Then he looked down at Gabe's hands, around the crossbar of the pitchfork, and something went loose in his face. The right hand had been pierced through the palm so that the long steel point seemed to grow out of the back. Price had trouble believing what he saw—thinking it had to be a trick of some kind—because Gabe wasn't acting like a man who had just had a steel point plunged through his hand. A momentary feeling came over the captain that he was dreaming.

It wasn't a dream for Gabe, and it sure as hell wasn't what he'd hoped for—he'd hoped to get his hands between the prongs—but he had accepted the possibility. His only thought now was to take the pitchfork away from Price, even when the captain started trying to yank it out of the impaled hand. Gabe clenched his jaw against the pain and kept a tight grip.

Price looked up from the hand and stared with fascination at Gabe's face. There was nothing there. No pain or fear, not even anger. It was like the face of a dead man. It crossed the captain's mind that the kid wasn't human, and the old feeling of panic came back to shame him again. He was trying to get the pitchfork back but he was scared, and his hands slipped and the kid was able to wrestle it free. Gabe took the shaft in his free hand, the other one still wrapped around the crossbar, and smashed the butt of the handle into the captain's chest, right above the heart.

Price stumbled back, still dazed by the feeling that he was in a dream—that none of this could really be happening—and Gabe had a chance to pull the prong out of his hand. It felt like a hot branding iron had been run through his arm from wrist to shoulder, but the pain didn't show in his face.

Price was suddenly struck by a memory of his own performance three years before, screaming and writhing on the ground as he tried to free his wrist. It drove the dreamlike feeling from his mind, replacing fear with shame and fury.

"Kill him," he yelled. "*Kill* the bastard!"

Gabe had already seen one of the officers reaching beneath the flap of his holster. He whipped the handle of the pitchfork against the man's forearm, hard enough to snap a bone. The officer cried out and gripped his wrist. Gabe felt a movement behind him and whirled around in time to drive the handle into another man's stomach, doubling him over.

They were all moving in now, and Gabe was using the handle of the pitchfork like a war lance, flailing and jabbing. The only way he could whip it around fast enough was to use the end of the handle, leaving the heavy steel prongs close to his midsection. It made things complicated, keeping the sharp points away from his body at the same time that he was fending off his attackers. He yelped like a wild man, startling the soldiers as he lashed out at them in a frenzied fury. He knocked a revolver out of another officer's hand—just as it was leveled—and smashed the handle of the pitchfork against the side of Price's neck. But then a gun barrel brushed by his ear and came down on his shoulder. He was spinning away, struggling to lift his numb arm, when he heard a sound from the shadows where no one was supposed to be.

The soldiers heard it, too, and froze.

It was a heavy metallic sound, in two parts: *klick-kluck*. It wasn't loud or frightening in itself, but everyone recognized it as the sound of a rifle's side hammer being eared back.

"That'll do 'er," said a voice that Gabe also recognized. "Yuh got no way o' knowin' where this thing is pointin', an' yuh won't have t'find out if yuh stay still."

Gabe and the soldiers were peering into the blackness, unable to see anything at first. Then they saw a ghostlike shimmer of movement just beyond the circle of lantern light. The shimmer came toward them, slowly taking form, until it turned into Jim Bridger.

He came out of the darkness like a vision.

CHAPTER FIVE

Gabe never forgot the magical feeling that came over him with the appearance of the old mountain man at the edge of the light. He thought for a moment that Bridger really was a vision, called up through the power of the spirit protectors given to him by his boyhood adviser. It seemed like nothing else could account for the scout's arrival at just this moment.

But Bridger carried a Sharps carbine as if he'd been born with it in his hands, and there was no mistaking the flesh and blood. He stepped into the light as if it belonged to him, wearing a buckskin shirt and fringed leggings that had grown soft with years of wear and molded themselves to the still hard muscles of his body. His neck was thick and strong like a bull's. His eyes were clear and thoughtful and very steady. There was also, now, a hint of amusement in them as they settled on Gabe.

"Don't be lookin' so hard at me, boy," he said. "I wasn't aimin' to take a hand unless I had to."

"You didn't have to," said Gabe. He had started resenting the intrusion as soon as he realized Bridger wasn't an apparition. He knew things were going badly in the fight, but he was sure he would have triumphed, and he regretted not having the chance to prove himself right.

There were also other reasons for Gabe's resentment, feelings that went back five years. This was the man who had taken him from his home by force, surprising him in sleep, then binding and gagging him to make him helpless. This was the man who had insisted that Gabe was unwanted among his people, and then abandoned him among the hated soldiers.

"Well, I for one am glad you're here," said Captain Price, recovering from his surprise. "The kid was about to kill someone."

The humor disappeared from Bridger's eyes. "Why in hell d'yuh think I stepped in?" he said. "That's exactly what he was fixin' to do. I figgered I'd save yuh the embarrassment, so's no one would know the five of yuh couldn't handle one unarmed man."

A couple of the officers looked at the ground, but Price appeared to be relieved, maybe even a little smug. "Then let's get on with it," he said. "Grab his arms, boys."

"Not so fast," said Bridger.

The captain stared at him with a new look of surprise. "I don't understand," he said. "I thought—"

"I know what yuh thought, Price, but things ain't always what they seem."

"But you said . . . I mean, it was your idea to . . ."

The captain ran out of words, stammering in confusion while Bridger watched him with a sly smile. Gabe looked from one man to the other, and suddenly he understood another piece of the day's puzzle: why it was that Price had gone to the colonel with a new story at this particular time, after three years of waiting. Moonlight had said it was a change of heart brought on by the arrival of Mrs. Eubanks in such wretched condition, but of course there had been no change of heart. That was only an excuse to cover up the captain's thirst for revenge.

Now it was clear to Gabe that Price's talk with the colonel and Bridger's presence at the post were no coincidence. He saw the old scout's hand at work in the day's events, and his appearance in the stable was a little less surprising.

"Goddammit," Price sputtered suddenly, tilting his head to indicate the scene around him, "this whole thing was your *idea*."

"It was?" said Bridger, his eyes wide with innocence. "You mean, I tol' yuh to try an' run the poor boy through with a pitchfork?"

"Well, not exactly . . ."

"All I remember sayin' is, he weren't doin' no one no good

sittin' around in a cell.''

"But the way you said it, Jim, I thought—"

"I can't help what you thought, Captain.'' Bridger looked at Gabe. "Sorry t'spoil your fun, boy, but if you'd o' kilt one o' these *brave men*, yuh mighta wound up hangin' alongside Two Face and Black Foot up on the hill. It's better that yuh light out o' here instead.''

"What the hell!" said Price.

Bridger's head swiveled on its thick bull's neck, and Price paled a little beneath the scout's bright stare. "You're right," said Bridger. "This here set-to ain't settled yet, is it? Boy, get the pistols off their hips.''

"Now just a goddamn minute—"

It was another of the officers, slipping his hand under the flap of his holster while he opened his mouth to protest. Gabe raised his pitchfork, but Bridger had already swung around as if to see who was speaking, the barrel of his Sharps swinging with him. It was a casual motion, but when the Sharps had finished its arc, the muzzle was aimed dead center at the officer's belly. The officer froze, then slowly took his hand away from the holster.

"Yuh want me to tell ol' Colonel Moonface the reason I had t'shoot yuh,'' said Bridger. "Want me t'tell 'im Lieutenant Boorman and four other officers couldn't handle a twenny-year-old kid?''

The lieutenant scowled and looked away. Bridger nodded at Gabe, gesturing with his Sharps, and Gabe leaned the pitchfork against one of the stalls before circling around behind the soldiers. He was careful to leave the scout a clear line of fire while he lifted the revolvers from each man's holster. When he had all five, he glanced at Bridger again.

"Toss 'em in the trough by the door,'' said the scout.

Lieutenant Boorman cursed bitterly and Gabe gave Bridger a questioning look.

"Go ahead,'' said the old man. "The water'll jes' ruin the charges. By the time they get new powder in the cylinders, mebbe they'll be cooled down enough to think twice 'afore comin' after yuh.''

"Evidently you've thought this out pretty well,'' said Price, wincing a little when he heard the splash of the revolvers in the trough. "But didn't it ever occur to you that this could lead to charges of treason, Bridger? A man your age would find it hard going at Leavenworth.''

The scout's look was mocking and scornful. ''A man my age,'' he said, ''has been on this earth long enough to outwit the likes o' you. *Evidently*, Captain, yuh ain't thinkin' too sharp on where yuh stand right now. To this chil' it looks like yuh was attemptin' cold-blooded murder. That's a hangin' offense.''

''First there'd have to be a court-martial,'' Price said. ''Who'd believe an old liar like you?''

Bridger shrugged. ''There's always the feller that hired me, Mr. Grenville Dodge. Have yuh heard o' him, by chance?''

Price looked disgusted. Grenville Dodge was the supreme commander of the Department of the Missouri, and everyone knew he had a high opinion of Jim Bridger—even if Price couldn't understand why the general had been taken in by all those tall tales. Any single graduate of West Point was worth a dozen ruffians like Bridger.

''Good,'' said the scout. ''Cause I don't want yuh raisin' any fuss when the boy and me ride out tonight.''

''Are you deserting, then?''

''Deserting?'' said Bridger, all full of innocence again. ''It's jes' now comin' t'mind that there's somethin' yuh don't know. Ol' Gabe here is *workin'* for me. Colonel Moonlight give him a job in the scouts.''

''I don't believe it!''

''Yep, the colonel thought it were a right good idea when I mentioned it this afternoon. He said—''

''You bastard,'' said Price. ''You've been playing me for some kind of sucker.''

''—said it's the smartest thing we coulda done, since there ain't no one who knows the country the way he does.'' Bridger frowned suddenly at Gabe. ''Yuh did take the job, didn't yuh?''

''Yes, sir,'' said Gabe. ''I was going to report to you after supper.''

''Well, I'm glad yuh didn't get hurt here, 'cause I got a scoutin' job for yuh. Startin' tonight.''

''You bastard,'' Price said again. ''I don't believe it.''

Bridger shrugged. ''That's why I had the boy lift your six-shooters, so's yuh wouldn't do anything till yuh talked to Moonlight. Now I believe yuh was wantin' to fight the boy?''

Both the captain and Gabe looked at him with surprise.

"Yuh wanted a fight three years ago," Bridger said to Price, "an' he obliged yuh nicely. Same thing tonight. So if yuh wanna have at the boy again—without the pitchfork, of course —well, hell, I sure won't stop yuh."

Price was looking back and forth between Bridger and Gabe, not sure whether to believe the scout, and not excited about tackling the kid. It was also hard to work up the same kind of rage while everyone was staring at him. He half wished Gabe would do something to start the ball rolling, but the kid was only watching him, waiting for him to make the first move.

"I guess I was mistaken," Bridger said mildly. "I thought yuh wanted a fight."

Price looked annoyed. Bridger was being stupid if he expected anyone to just start in swinging.

"Well," said the scout, "mebbe yuh changed your mind. Mebbe you're feelin' more kindly all of a sudden."

The captain stared at him. One of the candles hissed in the silence, and a horse nickered softly from the back of the stable.

"Well, glad it's over, then," Bridger said with shrug. "Course, your friends here'll think you're jes' skeered of a fight where the odds're even. They won't *say* so, o'course, but that's the story that'll get around. That's why people will be lookin' at yuh funny when—"

"Jesus Christ," said the captain. He rolled his eyes toward the rafters in irritation, but when he looked down again, he saw an arrogant, superior gleam in Gabe's eyes. It filled him with a familiar rage, and he brought his fists up in front of his face.

Price circled in on Gabe like a boxer, and Gabe watched him come for a moment, studying him with curiosity. He had seen white men fight before, but he had never really understood this matter of showing your hands and approaching with caution. Either you were fighting or you weren't. Before the captain was close enough to strike, Gabe bent low and rushed in on him, driving him to the ground and raining heavy blows down on his head. Gabe had to be careful with his right hand, which was refusing to close into a tight fist, but his left smashed solidly into Price's nose and brought a gush of blood.

Price arched his back in pain and surprise, bucking Gabe off to the side and ignoring his own blood to grab hold of Gabe's right wrist. He tried to smash the wounded hand into the ground. Gabe resisted but quickly realized that he couldn't overpower the captain directly, since they were of nearly equal strength. Gabe twisted around and used his left fist again, bringing it down on the back of the captain's neck. Price grunted and loosened his grip just long enough for Gabe to free his wrist.

Price also threw his head back in an automatic effort to protect the nape of his neck. Gabe chopped savagely at his exposed throat. The captain made a choking sound and scrambled to his feet, trying to get away. Gabe pressed in on him, throwing him against a wall with a forearm pressed against his windpipe. Price gripped the arm with both hands, trying desperately to release the pressure while his mouth fell open in a hopeless gasp for air.

From the corner of his eye Gabe saw that one of the officers was edging closer, but the officer glanced at Bridger and stopped.

Gabe bore down on the captain's throat. Price brought up a knee, but Gabe was expecting it and turned slightly to deflect it off his thigh. The two men stared at each other with bitter hatred, their faces only a few inches apart now. The captain's eyes fluttered and Gabe pressed harder, anxious to end the fight quickly. But Price felt along Gabe's arm to find his hand, wedging a knuckle against the back of it about where the wound should be. He rolled the knuckle over the small bones until he found a place that made Gabe's head spin.

Price saw the glazed look in Gabe's eyes and brought his knee up again, finding his target this time. It wasn't enough to drive Gabe back, but some of the heart went out of his effort to strangle the captain. Price was able to slide Gabe's arm off his neck and onto his chest, holding it there for a moment while his lungs swelled with air. He was still clutching the arm to his chest when he snapped his forehead down onto the bridge of Gabe's nose.

Gabe took a step back then, and Price came after him with a hard blow to the stomach, followed by a wide, swinging punch that landed on his ear. Gabe stood his ground, accepting the punishment and blocking a third swing with his right arm as he landed a left hook against the captain's chin. Price staggered, his knees buckling a little, and Gabe saw that it would be smart to concentrate on the captain's jaw. Gabe circled him, imitating the boxer's stance, even though he still couldn't close his injured hand into a tight fist.

The two men were breathing hard, watching each other with wary expressions, and the sharp smell of dust pinched at Gabe's nose. It made him think of their long-ago fight for possession of the pitchfork. It seemed like this was the same fight, for a moment, as if there hadn't been a three-year interruption. In that moment it also seemed like the fight would continue forever, and that Captain Price would be a constant part of Gabe's life. It made him tired and angry, and it made him want to end this thing once and for all.

Gabe tried feinting with his right, but Price expected that and was ready for the left hook this time. He blocked it and landed a fist over Gabe's right eye. When he tried to press his advantage, however, Gabe surprised him by moving inside and lashing out with a flurry of stinging blows. The captain wasn't expecting a sudden rage. He'd been thinking he would be safe as long as he watched that left hand, assuming Gabe would try to protect his right.

But Gabe had a feeling. He wanted to finish the captain quickly, and he had a feeling about how he might do it. He feinted with his right again, as he knew Price expected, and reached out with his left. But while the captain blocked him and countered with another blow, Gabe was gathering all his will and strength in the right hand that wasn't being watched. It still wouldn't close up, and it seemed to take forever coming up from someplace down near the floor, but Price had opened himself up. He never expected the right fist that smashed into his jaw. His head snapped back, his eyes closed, and his body crumpled to the ground.

Gabe looked down at Price, holding his right hand against his belly. Something had snapped when the blow landed, and now the lights in the stable seemed to be swirling around him. When Gabe looked at his hand, he saw the crusted blood around the angry red hole in his palm, but he also saw that the top part of his index finger was pointing over at his thumb.

His hand had been half open when it landed, and his finger had been caught above the ridge of Price's jaw. It was broken at the lower knuckle. Gabe tried to straighten it out but the bones grated against each other, and the pain almost made him cry out. He was disgusted with himself. His eyes watered a little when he tried to straighten the finger again, but still he couldn't do it. The finger kept its sharp angle, leaning over toward the thumb.

Gabe gave up and went toward the stall where he'd left the pitchfork, never taking his eyes off the captain. His eyes glittered when he came back into the circle of candlelight.

"Gabe," said Bridger, taking a step toward him.

Gabe lifted the pitchfork above his head, his eyes on Price's chest.

"I'd hate t'pull this trigger," the scout said.

Gabe looked around with a puzzled expression. "This man is my enemy," he said. "He lost the fight and he deserves to die."

"Sorry, but it ain't everyone who'd agree."

"He tried to kill me, Bridger. He'll try it again."

"I hope not, son, but that ain't the point. Yuh gotta learn the white man's way o' doin' things."

Gabe threw a scornful look at the four officers left standing between them. "You want me to learn the way of cowards who can't stand up by themselves?"

"I ain't sayin' I like it any more'n you do," Bridger said. "But the soldiers are here to stay. Yuh can't ignore 'em. They'd call it murder if yuh kilt the cap'n, an' they'd never forget it. They'd be lookin' for yuh the rest o' your life."

"I'm not afraid."

Bridger sighed and said, "A young-un can talk that way. But the rest o' your life is a long time."

"But it's *my* life," Gabe said harshly.

"That still don't mean yuh'd be doin' the smart thing. Now put 'er down, boy."

Gabe hesitated, still holding the pitchfork above his head while he frowned down at Captain Price. "I don't like it," he said. "It gives me a bad feeling to think of letting this man stay alive."

"It ain't your choice, boy. One move out o' you an' I squeeze this trigger."

"But he's an evil man," Gabe pleaded. "Something bad will happen if—"

"Put 'er down, boy."

Gabe looked closely at the scout, seeing regret in the old man's eyes but also a growing resolve as the silence wore on. Gabe slowly lowered the pitchfork.

"Good," said Bridger, turning to look at the other four officers. "Now don't forget it were a fair fight," he warned them. "The boy ain't done nothin' wrong, an' there ain't no reason to pester him. The thing is, he's got a job to take care of—a secret scoutin' mission—an' anyone goin' after him will answer to me an' Colonel Moonlight. Is that clear?"

The officers nodded, some more reluctantly than others. One of them was still holding his broken wrist.

"Good," Bridger said again. He was backing away, covering their retreat through the blackness that swallowed up the rest of the stable. He led Gabe down between the stalls and through a door at the other end. There were three horses tied up just outside, two of them wearing saddles and the third loaded with packs. Gabe had the magical feeling again, as if the ponies had appeared there merely because they would come in handy.

But the feeling didn't last this time. He knew that Bridger must have brought the horses with him, as part of some large plan he had in mind. Gabe wasn't disappointed over the loss of the magical feeling. Instead he was thinking of the old mountain man in a new way, with a new respect. There were still things that Gabe did not understand—questions he wanted to ask—but he knew the questions would have answers. He tried to think about them as he climbed onto one of the horses, but there was a steady pain shooting up from his hand now, and his mind seemed to stumble uselessly in a fog.

Then he heard the squeeling of the rusty iron wheels on the stable's front door, and a moment later the sergeant's angry voice sounding loudly through the length of the stable.

"What the hell," the sergeant yelled. "Is he dead? Did the kid kill Captain Price?"

"Christ A'mighty," Bridger murmured under his breath.

"He just left!" one of the officers was saying. "Out the back!"

There was the sound of men running through the stable as Bridger adjusted himself in the saddle. "Boy," he said, kicking his pony in the ribs, "I sure hope you ain't forgot how to ride."

CHAPTER SIX

The horses were nimble and quick to run, but they'd only covered fifty or sixty yards before the back door of the stable crashed open with an explosion of violent curses, followed by the greater explosions of gunfire. Some of the shots came so close together that Gabe knew there were at least two men with guns. Either the sergeant had brought help when he came looking for Gabe, or he'd been carrying an extra weapon and given it to one of the officers.

Bridger folded himself forward with the first shots, down over the neck of his pony, while Gabe had slipped over to the off-side. Not that it would put him completely out of danger, Gabe knew. The horses were much bigger targets than he was, and if one or two of them went down, he and Bridger wouldn't stand much chance of getting away. But Gabe also noticed that the scout was leading them toward a small hill behind the stables, and he appreciated the old man's instincts. There would be no skyline to silhouette the riders, and without a moon they were invisible against the black bulk of the hill. The shooters at the stable could only empty their revolvers in the direction of the sounds of the horses and hope for the best. As it was, Gabe felt the breeze of one ball passing just above his head and heard another one *spang* off a rock not far away.

Then the shooting died off and Gabe let out a wild, whooping cry that carried across the prairie. He thought he saw Bridger looking at him, but it was something he couldn't have held back. He was free of Fort Laramie and the hated soldiers, and he was on a horse again, riding flat out with his long hair streaming behind him in the wind.

Bridger held up his hand a minute later and brought them to a stop, sitting very still in the saddle and listening for the distant thunder of other riders coming after them. Gabe's horse shifted its footing with a restless thump of one hoof and the squeek of saddle leather, but no other sounds came drifting over the prairie. Bridger nodded his head in satisfaction and put his horse into an easy lope, holding the pace for about a mile until they topped a low ridge that gave them a view of the post.

There was very little to see, even now that their eyes had adjusted to the glow from the endless stars hanging above them. Gabe had to stare hard to make out a few pinpoints of light—much dimmer than the stars—flickering from the buildings around the parade ground. The buildings themselves looked like a small bunch of dark stains on the grass, and Gabe was a little surprised at just how small the post looked from the ridge; it was an insignificant speck in the dark, empty stretch of grass that swept off to the horizon. Gabe knew that even from this low ridge he could see eighty or ninety miles in any direction—five or six sleeps in Indian thinking—and in all that space there were only these few soldiers. He sat a little straighter in the saddle, feeling that they could not be a serious threat to his people.

"Mebbe we'll get lucky now," Bridger said, breaking the deep night silence of the prairie. He was almost speaking in a whisper, which suddenly became a dry laugh. "Mebbe the sergeant'll calm down long enough t'hear the story about me sendin' yuh on a secret mission."

Gabe wanted to ask about the scout's real reason, but there was something else that troubled him. "Maybe he won't hear it," said Gabe. "Captain Price will be angry when he remembers how you tricked him," said Gabe.

The scout peered at him in the darkness. "Yuh got a point," he admitted.

"You should have let me kill him, Bridger. Why didn't you?"

"Dammit, boy, use your head. If yuh'da kilt 'im, we'd have a patrol on our tails right now."

"You didn't have to come. I could have gotten away by myself."

"Mebbe so," said Bridger, "but it woulda been risky. I didn't get yuh sprung jes' t'get yuh shot."

For a moment Gabe only scowled down at the post. Then he said, "But it was your idea to get me free, right from the beginning? *You* went to Price?"

Bridger chuckled dryly again. "He never woulda thought of it hisself. An' ol' Moonlight never woulda listened to me if Price hadn'ta changed his story."

"But how did you even know about me? Was it Two Face?"

"He got word to me afore they hung 'im. Then I had to ask around 'bout why you was in there." The scout turned in his saddle to face Gabe. "Talk about foolish," he said. "What possessed yuh t'pick a fight with 'im in the first place?"

"I didn't. He's the one who started it."

Bridger didn't say anything, just sat and stared in his direction.

"Well," said Gabe, "I was angry. It caused me to be careless."

"Glad to hear yuh say it, boy. I wish I could think yuh'd learned your lesson."

This time it was Gabe who remained silent.

"Yeah, well," said Bridger, "I weren't always the soul o' discretion when I was your age, either. In fact—"

The scout stopped talking and leaned forward in his saddle, looking at a new glow of light coming from the fort.

"Torches," he said, putting out a hand when Gabe took up his reins and started to ride away. "Wait up a minute. Mebbe they'll turn back. I gotta know if they're really comin' after us."

"Why, Bridger? What is this all about? You didn't really think I would work as a scout, did you?"

"Not hardly," said the scout. "Lissen—" But then he only stared down at the fort for a long time without saying anything. "Lissen," he finally said again. "I think we done a terrible thing to yuh, your mother an' me."

Gabe had a sinking sensation in his chest. "Then it was her idea to send me away, just as you told me five years ago."

"Yes it was," Bridger said with a sigh. "But it broke her heart to do it."

"You said she didn't want me in the camp," said Gabe,

remembering the story Two Face had told him. "You said I had become a burden to her."

Bridger shook his head. "That were the lie. That were the part that gave me bad dreams, boy. I could see what it done to yuh, an' it made me sick, but your mother begged me to make it so's yuh'd never think o' goin back."

"But *why,* Bridger?"

The light of the torches had moved slowly away from the post, spreading out over the hillside that Gabe and Bridger were heading for when the shooting started.

"Lookin' fer sign," said the scout. "Mebbe hopin' we stopped somewheres close by." Then he answered Gabe's question. "She seen bad times ahead, son. Yore maw heard about the gold in Arapaho country—what they're callin' Colorado now. She'd heard about the strikes in Montana, and the signs o' gold Raynolds was findin' in the Black Hills. Dammit, she knew the whites was gonna come in big numbers, boy, an' someday there wouldn't be no room for the Indians. She knew there weren't no *future* for yuh, so she wanted yuh to grow up a white man. Even if it meant losin' yuh forever."

Gabe felt a terrible emptiness, mixed with feelings of anger and betrayal that confused him. "She should have asked me," he said. "She should have asked what *I* wanted."

"You was fourteen," Bridger said patiently. "An' yuh hadn't never lived in the white man's world. She figgered she knew some things you didn't."

"Why didn't she come with us?" said Gabe, as if he hadn't conceded the first point but had plenty of other objections. "We could have left together."

"I wanted her to," said Bridger, his voice full of sadness. "But she didn't think there were anyplace left for her in p'lite society. She figgered she'd be an outcast after livin' with the Injuns."

Gabe was silent for a time, trying to imagine the way his mother must have felt. He remembered suddenly the way her mood had changed in the winter before he was taken away from her tepee. She had become quiet and unhappy, tears springing up in her eyes for no reason. Now he wondered if that was when she had lost hope in the future of the Lakota people and made the decision to send her son away.

Gabe noticed that the torchlight seemed to be pulling in on

itself, getting smaller. "Gettin' together for a parley," said Bridger. "Mebbe somebody come out to give 'em orders." A minute later the procession of lights began moving back toward the post, and the scout breathed a sigh of relief. "I have a feelin' Moonlight finally took a hand," he said, gigging his horse into motion. "Thank God fer simpleminded fools. With any luck there won't be no one comin' after us."

"But I still don't understand where we're going," said Gabe. "Why did you go to all this trouble? Just to tell me the story?"

"That were jes' part of it, boy. I had to clear my conscience. But I figger it's time yuh return the favor your maw tried to do. I want yuh to go an' get 'er."

A half-moon appeared on the horizon sometime after midnight, bringing a pale glow to the rolling prairie and to the frosty vapor that appeared before their lips in the chilled night air. The half-moon was still visible when the sky turned gray and then blue-white, and even when the giant ball of the sun loomed up in the east. Jim and Gabe lost the sun again when they rode down off a ridge and walked their mounts into a winding stream lined with cottonwood and willow trees. Bridger was half dozing in the saddle, listening to the horses sucking up the water, when Gabe said something that woke him up.

"Yuh wanna do what?" said the scout.

"This is a good place for *inipi*," said Gabe. "Everything required for purification can be found here."

Bridger looked at the boy to make sure he was serious, then glanced up at the ridges around them. "This is a helluva time to take a sweat bath."

Gabe looked puzzled. "I don't want to take a bath in sweat," he said. "It's the inside of my body that must be cleaned. I lived in chains in a white man's prison and my"—he was frowning now, searching for the word—"my *ni* has become very weak."

"Your what?"

"I don't know what the white man calls it, Bridger. It is the same thing as my life. I take it in when I breathe." Gabe inhaled deeply and let the air out slowly, shaking his head. "I can feel the weakness, Bridger. My *ni* must be strong, to travel through me and put out the bad things."

The scout was looking at Gabe with his head cocked a little to one side, either trying to understand Gabe's words or trying to figure out whether he really believed them. Gabe held up his right hand to show the crooked finger and the swollen, crusted hole in his palm.

"Christ A'mighty," Bridger breathed. "We should've set that finger last night."

"I tried, but I don't think it will go straight again."

"The puncture ain't lookin' none too good, neither."

"Because my *ni* is not strong enough to fight the sickness!" Gabe said, still holding up his hand. "That's what I'm trying to tell you."

Bridger dug into the saddlebags behind his thigh and came up with a couple of bandannas and a tin flask. "Then it oughta have some help," he said.

Gabe gnawed at the inside of his lip while the old mountain man poured whiskey on both sides of the puncture and wrapped his hand in cloth. Then he squeezed his eyes closed to fight the tears when Bridger pulled roughly on the tip of the broken finger, making it wobble above the last joint.

"Goddamn," he said. "Feels like the joint's shattered all to hell. Maybe a piece o' bone is gettin' in the way."

The scout slipped off his pony and went crashing through the trees along the stream, coming back with a small branch that was bent at more or less the same angle as Gabe's finger. He sliced the stick in half with a keen-edged Green River knife, then wrapped the broken finger between the two halves.

"Yuh know," he said, glancing again toward the ridges of the little valley, "that sergeant jes' mighta talked Moonlight into comin' after yuh. Not to mention what a band of Oglala'd do if they caught us here."

Gabe shook his head. "The colonel will not listen to the sergeant. And the Oglala are my people."

"Christ A'mighty—"

"And if you're right," said Gabe, "then it's even more important to prepare myself. *Inipi* will make me strong for a fight, if there is one, and it will help me have the power to receive dreams and visions, so I may know what to do." Gabe studied Bridger's face while the older man tied a final knot in the bandanna around the splints. "Do you find the Indian ways foolish, Bridger? Is that what bothers you?"

"Hell, no!" said the scout. "Ain't nobody ever made sport of 'em without gettin' a good dressin'-down from me. I even hired me a Snake medicine man once, when ol' Fitzpatrick was late bringin' trade goods to the rendezvous.'' Bridger's eyes had a dreamy, faraway look. "Them was the days," he said with a long sigh. "We was *all* free redskins back then." The faraway look changed slowly to one of sadness. "But those days're gone, boy. That's one o' the things I been wantin' to say. The wild Injuns are gonna get swallowed up by the white man, an' things ain't never gonna be the same. It's comin' on a bad time to be an Injun.''

Gabe frowned at his bandaged hand. "The finger feels better," he said thoughtfully. "It's a strange thing, Bridger. Two Face told me the same thing.''

"'Cause he saw the way it's gonna be, boy. That's why I got yuh off the post.''

"To go back and help my people?''

"No! To get your mother *away* from them.''

Gabe remembered the way Fort Laramie had looked from the ridge the night before, so small in the middle of the great prairie. "I think you are wrong," he said. "The white men are few, the Lakota many.''

"Mebbe so, right now, in this here part of the world. But there's more of 'em where I come from than you can even think of, boy. An' now that they're done fightin' each other, half of 'em is comin' this way. Believe me," Bridger pleaded, "the white man has great power—big medicine that will defeat the Indian. Your mother's in terrible danger.''

Gabe was clearly finding it hard to believe. "You told me yourself she will not want to leave the People.''

"Prob'ly not," Bridger said with a dark look. "That's why yuh gotta force her. Take her away the same way she told me to take you.''

Gabe looked down at the old mountain man standing beside his pony. "My thoughts run around and around like the whirlwind," he said. "I must take care of *inipi*, so I can hear what you say with clear thoughts.''

Bridger wanted to argue, but he was tired and his bones were aching, and one look at the boy told him that any effort to change his mind would be wasted. "Goddammit," he growled, "I hope you know what kind o' rocks to use. I don't want nothin' blowin' up in my face.''

* * * *

They staked the horses on a patch of good grass on the other side of the stream while Gabe crisscrossed the hillside looking for small stones about the size of two fists put together. He ignored the ones that would crumble, as well as the ones that would explode and cause serious burns. By the time he had gathered a dozen proper stones, Bridger had chopped up some of the driest wood he could find. The scout didn't want a lot of smoke marking their position for any curious individuals who might be in the area.

Gabe laid the firewood, four pieces pointing east and west beneath four more running north and south. Then the two men piled the stones on top of the wood and set it afire. With a glance at Gabe's bandage-covered hand, Bridger volunteered to prepare the ground while Gabe went to chop willow saplings along the stream. The scout used his knife to cut through the sod and scoop out a dozen small holes in a seven-foot circle near the crackling fire. It wasn't long before Gabe came back with the same number of saplings and asked for Bridger's knife.

"What for?" said the scout.

"To remove the bark."

"The hell with that," said Bridger. "We can tie the frame with ropes."

"But the poles are supposed to be peeled," said Gabe. "That is the way."

"It ain't like you're goin' on a vision quest, boy. Everything don't gotta be perfect. Here, hand me one o' them poles." Gabe hesitated, and the scout put out his hand. "There ain't no time for this," he said.

Gabe knew it was sometimes necessary to alter the sacred ceremonies, but it was never easy to know which changes would be satisfactory to the spirits. "If I do something to displease Wakan-tanka," he said, "then I will not be granted the power of my *ni*. Something bad might happen."

"It's breathin' in the steam, boy, that's th' important thing. An' goin' in there with the right frame o' mind. The Great Spirit'll know you're in a hurry. Now give me the damn pole!"

Gabe hesitated a moment longer before giving it up. "All right," he said, picking out another sapling and beginning to peel off long strips of bark. "I won't scrape them clean. But we won't use rope, either. I'll take off just enough to tie the poles. I don't want anything from the white man's world inside the lodge.''

"Christ A'mighty, *you're* a white man!''

"I had white parents,'' said Gabe, his face closing up in a stubborn way. "But the white world is not my world.''

Bridger only groaned, jamming the butt end of a slender sapling into one of the holes. He filled in around it and tamped down the loose dirt with his foot, repeating the procedure in the next hole while Gabe continued to accumulate strips of bark. When he felt he had enough, Gabe used the knife to begin scraping a shallow pit at the center of the ring of poles that Bridger was creating around him. The pit had to be large enough to hold the dozen stones heating on the fire.

Bridger noticed that Gabe was scooping dirt with his injured hand, and switched jobs with him again. Gabe finished planting the saplings while the scout dug with his knife. In the deep silence of the prairie there was only the scraping of the knife and the crackling of the fire and the sharp sound of the horses ripping up grass across the stream.

Then Gabe took a deep breath and asked, "Are you in love with my mother?''

Bridger didn't stop working. "Always have been,'' he said matter-of-factly. "Ever since I fust laid eyes on 'er in St. Louis. But she were married to your paw already.''

"Do you want her now?''

Bridger nodded, rocking back on his knees for a moment and looking into the distance with sad eyes. "But it's no good,'' he said after a while. "I got me a wife an' two young-uns, waitin' on the farm back in Missouri. I'm doin' this for you an' your maw's sake, an' that's all.''

Gabe turned away and began pulling one of the saplings down over the stone pit at the center of the circle. Bridger jumped up to bend one from the other side, until they met in the middle to form an arch. The scout held them there while Gabe retrieved the strips of bark, which he used to tie the saplings together. Then the men pulled two more saplings across the circle and tied them with the first two, repeating the procedure four more times until they had formed a small dome about four feet high.

Bridger watched the boy, trying to read his thoughts as Gabe began roaming the grass near the lodge, pulling up clumps of sage. When he had a handful, he spread them across the north side of the circle enclosed by the framework, then stepped back to survey his handiwork.

"I hope the Great Spirit comes and talks to you in there," Bridger said with a frown. "An' I sure hope he knows what he's talkin' about."

CHAPTER SEVEN

Gabe was forced to accept two compromises in his desire to ban objects from the white world. He covered the dome-shaped frame of his lodge with blankets from Bridger's packhorse, since no animal skins were available, and he carried water in a canteen as a substitute for a buffalo bladder. But he stripped off his new uniform and left it in a pile in the yellow grass. He was completely naked when he crawled inside to prepare for purification.

Bridger used a pair of heavy forked sticks to lift the heated stones out of the embers and pass them into the lodge one by one, where Gabe arranged them in the shallow pit in a sacred pattern. The scout also handed in one of the embers, which Gabe added to the pit. He covered the coal with sage so he could breathe the sweet-smelling smoke and rub it over his arms and body. He also held his pipe in the smoke, to purify this last gift from Two Face. Attached to the pipe was a small deerskin bag filled with *chanshasha*, or *kinnikinnik*, the tobacco that Indians shredded from the inner bark of the red willow. Gabe offered up a twist of the tobacco to the four sacred directions as a sacrifice, then laid the twist on the ground near the pit and the pipe. Finally he settled himself on the small blanket of sage he had prepared and asked Bridger to cover the entrance of the lodge.

Several minutes went by while Gabe's eyes adjusted to the blackness, which was relieved only by the glowing coal and two or three pinpoints of light leaking through the blankets. Gabe told Bridger where the leaks were so the scout could cover them. By then the coal had extinguished itself, and after another minute or so Gabe could see the dull red glow of the rocks themselves. They had become the only source of light in the lodge, and Gabe called out that he was satisfied. Bridger mumbled a reply and went off toward the ridge to stand watch.

Gabe felt for the canteen by his side and drank some of the water, then splashed more of it over his face and hair before he soaked a kind of dipper he'd made from sage and willow sprigs. He used the dipper to sprinkle water on the hot stones—four times—and immediately there came a sharp cracking sound, like a rifle shot. Just as suddenly the lodge was filled with steam, and for an instant Gabe thought he had made a mistake.

He had forgotten how frightening purification could be. The steam pressed in all around him and felt as if it were burning his skin. Instinctively he tried to escape it by folding his body down over his knees, but the air near the ground was just as oppressive as the heat collecting near the roof only a few feet above his head.

Sweat started pouring from his face and stinging his eyes at the same time that the rocks stopped glowing, blinding him in his confinement. There was only the blackness and the continuous, ominous hissing of steam as the water hit the stones. It seemed to take the air out of the lodge, leaving Gabe with nothing to breathe except the steam that seared his lungs. The smell of the sage was overwhelming now, tasting bitter on his tongue, while the rocks hissed and the steam heat pressed down in the darkness, and the urge to escape almost overwhelmed him.

But Gabe mastered his impulses, chanting the sacred songs he remembered. He asked Grandfather and Wakan-tanka to take pity on him in the Lakota meaning of the word—that his prayers be heard and answered. Then he sprinkled more water on the stones and braced himself for another onslaught of steam. This time it wasn't as bad, and he knew he would get through the purification without making an opening for fresh air, as some did. There was even something pleasant about it by the fourth and last time he sprinkled water on the rocks. This was the feeling he remembered, the feeling of purity and well-being. There was less pain in his hand, and he could tell that it would begin to heal itself. He prayed to the Great Spirit for wisdom and understanding, and the power to do the things that are right. Then he gathered up the canteen and his pipe and went outside.

There wasn't much left to do. Gabe pulled up more sage and rubbed it over his body while he watched Bridger begin the long walk back down from the ridge, his big Sharps carbine settled in the crook of his arm. The scout had come about halfway when Gabe went to the stream and plunged into the snow-fed water. Its currents swept over his skin as he lay in the stream with his eyes closed. He felt as if there were no weight in his body, and no bones to hold it together or hold it down. He almost felt like he could float into the air and soar with the eagles.

It was a blissful sensation of peace and harmony and strength. The morning sun shone red through his eyelids, and the bad years of Fort Laramie fell away from him like dead skin from an old wound, leaving only the fresh growth of his new spirit. He was reborn in the ways of his people.

"Have any visions in there?"

Gabe opened his eyes to see the scout standing over him at the edge of the stream. He shook his head, the long strands of his hair swirling about him in the flow of the water. "I was asking for strength, Bridger, not visions."

"Mebbe so," said the scout, staring down at him, "but a vision or two wouldn't hurt yuh none, after all them years in white man's clothes. Yuh sure look different from when I brung yuh to the fort, Gabe. The Oglala might jes' kill yuh right off, soon as they see that white skin."

Gabe stood up and climbed out onto the bank, aware of the way his pale arms and legs almost glowed in the sunlight. He'd been much darker when he'd arrived at the fort, his skin deeply bronzed after many years on the open plains. Life at the post and three years in a dark cell had taken their toll, but he still didn't think he looked as bad as a real white man.

"It *isn't* white," he said. "Not like the soldiers."

"That's true," Bridger admitted. "Nobody'll ever be convinced yuh ain't part Injun. But yuh better be damn careful if yuh plan on headin' north."

"I will travel slowly, exposing my flesh to the sun."

"What about your hair? It ain't no darker than the sand along the stream there, and *that* sure ain't gonna change."

"My people will know me by my hair. 'Here comes Long

Rider,' they will say. 'Let us give thanks for his return.'"

The scout rolled his eyes toward the sky. "Lissen, boy—"

"I am not a boy."

"Then act like a man, dammit, an' do the thing yuh know is right!"

"You're thinking of my mother again."

"She needs to be someplace safe, an' you're the only one who can go into that country an' bring 'er out."

"I have thought on this matter, Bridger. I remembered that you yourself said there would be no place for her in the white world."

"I said that's what *she* thought."

"Is it not true?"

"It mighta been. Once. But people are movin' West now that the war's ended. There's gonna be whole new towns out here, with folks comin' from all over. Everyone'll be strangers. That means someone like your maw could start fresh. There ain't nobody'd have to know what she done or where she been."

"We would still be living among the whites," said Gabe. "We would still be among our enemies."

"They wasn't always your maw's enemies. Go ahead an' ask her about it why don't yuh. She'll tell yuh there's good whites an' bad whites, jes' like there's good redskins and bad 'uns."

Gabe turned away with a thoughtful look and started walking slowly toward the pile of clothing he'd left near the sweat lodge.

"She'll prob'ly end up with the whites, *anyway*," Bridger persisted, following along behind. "They'll find her as soon as the wild tribes get rounded up an' sent to reservations. What's gonna happen then, do yuh think? The soldiers'll take her back, o' course, an' by God, the whole world'll *know* she were livin' with the savages."

Gabe turned around with a sharp look.

"*I* know they ain't savages," said the scout. "I'm talkin' about the way other folks'll see things."

"But none of that will ever happen," said Gabe. He had reached the pile of clothes, light and dark shades of blue in the tall yellow grass, and he was looking down at them with obvious distaste. "The Lakota will never give up the Powder River country. It's our last free hunting ground."

"That's exactly where you're wrong," Bridger said, as if he were pleading. "It's the thing I been tryin' to get through to yuh. The Sioux won't have no *choice*, 'cause the whites are gonna overrun 'em like a plague o' locusts. Yuh can't imagine how many there are. There's more whites back East than all the buffalo yuh ever seen.''

Gabe shot him a skeptical look, and Bridger threw up his hands.

"It's true, bo—Gabe. It's true, an' yuh gotta believe it. They got powerful medicine too. Yuh seen some of it at the post, like the new gun that shoots many times without reloading. Plenty of young women will cry in their lodges if more soldiers get their hands on those guns. There's even stuff yuh ain't seen yet, like the long metal rails they're gettin' ready to run across the country. They're gonna have these big locomotives . . . big engines made of iron that'll run over the rails, draggin' along these . . . well, these little houses on wheels. Pull 'em right along like a pony pullin' a travois.''

Gabe was pulling on the sky-blue uniform trousers with thin yellow stripes on the side, still squinting at the old mountain man.

"I swear it's true," said Bridger. "Ever' las' word. There ain't no way o' tellin' yuh how bad it's gonna be if the Oglala keep fightin' the whites.''

"Then my place is with them. I must help my people fight.''

"Christ A'mighty," Bridger roared, "*they ain't yore people!*''

Gabe slipped into the heavy flannel tunic, then looked at the sun above him and took it off. He threw it to the ground. "You would rather I live among the whites?" he said with contempt. "The same ones who steal land and kill human beings for the yellow metal?''

"Yellow metal, horses, good hunting grounds—what's the difference what people die for? 'Sides, that's the way your mother wanted it.''

Gabe tried not to show the emptiness that came into his heart. "I can't believe that, but I will find out," he promised, pushing his feet into the stiff black army boots. "I will meditate on this some more and seek guidance from the spirits.''

"Well, make sure yuh mention that it's your maw you're talkin' about," Bridger grumbled. "The one who gave yuh birth an' brung yuh up, an' sent yuh off with Ol' Gabe even if it tore her heart to pieces.''

Gabe stopped struggling with the boots for a moment, giving the scout a thoughtful look. "That name," he said. "The sergeant used it too."

"Jed Smith was the one who started it," Bridger said with a laugh. "I took things pretty serious back then, an' Ol' Jed said it tickled his funny bone, seein' me so solemn all the time. Said I looked like the world was comin' to an end, an' I was jes' like Gabriel—"

"Sure!" said Gabe. "I remember him. The archangel was a messenger from God!"

Bridger's look of surprise lasted for only a moment. Then he smiled. "I forget you're a Bible reader, too, jes' like ol' Jed. Your mother told me she used it to teach yuh how to read."

"I think she also wanted to teach me about the white man's spirit world," said Gabe, "so I would be ready when the time came. I can see that now. But why do we have the same name, Bridger? Is it just an accident?"

Bridger's smile turned wistful. "No, it weren't no accident."

"Was it her idea or yours?"

The old scout lowered his eyes. "It were hers," he said modestly. "I guess she figgered some o' my good luck would rub off on you."

"Perhaps she thought of more than luck," said Gabe. "You have lived a long life, and other men honor your bravery. Among the Oglala you would be called Grandfather. Your words would be listened to with respect."

"Then listen to 'em," said Bridger, his sharp blue eyes flashing with humor. "I'm tellin' yuh to go find your mother an' get her out of the Powder River country afore it's too late. Take her someplace where she can live in peace."

"I will think on it," Gabe assured him. "But there's still something I don't understand. Aren't you afraid I'll warn the Oglala of General Connor's plans?"

"I'm hopin' yuh will," said Bridger, smiling at Gabe's look of surprise. "Hell, their scouts'll prob'ly see the soldiers comin' in plenty of time, anyway. But I think the government's makin' a terrible mistake, sendin' the troops out with one hand while they're tryin' to make peace with the other. I'm hopin' fer peace, myself, so I figger if there ain't much fightin' this summer, an' things has a chance to simmer down a bit . . ."

Gabe looked even more surprised. "You think the Oglala will

run away from the soldiers?''

''I'd rather have 'em *stay* away. That'd be the smartest thing. There's gonna be more'n two thousand soldiers. I'm hopin' they'll jes' march around a while an' leave. Then a peace commission will come out in the fall, lookin' to make a treaty.''

''But there will be no treaty,'' Gabe said. ''The Oglala won't allow a road.''

''I know they won't *like* it,'' Bridger said with a scowl. ''Hell, that's why I staked out another road on the other side of the Big Horn last year. But the gov'ment's pushin' the Bozeman Road 'cause it's shorter.'' He looked pleadingly at Gabe. ''It's jes' a road, Gabe. Jes' people passin' through.''

Gabe shook his head firmly. ''The Oglala will fight.''

The scout's forehead creased in a troubled frown. ''Mebbe you're right,'' he said, turning away, ''an' mebbe this is a bad mistake I'm makin'. But I got somethin' from the sutler when I knew I was gonna get yuh out o' the guardhouse.''

Bridger started walking away, and Gabe followed him after a moment, as soon as he'd recovered from his surprise. They crossed the stream and headed toward the horses. The scout unlaced the flap of one of his saddlebags and took out a flat wooden box, giving Gabe another thoughtful look before he opened the top of the box.

A brace of Remington revolvers lay inside, fitted into a green felt lining. There was also a small powder flask in the box, and something else Gabe couldn't identify. He touched it with his fingers.

''That there's a bullet mold,'' said Bridger. ''Any kind o' metal yuh can melt, yuh can pour in there to make a ball.''

Gabe's fingers moved away from the bullet mold and closed around one of the revolvers, lifting it from the case. ''You bought these *for me*?''

''I figgered I owed yuh, boy. Gabe. Mebbe I made another mistake when I brung yuh to the post five years ago. Who's to say? But I'm gonna leave yuh with one o' the horses an' these here six-shooters . . . an' a few pointers that might come in handy.'' He nodded at the one in Gabe's hand. ''I assume yuh ain't had much experience with 'em.''

Gabe shook his head. ''The warriors have captured only a few of them,'' he said with reverence, ''and guarded them closely.''

''That's what I thought,'' said Bridger, squatting down to

place the wooden box on-the ground. He pulled out the other weapon and the tin powder flask, which had the teardrop shape of a miniature bellows. Holding the revolver with the barrel pointed straight up, he uncapped the flask and tilted the nozzle toward one of the chambers in the upended cylinder. "I already got some powder in the horn," he said. "But there's another half keg packed away. You'll get used to how much yuh gotta put in. Yuh jes' dump it in the chamber like this. Then yuh put in a ball." He reached inside a pouch on his belt and pulled out a rounded chunk of lead, holding it up against the sky. "Yuh gotta make sure it's clean, an' make sure there ain't no chips or dents that'll make it fly off-true. Then yuh shove it into the chamber. It'll be a tight squeeze, which is how it stays where it's supposed to. But that means yuh gotta push it in hard an' ram it home with this contraption."

Bridger rotated the cylinder until the chamber he'd just filled was in line with the bottom of the frame, then pulled at a rod beneath the barrel. The rod was actually a lever, mounted on a hinge in such a way that it pushed a plunger through a hole in the frame of the Remington and into the chamber. Bridger pressed down hard on the plunger, then moved the rod back to its original position beneath the barrel. Then he handed over the revolver and the flask and watched Gabe fill the rest of the chambers, spilling powder and feeling generally awkward as he struggled with his stiff right hand.

Gabe was also thinking about trying to load the weapons in the middle of a fight.

"Yuh'll get used to 'er," said Bridger, guessing Gabe's thoughts. "An' yuh won't always have your fingers bandaged up like that. Won't be long afore yuh can do it with your eyes closed. But she still ain't ready to fire. Yuh still need somethin' to set the powder off."

The scout took back the Remington and reached once more beneath the stiff flap of his belt pouch, coming out with a handful of tiny metal stubs that gleamed in his palm.

"Copper caps," he said. "They blow up when somethin' hits 'em, so they go here."

He pressed one down over a protruding nipple on the back of the cylinder, then gave the revolver back to Gabe. A minute later Gabe had five more caps in place.

"Now yuh gotta be careful," said Bridger, " 'cause one o'

the chambers could go off if anything hits the hammer. Some folks keep an empty chamber under the hammer, but I like havin' all six ready to go. Yuh never know when one of 'em'll go bad on yuh. Mebbe the powder gets damp, or it pulls away from the back end o' the chamber, where the fire from the cap goes through. Yuh might even get a bad cap. Anyway, I feel safer if I put in new loads after a hard rain, say. Or a long, bouncy ride.''

Gabe only nodded, concentrating on every word as Bridger went on to talk about straight shooting.

"Yuh gotta decide what works best for your ownself,'' he said. ''An' even that'll depend on what the other guy is doin'. If he's any distance away—say, six yards or more—why, then yuh oughta aim across the top o' the gun. Yuh don't wanna rush things, either, 'cause that first shot's the one that counts. But any closer than six yards—especially when the other man is goin' for a weapon at the same time—then shootin' from the hip starts to make some sense. Yuh get so it's like pointin' a finger. All yuh need is practice, Gabe, an' lots *of* it. Try shootin' at big trees an' watchin' where the balls go. I wish I could stay to help yuh out, but things'll go a little easier if I head back to the post.''

Gabe shook his head. ''Don't worry,'' he said. ''I'm grateful for the things you've done already. I could still be in the guardhouse. What will you tell the soldiers?''

''I'll jes' keep sayin' I sent yuh on a special scouting mission to take a look-see aroun' the country. An' if yuh don't come back''—the old man shrugged—''well, it's a dangerous business. Moonlight won't like it much, mebbe, but he ain't gonna last much longer, anyway.''

''Why do you say that?''

''He'll make one mistake too many, an' somebody's bound to notice. I jes' hope it happens afore he gets somebody killed.''

''Make sure it isn't you, Bridger.''

The scout tilted his head to one side, his keen blue eyes locked with Gabe's, and after a moment he realized he was looking up. ''Yuh sure grew into a *big* sumbitch,'' he said with a smile. ''Your mother'll be right proud to see yuh again. Tell her I was askin' for her.''

''I will.''

''An' there's one more thing I wanted yuh to have,'' said

Bridger. He picked up the well-worn Sharps carbine he'd propped against a tree and held it out with a little flourish, but Gabe only stared at the rifle and didn't move.

"Go ahead an' take it," said the old man. "I been wantin' to switch to a Spencer, anyway, or maybe one o' them Henrys. Repeaters are gonna come in handy, I bet. The Army woulda issued yuh one to carry as a scout, but where you're goin', it won't be easy comin' up with them new metallic cartridges. The Sharps'll make a lot more sense. An' yuh can't beat it for hittin' what yuh aim at."

Gabe finally accepted the rifle, afraid that a foolish grin was about to appear on his face. He lifted the stock to his cheek, as he had seen the soldiers do, and lined up the front bead in the sight.

"That there's called a leaf sight," said the scout. "Makes it so yuh can hit things way out. But it's marked in yards, which ain't gonna mean much till yuh get used to it. It's mebbe fifty yards back to the sweat lodge, say, an' about three hunnert up to the top o' that ridge." Bridger kept his eyes fixed on the ridge while his expression turned thoughtful. "I jes' hope yuh don't put no soldiers in them sights," he said. "I hope yuh use it to take care o' your duty."

Gabe lowered the rifle and looked at the scout. He understood the meaning of Bridger's words, but he didn't know how to answer.

Bridger tilted his head again, studying Gabe's eyes. Then he clamped a leathery hand on his shoulder. "Anyway," he said, "I'll wish yuh good luck an' easy travelin', young Gabe."

"Thanks, old Gabe."

Both men were smiling, but the scout turned serious again. "Have yuh got any ideas on what you'll do?" he said.

Gabe looked down at the Sharps, thinking of the power he held in his hands. "I wish I could tell you," he said softly, "but I just don't know."

CHAPTER EIGHT

Gabe had been trailing an Oglala hunting party for more than half a day when he brought his pony to a sudden stop, leaning forward a little to study a second trail that joined the one he'd been following.

The new path of trampled yellow grass was wide enough to show that the second group was much larger than the first. Seven or eight riders had come in from the west, and they had changed direction when they came across the older trail. They had also lashed their mounts into a sudden gallop, leaving half-moon cuts in the prairie sod. Gabe frowned at the cuts with a growing sense of urgency, hoping he was wrong about their meaning. He imagined that the air had been filled with war whoops and high-pitched cries of defiance when the new arrivals lashed their horses into a flat-out run.

There was always the possibility that the second trail had been made by other Oglala, or members of a neighboring Sioux band like the Brule or the Hunkpapa. Perhaps they were even friendly Shyela or Blue Cloud—known as Cheyenne and Arapaho to the whites. But it wasn't likely that one party would change direction and gallop off to follow another. War and hunting expeditions tended to be individual, independent operations. It also worried Gabe that the second trail came from the west and a little to the north—from the land of the Lakota's traditional enemies, the Crow.

Gabe mounted his horse and urged it into a gentle lope, even more alert than before, and feeling more uneasy about the meaning of the two trails. He believed there were only three Oglala hunters in the first group, who would be outnumbered more than two to one by the second group. He also knew that the war party—he was pretty sure of this now—would have the advantage of surprise. Gabe pushed the pony to a faster pace, feeling a little easier in his mind when it responded with an eagerness to match his own.

Jim Bridger had given him his pick of the three mounts they'd brought along, and Gabe felt he had chosen wisely. It was a small horse, even for a mustang, but it had a deep chest and a restlessness that hinted at durability and spirit. It was also bred and raised for a life on the plains. Bridger had said he bought the mustang from a tame Oglala who'd never fed it grain, and after seven days of travel Gabe was willing to believe the story. The pony was still going strong on nothing more than the well-cured grass of early summer.

Gabe had moved slowly after parting with the old mountain man, covering only a few miles each day and being careful to avoid contact with Indians while his broken finger healed and his skin turned dark under the sun. He got into the habit of stopping late in the afternoon to cook supper, building his fires under trees or rock overhangs to diffuse the smoke. After supper he would practice shooting and loading the Sharps and the Remingtons until sunset, making sure that he never emptied all three weapons at once. Then he would move on under cover of darkness to set up a cold camp somewhere else, so anyone who might have seen his smoke or heard the shots would not be able to find him.

His practice with the weapons proved to be awkward at first, since it was the trigger finger of his right hand that he'd broken on Captain Price's jaw. He hoped it would be usable someday —that he could learn how to curl the crooked joint inside a trigger guard—but for the time being, he was forced to use his middle finger. That meant he had to grip the butt of a revolver with only two of his remaining fingers, which also happened to be the weakest and the smallest. He felt so uncertain about the fragile grip that he began to practice with his left hand as well as his right, and by the seventh day the weapons had begun to feel natural to him. He had also become fairly accurate with a

Remington in either hand.

Gabe had learned enough about the Sharps by the third day to bring down a young mule deer, which affected his appearance as much as the sun did. Gabe soft-tanned the hide and cut a wide strip to make a comfortable belt, replacing the stiff army belt that had been cutting into his skin. He decided to keep the holster, however, as well as the pouches that were designed to carry caps and balls. He had to admit that the white man made some useful things. On the other hand, he was glad to abandon the heavy army boots after he'd spent several hours sewing a pair of moccasins for himself—long and tedious hours when he began looking forward to finding a wife of his own.

He tried to think of something else almost immediately. The thought of women always led him to remember one in particular. Her name was Yellow Buckskin Girl, and her image had formed in his mind a thousand times during his captivity at Fort Laramie, bringing with it a painful longing and an inability to concentrate on anything else. There was no relief from the longing, even now that he was returning to the Oglala, since it was almost certain that she would already be taken by another man. For a moment he allowed himself to hope that Yellow Buckskin Girl had spurned other suitors, until he remembered that five years had passed since his unexplained disappearance. She would not be expecting to see him again. He turned to his other tasks with a heavy sadness in his breast.

Making a breechclout was easier than sewing the moccasins. Gabe only needed to cut a wide strip of hide that he could fold under his belt in back, then pass between his legs before folding it over his belt against his stomach. That left a long flap that gave him a second layer of protection in front. Eventually he would paint designs on the flap, when his visions had taught him more about the animals and spirits that governed his life. For now he was content to wear only the breechclout and the moccasins as he rode, enjoying the warm sun and cool breezes against his skin.

It was mid-morning of the seventh day when Gabe came across a kill site on the upper reaches of Spotted Horse Creek, marked by two broken arrows and a stain of fresh blood in the grass. Gabe recognized the arrow shafts as Oglala and saw that the hunters' trail led toward the traditional Lakota camping places along the Powder River. He guessed that the hunters had left the site that same morning, and he decided to follow them, hoping to catch up by nightfall. He was filled with excitement as he rode, eager for a chance to hear news of his friends. He also realized it would be easier to fall in with a small hunting party that could take him safely into one of the Oglala villages.

Now the Oglala hunters had become the hunted, and Gabe was driving the mustang to its limits. The sun had traveled about the width of his hand when he came to a place where the newer path ended in a large circle of crushed grass. The stopping place was just behind the crest of a low rise, and it was clear to Gabe that the riders had waited here while one of their number went ahead to observe the Oglala. Then the larger party had veered off to the right, still hidden by the ridge that ran beside Spotted Horse Creek.

Gabe felt sure that if he continued over the rise, he would find the Oglala making camp on the creek not far ahead, but he decided against going to warn them. It would remove only part of the surprise, since the time and manner of the attack would remain unknown. The Oglala would also still be outnumbered and on the defensive.

Gabe turned off to follow the enemy trail behind the ridge.

The trail angled up the ridge and disappeared over the top. Gabe stayed behind it, sliding off his pony and crawling the last few yards to the crest, where he finally saw the enemy war party across a wide and shallow wash. The warriors were concealing themselves from the Oglala on the side of an earth mound that lay between them and the creek. They appeared to be Crow, although Gabe couldn't be sure at this distance. He let his eyes sweep across the wash, and then he squinted again at the warriors, guessing that they were about four hundred and fifty yards away. The number came to his mind automatically. He had been forming the habit of estimating distances as he traveled. He wanted to learn the white man's measure of distance so he could use the white man's rifle.

Gabe counted seven Crow. Six were lying in the grass at the top of the mound, watching the Oglala just as Gabe was watching them, while a young boy held their horses near the bottom of the wash. There were nine mounts altogether. The Crow either had lost two warriors or had managed to steal two horses. Now they were expecting to acquire more horses, probably in a night raid, and perhaps even take a few Oglala scalps in the bargain.

Gabe saw only one rifle among the Crow, an old smoothbore musket. He assumed there might also be a revolver, but it was more likely that the other warriors would be carrying bows and arrows and clubs.

Gabe also saw, however, that he would not be able to surprise the Crow if he used his horse. There was nothing but grass as far as he could see—not a single tree or even a large rock—and the land rolled in long, steady swells that allowed for unbroken views. He might have had better luck in the dark, but he knew he couldn't wait. The Crow were waiting for the same thing.

His only choices were to mount a bold assault on horseback or try to sneak up on the war party through the grass. He knew that if he tried approaching on foot and was discovered too early, he would be helpless against seven mounted Crow. It was not a pleasant thing to think about. But if he attacked on horseback, the Crow were sure to reach their horses no matter how fast he rode. They would still be very dangerous to him, and to the small party of Oglala on the other side of the mound.

Gabe crawled back from the crest of the ridge and staked his horse so it wouldn't run away, then carefully examined his weapons. He glanced at the sun and decided there wasn't time to reload the revolvers as Bridger had suggested. Instead he used the ramrod on each chamber to make sure the powder and ball were tightly packed. He also made sure that each cap was in place before he put one of the revolvers back in its holster and tucked the other one inside his belt. He slung the Sharps carbine across his back.

A white man would have been ready to fight now, but an Oglala warrior felt better if he'd asked for help from his protector spirits. Gabe retrieved Two Face's pipe from the saddlebag and offered it to the powers of the four directions. He set fire to a twig with a white man's lucifer, then used the twig to light the pipe. Breathing in the smoke of the *chanshasha*, he felt the power of the spirits enter his body. It was a physical sensation. He knew he had pleased Wakan-tanka by the offering of his prayer, and he sensed the spirits' presence in the smoke. It made him feel strong, and drove out any fears or thoughts that might distract him.

There was no change in the scene below when Gabe went back to the crest of the ridge. With another anxious glance at the sun he began crawling down through the tall grass on the other side. The air had fallen very still, forcing Gabe to stop whenever the horse holder looked around. It was part of the boy's job to act as a guard, so he would be alert for any unusual movement in the grass. But the boy spent most of his time watching the other warriors on the hillside.

The sun looked like a dusky red ball resting on the rim of the prairie by the time Gabe had come close to the boy and the horses. He lay very still in the grass while he eased the Sharps around to his shoulder, thanking the spirits that the boy had failed to detect his presence. Gabe was feeling a little sorry that the horse holder would have to pay such a high price for this failure in his duty. He looked small above the bead in the notch of the leaf sight. But Gabe told himself that the boy was thirsting for the chance to kill an Oglala, and a coldness came into his heart as he pulled back the heavy side hammer of the Sharps.

The boy turned when he heard the sound, and their eyes met as Gabe pulled the trigger. The boy had opened his mouth to call out a warning, but his voice lifted into a scream when the ball tore through his chest. The force of the huge bullet knocked the boy backward, and he threw up his hands as he fell, releasing the horses and clutching at his heart.

Gabe was on his feet and running while the explosion still echoed down the wash, sliding the Sharps around to his back and out of the way. The Crow were also running, but he had made sure that he was closer to the horses than they were. Through the ringing in his ears their war cries sounded even farther away. A couple of arrows arced toward him and thudded into the ground.

The boy rolled over onto his belly among the milling horses, his legs twitching and his fingers digging into the grass. The ball had torn a fist-sized hole through his back, and blood was bubbling up through the ragged flesh. Gabe stepped over him and jumped onto the nearest pony, seeing that the boy's spine gleamed white through the hole. Gabe felt nothing but the cold rage that had overtaken him. He shouted a fierce, animal cry and wheeled the horse around to drive the rest of the horses away from the oncoming Crow.

One of the ponies bolted in the wrong direction. A warrior

leapt onto its back and came toward Gabe with his war club raised high. He was only a few feet away when Gabe pulled the Remington from his belt and shot the Crow off the horse. The revolver exploded almost above the pony's ear, and it ran back toward the Crow. They tried to surround the animal but it skittered away.

One warrior was still running downhill, quickly closing the distance. Gabe aimed the Remington again, but the cap snapped harmlessly on a bad load. The Crow let loose with a taunting scream, lowering his lance and never breaking stride. Gabe pulled back the hammer again with the web of flesh between his thumb and broken trigger finger, just as Bridger had shown him, and he had a fleeting picture of himself. It was a moment of cool pleasure when he realized how calmly he was facing the warrior. It seemed as if he lacked the part of a man that feels fear. There was no trembling in his arms, no weakness in his legs as he cocked the pistol and pulled the trigger.

This time he didn't have a chance to aim, however, and when the smoke cleared, the warrior was still running at him, trying to impale him with the lance. Gabe cocked the revolver again, looking puzzled. Then he saw a smear of blood on the warrior's naked belly. The Crow's legs faltered, and he tumbled into the grass. He rolled over to stare up at Gabe with eyes that were briefly alive with hatred and determination and anguish over his helplessness at dying.

The other warriors had given up on the stray horse. It danced nervously just behind them as they came running toward Gabe again. The Crow with the old musket stopped suddenly, farther back on the side of the hill, taking careful aim now that there were no other Crow in the line of fire. Gabe snapped a shot at him and emptied the rest of the chambers at the others while he kicked his pony into a sprint, hearing the crash of the musket just as he slid over onto the off-side.

The ball whistled across the back of his pony, where he'd been sitting a moment before. It was followed by the soft hiss of three or four arrows. But Gabe was already racing away to make another pass at the horses, sticking to the strategy he'd decided on even before he started his crawl through the grass. He drove the ponies farther down the wash until he thought there was enough distance between them and their owners. Then he made a wide circle around the enraged Crow, heading back toward the top of the hill. He thought it was time to see if the Oglala were coming to investigate—and maybe give him a hand.

He met three warriors riding hard up the other side. Gabe didn't recognize them, and they changed direction as soon as he appeared on the ridge, eyeing him with wary expressions, but his heart filled with pleasure.

"Come help me whip the Crow!" he cried.

Gabe continued his circle around the crest of the hill, knowing that the Oglala wouldn't be too far behind. They'd be wary of a trap, but they would also be eager for any chance to fight their old enemies. Gabe slipped the empty revolver into his belt as he rode and pulled the other one from its holster. He figured he had time to get around to the west of the Crow, so he could sweep down on them out of the setting sun.

The Crow had surrounded the skittish horse again, watching Long Rider to see what he would do. It looked like they weren't sure whether to wait for him or to try to reach the other ponies. One of the Crow finally managed to mount the skittish stray, which ran away with him while the other three warriors ran to meet Gabe's attack.

One of them got off two arrows, then made a grab for Long Rider's horse as he rode down on them. The Crow with the empty musket was using it to try to knock him off. Long Rider dodged the musket and swerved his horse into the third warrior, who was swinging a stone-headed war club. He shot the bow carrier in the face.

It was an instant of savage fighting, and then he was past them, running his horse on down the hill. He turned back for another rush, but the Oglala had come over the hill and were about to fall upon the two remaining Crow. The war party would be wiped out in a few more seconds, except for the lone warrior whose horse was still carrying him away from the battle. One of the Oglala had veered off to go after him, but Long Rider saw that the Crow's lead was too long. He felt a moment of disappointment that the enemy would escape, perhaps bringing reinforcements if there was a Crow village nearby.

Then Long Rider was aware of the Sharps carbine slung across his back, its hard steel barrel pressed against his shoulders. The Oglala were fighting the Crow now in a swirl of blood-red dust, but he ignored them, sliding to the ground while he reached beneath the flap of the cartridge pouch on his belt.

The Crow warrior was already a hundred yards out, Long Rider guessed, and he was racing off at an angle that put a few more yards between them every second. But Long Rider worked with a steady, cool precision born of practice and confidence. He had learned to make the bullets go where he wanted them to go, and now his fingers felt at home as they levered the Sharps' trigger guard down away from the stock. The guard operated the breechblock behind the carbine's barrel, sliding it up on a set of grooves to expose the chamber in the rear end of the barrel.

Long Rider already had a cartridge in his hand, a half-inch ball packed into a linen sleeve along with plenty of powder behind it. He pushed the cartridge into the chamber and quickly closed the guard over the trigger again, which lowered the breechblock into place. Bridger had told him that the sharp edge of the breechblock cut open the back of the cartridge as it came down, exposing the powder. Long Rider eared back the big side hammer with a satisfying *klick-kluck,* then put a fresh cap on the nipple above the breechblock. Finally he squinted once more at the Crow warrior, still far out in front of the Oglala brave. He gave himself another second to make sure, then set the carbine's leaf sight for a little less than three hundred yards.

Long Rider planted the butt plate of the Sharps against his shoulder, tracking the far-off pony above his sight. He would not try to shoot the rider—not at three hundred yards. He had confidence in his instincts, but they were no substitute for practice, and he had never tried to shoot anything that was moving fast over uneven terrain. Long Rider knew he would have to guess at how much ground a horse would cover in the time it took a ball to get there. His only hope was that the length of the horse would give him room for error, since the huge Sharps bullet could probably knock the horse down no matter where it hit. He took in a quick breath and held it while he moved the bead a few yards ahead of the pony, leading it as it ran. Then he implored the spirits to guide his instincts and squeezed the trigger.

There was a small snap, followed by a larger explosion, and then a billowing cloud of white smoke was hanging in the still air. Long Rider stood up and moved away from the smoke so he could see, and still it seemed as if a long time went by while he waited. Then the far-off horse stumbled and fell, pitching the Crow warrior over its neck.

The horse lay on its side, squeeling and thrashing in terror. The Crow was already on his feet, facing the Oglala who bore down on him, but one of his arms was hanging uselessly by his side. The Oglala's war club rose and fell only three or four times before the Crow sagged to the ground and lay still.

The Oglala jumped off his horse and kneeled over the dead Crow. Then he stood and held the enemy's scalp high above his head, turning his face toward the sky. A wild cry of victory came floating across the prairie. Long Rider could hear it even above the screaming of the horse and the ringing in his ears.

An answering cry came from the hillside above Long Rider. When he looked, he saw the bigger of the two Oglala braves turning to give him a quick, curious glance before he pulled a knife from his belt and bent down to take his own trophy from the dead Crow lying at his feet.

The smaller brave didn't seem concerned with the trophies of battle. He was studying the hillside itself, his gaze sweeping up from the dead boy in the wash to the bodies of the three Crow warriors who had died before the Oglala had arrived. Then he looked at Long Rider and started walking slowly down the hill. The big Oglala came behind him a moment later, leaping from one body to the next and touching each one with his coup stick. The smaller brave was ignoring the fallen warriors, stepping over their bodies as if he didn't see them, his eyes fixed on Long Rider as he walked.

Long Rider met his scrutiny with equal curiosity, intrigued by this peculiar behavior. The sun had disappeared, and it was getting harder to see, but something about the quiet Oglala drew Long Rider's attention. He was a young warrior of eighteen or nineteen winters, and his hair and eyes were lighter than usual—more like a dark shade of brown. Long Rider also noticed that there was a small stone tied into his hair, just above one ear. But it was more than his physical appearance that set him apart. There was a deeper strangeness that Long Rider sensed in this quiet Oglala who was approaching him in the twilight with such solemn gravity.

"Have you come alone?" said the young brave.

Gabe nodded, and the quiet Oglala frowned at the battlefield.

"You alone are responsible for this destruction of our enemies?"

"No one else is with me."

The strange young warrior looked down at Long Rider's carbine for a moment, then lifted his gaze to the fallen horse three hundred yards away. The horse was still kicking, but the brave who had taken the first scalp was sawing at its throat with a knife. Suddenly there was an end to its screams, and the warrior with the knife was leaping away to stay clear of the blood. The quiet Oglala turned his attention back to Long Rider.

"Do you have some kind of magic?" he asked, tilting his chin toward the rifle.

"No," said Long Rider. "It is only a gun that works well."

The young brave looked into Gabe's face, considering his words carefully. "You have saved our horses and perhaps our lives," he said, "and you have helped us rub out our enemies. But you are not Oglala, and you carry a white man's gun."

"I *am* Oglala," Gabe said. "I am Long Rider."

There seemed to be recognition in the young brave's face, and a fair amount of surprise. He started to say something, but the big Oglala was calling out to them.

"Who will count second coup?" he said, as if he were tired of enjoying the victory alone. "Will those who rubbed out the Crow come and take their hair?"

Long Rider hesitated. He had never been comfortable with taking scalps, even before he'd been carried away to live with the whites. He had often wondered what he would do when the time came that he was expected to lift an enemy's hair. Each warrior was a free man, in theory, free to act according to his own ideas. But he had worried about the opinions of other Oglala if he did not participate in such a common ritual of war.

Then Long Rider realized that the younger brave was doing exactly that.

"The hair is yours," the younger brave was saying, his tone almost weary. "Runs Alone may count second coup when he returns."

The big Oglala gave the young brave a hard look, but Long Rider saw that he was not surprised. Apparently he was already familiar with the young brave's odd behavior, and his expression contained more bafflement and curiosity than anger.

"I do not understand this indifference," said the big Oglala. "You show the promise of a great warrior, Crazy Horse, but I fear you will not be honored or remembered."

CHAPTER NINE

The big Oglala was called Hump, a name that Long Rider had heard many times. He was considered a great warrior among the Lakota, and it was an honor to share his camp, even if he didn't seem to return the high opinion. Hump sat across the fire from Long Rider, staring hard at him with a look full of doubt and suspicion. Long Rider could see it even through the smoke of the burning cottonwood logs.

The Oglala named Runs Alone, the one who had pursued the mounted Crow, was squatting on Long Rider's left and chewing a piece of venison with great pleasure and a lot of noise. He didn't seem to be paying any attention to anything else. Crazy Horse sat cross-legged on the right, staring intently into the flames.

Earlier there had been feasting and dancing around the fire to celebrate the victory over the Crow. The Oglala had been on their way home after a successful hunt when Long Rider gave them the chance to add horses and enemy scalps to their collection of prizes. As a result, their spirits had been high.

Now the mood around the fire—except for Runs Alone—was somber.

"Could the bluecoats really be so foolish?" said Hump. "I hear you tell me of their plans, but it is difficult to believe the words."

"They will arrive in great numbers," Gabe said. "The

soldier-chief, Moonlight, told me they will come from three directions and meet in the Powder River country. More than two thousand all together, he said.''

Hump waved his hand with a grunt of dismissal. ''We have twice that number of warriors along the Powder and the Tongue. Would the bluecoats truly come to fight us in our own stronghold?''

''If they do, they will die,'' said Runs Alone. He made the remark offhandedly as he ate, and Long Rider decided he was the kind of warrior who was more concerned with fighting and eating than anything that might happen in the future. Runs Alone would take pleasure in the glory and prestige of his victories, content to let someone else worry about the hard thinking and planning.

Crazy Horse was not so easy to understand, partly because he had said very little since the battle. The slender young brave hadn't joined in with the others when they'd recounted their brave deeds of the day. While they danced he had gone off to be by himself. Hump told Long Rider that no one had ever seen Crazy Horse dance or sing. He always seemed to be thinking about something else, said Hump. Now it appeared that he was listening to the talk, but Long Rider wasn't even sure of that. Crazy Horse had a thoughtful expression on his thin face as he gazed into the fire, but his eyes seemed to be looking right through the flames.

''The bluecoats will surely die,'' said Hump, agreeing with Runs Alone. ''But I do not believe they are coming. Even they would not be so foolish.''

''Bridger told me it was so,'' said Long Rider.

''Then he lied! He is nothing more than a scout for the whites, after all.''

''Did the soldier-chief also lie? Moonlight talked of the plan when he asked me to work for the bluecoats.''

''It might have been a trick. To make you believe the story.''

''Why would they do that, Grandfather?''

Hump frowned. ''Who can know for sure? Perhaps they arranged to send you here to spread confusion and alarm among the People.''

''I don't believe that is true,'' said Long Rider, troubled by the look of suspicion in Hump's eyes. For the first time he began to see that his effort to warn the People might be met with resistance. Hump had suggested that Long Rider was being tricked by the whites, but it was clear that the old warrior was thinking of a second possibility—that Long Rider himself was part of the trick.

Long Rider had already explained his disappearance from his mother's village. When the victory dancing died down, he had told the Oglala about his abduction by the old army scout named Jim Bridger, and the hated life of loneliness he'd endured among the whites at Fort Laramie. He described the fight with Captain Price, and the years in the guardhouse, and the second fight in the stable. He showed them his broken finger, with its sharp and permanent bend at the knuckle. He let them see the open wound in his palm, still leaking its poison as it healed. He even displayed the sacred pipe that chief Two Face had given him. But now he saw that there would be lingering doubts he would have to overcome.

"Bridger told me how it was," Long Rider insisted, "and I think he was telling the truth. The white men were fighting among themselves, he said, but now the fight is over and many of them will come here to search for the yellow metal. They wish to make a road which—"

"A road!" said Hump. "We want to close the road they already have along the Platte. Now you say they plan to build another one?"

"It was scouted last year, Bridger said. It will cross the Powder and the Tongue on its way around the Big Horn Mountains—"

"This is the last hunting ground we own," Hump roared, his face turning dark with anger. "The whites have ruined our country along the Platte. They press in on us from the east. And now you say they will build a road here, driving away the buffalo and bringing more whites to slaughter the other animals. Our people will go hungry, and the children will starve."

Long Rider nodded gravely, seeing that Runs Alone had stopped eating so he could pay more attention to the conversation. It might have been the danger of going hungry that bothered him, but his eyes were also gleaming in the light from the fire. Long Rider thought it was a look of hatred for the whites. He glanced at Crazy Horse to see what the young Oglala's reaction would be, but there was still no change in his thoughtful expression as he stared blindly into the fire. Crazy

Horse had not even shifted his position.

"That is why the Lakota must prepare themselves," pleaded Long Rider. "Bridger said there will be more bluecoats to protect the whites who come. He said the bluecoats who fought in the war will come now to fight the Lakota."

"Perhaps you want the People to run away," said Hump, glaring at Long Rider. "Perhaps the People will make peace if they are frightened of the bluecoats. Then your friends the whites can take our country."

"They are not my friends," said Long Rider, a tone of bitterness coming into his voice. "I only wish to warn the Lakota so we can keep the whites out of our country." The older warrior's hand had gone to the butt of his knife, and Long Rider saw that his hatred might run away with him. "I know that my mother and father were white," he said quietly. "And my skin is also white. But I was born among the *oyate ikce*, the native people, and I consider myself as one of them. My heart belongs here."

"How!" Crazy Horse said in sudden agreement. "I believe Long Rider is speaking the truth. The soldiers will come as he has said."

Long Rider and Runs Alone stared at Crazy Horse in surprise, but Hump was studying the strange young warrior with respect and something like fatherly affection. Crazy Horse looked up at the older man.

"I have heard of this war," he said, "and we all know about this yellow metal. It would be wise for Red Cloud to hear the things Long Rider has to tell."

"Red Cloud?" said Long Rider. "My uncle?"

"He is one of the leading chiefs who talk for war against the Wasichus," said Crazy Horse. He tilted his head toward the Oglala across from him and added, "We are only a few of the Lakota who have gathered around his council fire, Long Rider. There are many more who want to drive the whites from our country. Red Cloud has gained great influence among his people, and his village grows strong."

Long Rider looked at Hump, who held his gaze for the space of several breaths. Then he nodded reluctantly and frowned at the fire. "Yes," he said, "the council will want to hear what you have to say, Long Rider—if it is true."

"Everything I tell you is straight, Grandfather."

"But will you have time to speak? When will you go to find your mother?"

Long Rider was not afraid to let them see his disappointment. The Oglala had already told him that Yellow Hair was absent from Red Cloud's village on the Powder River. They said she had journeyed with her husband to an Arapaho camp over on the Tongue, to visit the relatives of Little Wound's second wife. It would require another four or five days' travel to reach the Arapaho camp.

"I will leave for the Tongue as soon as I have spoken to the council," Long Rider said. "It is important that they have time to think about the coming of the soldiers. I also wish to counsel with my adviser, if he is still in the village."

"Who was your adviser?" asked Hump.

"High Backbone. Do you know the name?"

Runs Alone and Crazy Horse looked blankly at each other, but Hump said, "High Backbone was your spiritual adviser?"

"Yes, Grandfather."

"He will be there," said Hump, looking at Long Rider with new interest. "It is said that those he advises are strong in the ways of the people."

"I am glad to hear you praise his power."

But Long Rider kept to himself the reason for seeking out his old adviser. He was hoping for careful instruction in a vision quest, so that Wakan-tanka might provide him with insights that would help him make a decision concerning the future of his mother. He still couldn't imagine that she would be happy among the whites, and he was beginning to think that Bridger was wrong about the People being in danger, but the scout had begged Long Rider to take his mother away from the Powder River country, and he had promised to give the matter careful consideration.

Hump was still staring directly into Long Rider's eyes, which was considered an aggressive act among the Lakota, but his words were friendly. "It is I who am glad to hear you speak so strongly for the People," said the warrior, "and I am grateful for your brave fight against the Crow. It is good that you come with us. The people will want to celebrate the return of Long Rider and the brave deeds he performed today."

"How!" said Runs Alone. "You have become a rich man in a very short time, Long Rider. You may compose songs in your honor, and the women will sing them for you." He was grinning with enthusiasm now that the conversation had turned to something in which he was truly interested. "Perhaps you will find one to your liking," he said with a laugh. "Five horses can buy a pretty good wife."

Long Rider laughed, too, but it pleased him to be reminded of his new wealth. By Oglala custom he was entitled to the belongings of all enemy warriors he killed in battle, and since he had killed four Crow, he now owned four of the horses rounded up after the battle. The Oglala had also given him the leftover mount as a reward for his bravery in preventing a surprise attack, and they had allowed him to choose his ponies before the others chose theirs. Counting his mustang, Long Rider could now boast of owning half a dozen horses of fine quality. He also possessed a new lance, a bow and several arrows, and some of the dried meat the Crow had been carrying.

Meanwhile Hump and Runs Alone were glad to have the extra scalps that Long Rider and Crazy Horse didn't want to bother with.

"I hope you are right," Long Rider told Runs Alone. "I'm ready to take a wife, and I'm already thinking of one young woman in particular among the Oglala."

"If that is so, then five ponies may not be enough," said Runs Alone. There was a glint of something like mischief in his eyes. "She must be a fine woman if you have remembered her through five hard winters."

"I thought of her often," Long Rider agreed. "It gave me much pleasure, and also much sadness."

"A woman so desirable might command a great price," said Runs Alone. "You would do well to have many more ponies."

"I will get them if I have to."

"Perhaps you can have them right now." The warrior looked down at the Sharps carbine by Long Rider's side and couldn't hide his desire. "I would give you ten horses for that rifle."

"Ten!" said Long Rider. "Do you have so many?"

"It is everything I have, but it would be a fair price. In time I could acquire many more horses with such a weapon. I could also take the scalps of many enemies, and the People would be sure to remember my name."

Long Rider hesitated, thinking of the girl he remembered and the way she must look now as a woman. He felt the familiar emptiness, and then he was ashamed of his temptation. "I am sorry," he said, "but I must keep the rifle."

"Fifteen horses, then! Perhaps seventeen, if none have been lost in my absence."

"No," said Long Rider, resting his hand on the barrel of the Sharps. "This was given to me in accordance with the vision of Two Face. It would displease Wakan-tanka if I gave it up."

Runs Alone nodded unhappily. "I would do the same if I were you," he admitted. "One can always find a woman, but not a gun with such powerful medicine." The warrior seemed to think of something that made him more cheerful. "But if the bluecoats come as you say, Long Rider, then I will have a chance to take such a weapon in battle. I will use a soldier's weapon to kill more soldiers, and we will teach them a lesson." He threw back his head and screamed like a hawk. "We will both perform well this summer, Long Rider, and perhaps you will win this woman with your great honor."

Long Rider smiled at Runs Alone's enthusiasm. "Do you think of anything besides women and war, Runs Alone?"

"What else is there?" the young Oglala said with a grin. "What else have *you* thought of these past five winters?"

Long Rider only shrugged. There was an answer to the question, but he saw no reason to mention it.

"Tell us the name of this woman who has occupied your thoughts," said Runs Alone. "Is she Oglala?"

"She is Oglala. She is called Yellow Buckskin Girl."

Runs Alone bobbed his head in sympathy with Long Rider's longing for a comely woman, but Crazy Horse looked up from the fire with a troubled frown.

"It is a good thing you did not trade your rifle for the horses," he said. "Yellow Buckskin Girl has already taken a husband, Long Rider. She keeps the lodge of a chief. One of the young men who serve Red Cloud."

Long Rider felt as if a buffalo had kicked him in the ribs. But even though he was surprised by the power of the feeling, he didn't let it show on his face. He merely shrugged, and after a while he said, "There will be others, then." His voice sounded strange to him, so he coughed. "If the village is as large as you say, many young women will be there to look with favor upon a returning warrior."

"How!" said Runs Alone, slapping his own chest with his

fist. "They will honor you, and also those who return with you."

But Hump and Crazy Horse were not so easily satisfied. The quiet young Oglala was staring into the flames again, as if he could see the future there, while Hump studied Long Rider's face with a look of concern.

"Iron Hawk is a brave warrior and a powerful chief," said Hump. "Also a man who is given to easy anger."

"He is the husband of Yellow Buckskin Girl?" asked Long Rider.

Hump dipped his head once. "He is a powerful chief and has three women, but I think there would be trouble if somebody tried to steal even one of them."

"It would not benefit the People if there was trouble among us," said Long Rider, wanting to assure him. "Do you know if she seems happy?"

Hump looked uncertainly at Crazy Horse, who only stared into the fire. "I don't know," said Hump. "But you are right when you say there are many young women who would be happy to live as Long Rider's wife. One of them will serve you well and bring harmony to your lodge. And to the village."

"I hear your words, Grandfather, and I will tell you this. Two Face said he saw in a dream that I would do good things for the People. That is why I have come."

Long Rider noticed a haze of smoke on the horizon many hours before the small hunting party crossed into the valley of the Powder, but he was still surprised by what he saw there. Even the Oglala description of the village had not prepared him for the vision that presented itself. When they rode over the divide late in the second day, Long Rider stopped his pony to stare in wonder at the lodges of the People, stretching for miles along the river.

"You spoke the truth," he said to the Oglala. "I have never seen so many of the People together in one place before."

"The village was even larger at one time," said Hump. "There were so many gathered here that the land could not support them. It's too bad that it was the Arapaho who moved to the Tongue for better grazing. Otherwise your mother would be down there to greet you."

"I have no regrets," said Long Rider, his gaze drifting across the valley. "There is too much happiness in what I see."

They were looking down on a formal winter village, a great collection of tepees winding along the river for many miles. The lodges were covered with weathered buffalo hides that looked white in the late afternoon sun, and they were arranged in circles where the tribes and bands had camped together. Hump had said that several Oglala bands had joined Red Cloud's Bad Faces, along with members of other Lakota tribes like the Sans Arc and Hunkpapa and Brule. Soon the People would start breaking up for the summer, roaming off in all directions to follow the buffalo herds or make war against their enemies. But now their lodges numbered in the thousands, and their horse herds darkened the prairie wherever he looked.

"It is good to see that my alarm over Bridger's words was unnecessary," said Long Rider. "I think we are like the columns of smoke that rise from the lodges. Each of them is small and easily blown about, but when they join together, they can blot out the sky."

"Just as we could wipe out the whites who try to enter our country," said Crazy Horse. "But first we must learn to *remain* joined together, Long Rider. I hope you will be equally convincing when you speak before the council."

Long Rider looked uncertain. "What have I said that will be useful?"

"I believe we must change the way we think about making war. The old ways will no longer work against the whites."

"What should be changed?"

Crazy Horse looked down at the village. "It is only something I *know*," he said, "but I do not understand it yet. The bluecoats fight in a different manner than we do, and I believe we will have to learn from them. Otherwise we will lose this country, and many of us will lose our lives."

Long Rider glanced at Hump, who shrugged his massive shoulders. "I am an old man," he said. "I only know the old ways. But my ears are open to the words of Crazy Horse, because he has been to the real world behind this one, and his vision has brought him great power."

"That is true," said Runs Alone. "In battle he can think of the other world and enter it, so the arrows and the bullets of the enemy cannot touch him."

Long Rider looked away, shamed by a stirring of envy. "It is a good thing to have a vision," he said. "My voice was just beginning to change when Bridger took me from the village— before I was prepared for my first vision quest. Perhaps that is why I lacked the power to behave well among the whites."

Hump nodded in sympathy, nudging his pony down the grassy slope. "We will find High Backbone as soon as possible."

Long Rider followed the old warrior down into the valley, keeping his face stiff so that he would not show his excitement. He was already thinking about the way his people would greet him after believing him to be dead for five winters. Not only was he returning from the grave, he was also coming back with one of the greatest Oglala warriors. More than that, Hump would praise his exploits in killing four of the hated Crow in one battle. It seemed like a boyhood dream of glory coming true, because on top of everything else, he was bringing the enemy's secret plans to the Lakota, information that might save a great many lives.

The Lakota lodges had the place of honor in the middle of the camp that stretched up and down the river, and they were arranged in a great circle with an opening that faced the rising sun. This was the entrance, according to Lakota custom. Only an enemy would come into the circle from any other direction. Hump led his party through the entrance and straight across to the circle of Oglala tepees, making a great commotion as they drove the captured ponies ahead of them. All of the Lakota bands were camped in smaller circles that formed the larger one, and the Oglala had the place of honor. This was the place opposite the entrance, just as the chief's lodge was erected across from the entrance to the Oglala circle.

They found Red Cloud in the council tepee next to his lodge, conferring with other chiefs. That was the way the headmen passed much of their time, discussing the geography of the country or the location of game or the best strategies against their enemies. But when Red Cloud heard Hump's story, he welcomed Long Rider to the camp with a show of great pleasure and immediately began preparing for a feast in his honor. He called the village crier out of the council lodge and told him to ride among the Oglala, announcing Long Rider's return and informing the People of the Oglala victory over a Crow war party. Red Cloud also announced that he would supply a dog for

one of his wives to cook, and Long Rider was honored that the
chief himself would offer the most highly prized delicacy among
the Lakota.

By now the voice of the crier was fading in the distance. Then
it was lost completely beneath the growing sound of laughter
and happy voices, and the barking of dogs as they felt the
growing agitation in camp. Men and women were coming out of
their lodges or returning from a swim in the river, talking among
themselves, excited by the killing of Crow warriors or the
sudden appearance of the youth they still remembered for his
daring ride through a winter blizzard.

Slowly they began to gather in front of the council lodge.
Long Rider's boyhood friends came to greet him joyously, and
he was happy to call them by name. They talked of their old
adventures while other men built a large fire and the women
brought food for the feast.

Then Long Rider noticed one of the women, who was placing
before the fire a large piece of meat from the buffalo hump. She
looked his way, and he stopped listening to his friends.

He thought he had never seen a woman who looked so
striking as the one who bowed her head to watch him from
beneath her lashes. He began walking toward her, his blood
turning hot when she smiled shyly at him. He saw that she had
recently applied vermilion to her cheeks, and understood that
she had done it for him.

"I can hardly believe it is you," the woman said when he
came close. "Your mother said she was sure you had been
killed."

"And perhaps I was," said Long Rider, "for only in the
spirit world could a girl grow into such a beautiful woman,
Yellow Buckskin Girl."

CHAPTER TEN

Yellow Buckskin Girl tilted her head back and laughed with pleasure, her dark eyes sparkling with the same affection and playful spirit that Long Rider had remembered many times while he languished in the guardhouse at Fort Laramie.

"I can see that Long Rider truly has returned," she said. "Also that he is the same as the boy who went away five winters ago. He still has the power of words."

"That is where you are mistaken," said Long Rider. "I have dreamed of this moment many times, but now I don't know what to say."

The woman's eyes began to shine with tears. "You did remember me, then?"

He nodded, troubled by her look of sorrow. "Many times," he said again.

"But why did you go away?"

"I did not want to go, Yellow Buckskin Girl. I was taken against my will. I can tell you more when the time is right, for I have come back to stay with the Lakota."

The big fire was burning well now, and Long Rider could feel its heat against his face. He also felt another kind of heat when he saw a wistful sadness in the woman's eyes. He glanced away for a moment and noticed that some of the people near the fire had drawn back, to give them privacy. The people were trying to pretend that they weren't watching the couple with great curiosity.

"I see there are those who still remember," said Long Rider, making a joke of it. "We will be the subject of gossip tomorrow among the women."

Yellow Buckskin Girl smiled, but it didn't hide her sadness. "They knew I never had an interest in anyone but you."

"Then they must have also seen that one day I intended to take you under my robe," said Long Rider.

"That is what they believed, that I would become the wife of the white Oglala named Long Rider." She turned suddenly and began walking away from the fire.

He watched her for a moment, with a stirring beneath his breechclout. Her rawhide belt was drawn tight around her waist, and Long Rider admired the way her soft-tanned gown clung to the swelling curves of her body. He was also stirred by the gentle sway of her movement, and the leather leggings that hugged her calves from knee to ankle.

Long Rider sighed deeply and shook his head, hurrying to catch up with Yellow Buckskin Girl. Only when he fell in beside her did he notice something that made him feel troubled again. While they talked, she had been standing with her head turned to the side, showing only one of her long braids. Now he saw that the other one was missing. It had been chopped off, which was considered a man's privilege if his wife had been lying with another man.

She looked back and saw his frown.

"You have noticed the mark of adultery," she said.

Long Rider nodded.

"Then you know that I have a husband."

"I knew it before. Crazy Horse told me when I asked about you."

She showed him a faint smile, pleased to hear again that he had remembered her. Then she looked at the ground. "You must believe me to be a bad woman."

Long Rider shook his head, then realized she had not seen him. "I think of the girl I knew," he said, "and I am sure there was a mistake."

Yellow Buckskin Girl stopped walking, then turned to him with gratitude and despair mingling in her eyes. "I would give anything if Iron Hawk trusted me as you do. But he only calls me a liar and refuses to listen.''

"Then he is a fool," Long Rider said sharply.

They heard the beating of drums, and Long Rider looked back toward the council lodge just as several holy men began singing a consecration ceremony. The feast area was already crowded with people, some of them dancing around the large fire that glowed through the rising dust. Women watched their children and tended the meat cooking over the fire, while several *akicita*—the Oglala camp marshals—kept order during the preparations.

"Do you want me to go away?" said Yellow Buckskin Girl.

Long Rider looked at her in surprise.

"I see you wishing to be with your friends, and not with the woman who betrayed you."

"What woman are you talking about?"

"Don't make jokes, Long Rider. You are angry that I took a husband."

"Anger is not permitted during a feast. That would be bad behavior."

"I said don't make jokes! I know you are angry."

"But again you are wrong—"

"I would not have accepted Iron Hawk if I had known you were still alive, Long Rider. I promise you that is true."

"And I *believe* you," he said. "You could not know I would return."

"I turned my back when my father invited him to sit in front of the tepee," said the woman. She looked toward the fire, remembering how it was. "But Iron Hawk drove off all of the other young men who tried to woo me, and my father became angry that there was no suitor to bring horses and wealth to his lodge."

"You had to think of your duty," Long Rider agreed. "To your father and to the People."

She nodded slowly, but her sadness was greater than ever. "I believed Iron Hawk would be a good husband, at least. He is known as a warrior and as a hunter, and he is heard with respect in the council. In the end I smiled upon him and became his *tawicu*."

Long Rider set his face hard against the things he felt, for Yellow Buckskin Girl had used the word that meant she was not Iron Hawk's principal wife. She was only his *tawicu*, his woman. She would not be consulted in matters of family life, and it was likely that Iron Hawk didn't even share her lodge. She would have been supplied with her own tepee by her mother or her friends, and according to Lakota custom, she would own the lodge and everything in it, but as a *tawicu* she was also the same as Iron Hawk's property, to do with as he wished. Long Rider assumed that Iron Hawk had pursued her only for the purpose of giving him pleasure, and perhaps to provide him with more children.

This was the thought that made it difficult for him to speak. In his mind he saw Iron Hawk pushing himself down between the legs of the woman he himself most wanted to have. He saw Iron Hawk pumping up and down against her, and it brought a sickness into his belly. Yellow Buckskin Girl was still looking into his eyes, and he wanted to say something to reassure her, but he was afraid his voice would betray him.

"I know you are angry," she said. "I beg you to forgive me."

"There is nothing to forgive!" Long Rider shouted, trying to make his voice softer. "I am only wondering if it must stay this way."

Yellow Buckskin Girl put her and hand on his arm and looked up into his eyes, wanting to be sure she understood his meaning. Then she looked away. "I wanted to leave him when he cut my hair, but my friends weren't sure they could protect me. If he came for me and they couldn't offer a good reason for leaving him, they might have been forced to give me up."

"He shamed you in front of the People."

"It was his right."

"Only if he was correct in accusing you."

"He was not!" she said, her dark eyes flashing briefly with defiance. "But who would the People believe, a chief or his *tawicu?*"

"But I'm afraid for you if you stay with him. If he believes you have been with another man again, he will cut off more than your hair."

Yellow Buckskin Girl tightened her grip on his arm and clapped her other hand against the side of her head. "I have a friend whose husband took part of her ear," she said with a shudder. "Then he threw her away. I'm afraid of Iron Hawk,

Long Rider, but I don't know what to do. Lakota law is very strict.''

"Just tell me this, do you still want to leave him?''

"I worry if it would be the right thing." She avoided his gaze again, looking off toward the fire, and suddenly she pulled her hand away from his arm while her eyes went wide with fear.

Long Rider turned in the direction she was looking and saw a man coming toward them with a dark scowl on his face. He carried the wand of a chief and wore a scalp shirt as well as a ceremonial headdress studded with eagle feathers. "That is Iron Hawk,'' he said.

Yellow Buckskin Girl nodded and said, "Perhaps you should return to the fire.''

"That would only give him reason for suspicion.''

"He already has reason, Long Rider. I'm sure he has heard the stories of how I felt about you when I was young. He will not be happy that you have returned.''

"Even if that is true, he will cause no trouble today. Surely a headman would not go against Lakota custom.''

"You don't understand—''

But she was interrupted by Iron Hawk calling out from several paces away. "What is happening here?" he demanded roughly as he stalked toward them. "Why does my woman make a fool of me in front of all the People?''

Long Rider was surprised. "You make a fool of yourself," he said, "by showing anger in a time of celebration.''

Iron Hawk glanced at him only briefly, as if Long Rider's presence was nothing for a headman to be concerned with.

"Please, husband—'' Yellow Buckskin Girl began.

"I am only speaking with a friend from my childhood,'' Long Rider said. "Everyone knows this, just as they know there is no shame for Iron Hawk.''

This time the chief didn't even look his way, and Long Rider realized he had been wrong about Yellow Buckskin Girl's husband. She had tried to warn him, just as Crazy Horse had tried, but he had not understood what they meant. Long Rider had imagined a man who was quick to anger, perhaps, but who would still listen to reason. Now he saw that Iron Hawk was like a wounded buffalo bull. His fury could become so great that he would not think of anything else, or even see anything that stood in his way. Like the enraged bull, Long Rider thought, Iron Hawk would not be turned aside easily.

The chief was rubbing the skin beneath Yellow Buckskin Girl's eyes, where she had spread vermilion across the high cheekbones that helped give her face its striking beauty. "What is this?" Iron Hawk said. "You have painted yourself for the sake of a white man?"

The woman stood meekly under her husband's harsh prodding, glancing at Long Rider with a silent plea not to interfere. He nodded quickly to show that he understood.

"Why do you look at the white man?" Iron Hawk demanded, pinching the flesh he'd been rubbing. Yellow Buckskin Girl cried out in pain and covered her face, pulling away from him, but Iron Hawk grabbed her single braid of oiled black hair and gave a sharp yank while he glanced toward Long Rider with a scornful look of contempt. "See?" he said. "The frightened white man will do nothing to protect you."

Long Rider felt his teeth grinding together as he worked to mask the growing fury that threatened to consume him. "Now you show your own stupidity," he said. "I am trying to remember that Yellow Buckskin Girl is your *tawicu*. I am also trying to obey the custom that calls for harmony during feasts, but you are making it difficult. I warn you to be careful, Iron Hawk."

The chief only pulled the woman's braid again while he watched Long Rider with a taunting expression. "Return to your lodge," he told her. "I don't wish to see you again today."

Long Rider stepped between them, brushing Iron Hawk's arm out of the way. "Perhaps you would like to be rid of her forever," he said. "I will give you six ponies and plenty of meat in return for this woman who causes you so much trouble."

The chief's eyes flared with an even greater rage. "A white man offers to buy my woman?" he roared. "Move away before I kill you."

Long Rider didn't move, and there was an instant of time that seemed to last forever while he waited to see what the chief would do next. The two men stood so close to each other that their bare chests nearly touched. Long Rider had been threatened and he wanted to strike first, as he would have at any other time, but he had seen something that kept him still.

There was another man striding toward them from the

direction of the council lodge, carrying a heavy wooden stick. He also wore three black stripes on his cheek, painted diagonally from the outer edges of his eyebrows down to the corners of his mouth. This was the chief of all *akicita*, who had the power to punish offenders at his discretion. Avoiding punishment was the least of Long Rider's worries, however. As the guest of honor, he didn't want to spoil the feast on the first day of his return.

"I told you to move," said Iron Hawk, pushing hard against Long Rider and reaching out for Yellow Buckskin Girl. "And I told you to return to your lodge, woman."

"Don't go," Long Rider said over his shoulder.

The chief's head reared back, and then he lashed out with his wand. Long Rider caught it just above his head, gripping it hard while Iron Hawk struggled to pull it away. The chief's expression showed a flicker of surprise at Long Rider's quickness and strength. Then the rage and determination returned to his eyes, and there was no change when he heard the *akicita*'s stern voice behind him.

"Iron Hawk!" said the marshal. "Stop this desecration."

The chief continued struggling with Long Rider, each of them holding the wand with two hands now and circling for a better position.

"You will pay a stiff penalty," the marshal warned. "Already I will take two—no, three—ponies from your herd for disturbing the feast."

Iron Hawk didn't seem to hear the *akicita*. He stared at Long Rider with hatred as the two men pulled and twisted the wand, grunting with their effort. A cloud of dust began to rise around them, and Long Rider thought of his fights with Captain Stanley Price. He felt a sudden hopelessness, as if he never could expect to find peace in this world. It came to him that perhaps he would always be fighting with other men, struggling for possession of something that lay between them, just as he was struggling now for the wand.

"*Five* horses!" said the marshal, who stood beside them now. "And if you continue in this manner, I will make sure that your lodge and its contents are destroyed."

Still Iron Hawk refused to stop fighting. The marshal raised his stick and brought it down hard on the chief's shoulders, increasing the force of his blows as Iron Hawk ignored them. Yellow Buckskin Girl watched the scene with one hand over her mouth, her eyes full of fear. Long Rider was also starting to feel uncomfortable with the wild glow in her husband's eyes. He had never experienced anything like it. The chief's gaze bored into his as if Iron Hawk didn't feel the heavy ashwood stick cracking against his neck and shoulders—as if he didn't even know it was happening. Long Rider was relieved when Iron Hawk suddenly pushed hard and let go, tumbling him to the ground. The chief looked down at him with a last flare of hatred, then composed himself before turning to the *akicita* with an air of dignity.

"You will have your horses," Iron Hawk said.

The marshal nodded. Long Rider had gotten to his feet, and now he returned the chief's wand of office. Iron Hawk took it without looking at him, staring instead at Yellow Buckskin Girl. He commanded her to leave with a sideways movement of his head, then walked away without looking back. Yellow Buckskin Girl glanced at Long Rider before following her husband across the camp circle.

Only the *akicita* remained, watching Long Rider with a hard, suspicious expression. Then the marshal turned toward the council lodge, and Long Rider was alone.

He watched Yellow Buckskin Girl until she disappeared.

Long Rider's old friends saw his solemn look and tried to joke with him when he went back to the fire, making fun of Iron Hawk and saying Yellow Buckskin Girl had made a bad mistake when she agreed to be his woman. Long Rider tried to laugh with them, but their voices seemed to come from far away. He heard the People singing and beating their drums, the children laughing and dogs barking, but nothing could touch his heart. He had dreamed of returning to his people just like this, yet now he could feel no pleasure.

But Long Rider was slowly coming to a decision. He saw he couldn't be happy unless Yellow Buckskin Girl was by his side, and once he understood this, he also saw he had no choice but to take her from Iron Hawk. Once he had resolved to do so—no matter what the consequences—he was able to laugh with his old friends again and enjoy the feast in his honor.

Long Rider was doubly honored, since the Oglala included a sacred kettle dance in their ceremonies and chose his old spiritual adviser, High Backbone, to conduct it. This was possible because High Backbone had seen visions during a thunderstorm, signified by the red lightning designs that were painted on the old, weathered skin of his chest.

It was High Backbone's responsibility to make sure that everything was done in a proper manner. The women hung a buffalo stomach from four upright sticks, filling it with water and heated stones from the fire. Then the holy man strangled a young dog, washed its body, singed off its hair, and cut it into small pieces for the boiling kettle.

An assistant to High Backbone chose eight worthy men. The shaman led them in a dance four times around the kettle, after which they followed him as he circled off to each of the four sacred directions. He prayed aloud to the spirits they represented, asking them to provide all the things the Lakota needed, and then he divided the dancers so that four of them were on the east side of the kettle and four on the west.

The drumbeats came slower now as the dancers moved up to the kettle and backed away again. They did this four times, and on the fourth approach High Backbone plunged his arms deep into the boiling water. Many of the People cried out in awe and amazement when he came up with the dog's head in his hands.

High Backbone went among them and gave the head to a young boy, as a prayer that the boy would grow strong and have a family. Then the holy man plucked a piece of meat from the kettle and went off to bury it in the ground as an offering to Wakan-tanka, the Great Mystery who had made all other things.

Finally, when he knew by the look of the water that the dog had been properly cooked, High Backbone took out another piece of meat and brought it to Long Rider. To be served first at such a feast was among the highest honors among the Oglala, and High Backbone looked at him with pride before going back for more meat to serve the chiefs and high officials of the camp. The indigent and helpless came next, followed by everyone else. No one ate more than a small mouthful, since it was important that all who attended the feast should have at least a taste of the dog's sacred flesh.

But no one went hungry. There were great slabs of buffalo ribs roasting above the fire, and more boiling kettles full of turnips and wild potatoes. There were also wild plums and currants and sand cherries. The people ate until they could eat no more, laughing and dancing and singing songs and telling stories late into the night.

Long Rider thought often of Yellow Buckskin Girl, longing for her presence, but for now it was enough that he had determined to get her away from Iron Hawk. For now it was enough to be among the People again, singing the old songs as he filled his belly, smelling the wood smoke and cooking meat.

He was almost able to forget about Fort Laramie and the bluecoats who were coming to invade his country.

CHAPTER ELEVEN

"Long Rider lies!" Iron Hawk roared. "Where are these bluecoats he tells us about? Have we seen them? When the Cheyenne and Arapaho journeyed here from the south, they raided at will across the country. The bluecoats came after us, but they were like a pack of coyotes nipping at the heels of a great buffalo herd. This was only six moons ago, but Long Rider says they have found many more bluecoats to come into our country. I say the whites have sent him here to make us afraid, so the People will listen to Spotted Tail and the other weak chiefs who beg for peace. But we must not listen! We must rub out the whites who steal our land and kill our women and children."

A chorus of rough-voiced "Hows!" ran among the dark, stolid figures sitting around the council fire. Soaring above them were the buffalo-hide walls of the great council lodge that served the combined winter village. It looked like a large tepee that had been cut in half and pulled apart, with more hides stretched across a lattice of poles in the middle.

The village councilors were assembled here, along with the chiefs and members of the important warrior societies. They had come together around the council fire to consider how they should proceed against the whites. It was the job of the councilors and chiefs to make such decisions, but they listened to anyone who wished to come and speak to them.

They listened in the Indian manner, staring at the ground or at some other object with keen concentration, never looking the speaker in the eye. That would be very bad form. Nor did anyone interrupt. Each speaker was allowed to continue at any length, until he or she was finished, and then there was a respectful pause before someone else began to speak.

Iron Hawk sat down, and Long Rider could feel many eyes turning secretly in his direction. He started getting to his feet, hoping the others could not see his weariness, but a sharp voice spoke up behind him.

"Iron Hawk must believe we are blind and deaf," said Crazy Horse.

There was a murmur in the lodge as the thin, young warrior came toward the council fire, stepping carefully around the dark bodies of the men huddled on the ground. His hair and skin, by contrast, looked even lighter than they usually did, and Long Rider couldn't help wondering—as he had before—whether it was pure Lakota blood that ran in his veins.

There was no question about his reputation as a warrior, however. It was growing rapidly. Long Rider had learned that many people knew of Crazy Horse's vision and his power, and now they were looking upon him with respect as he came toward the council fire.

"We have already seen the wounds that the soldier-chief caused to Long Rider's hand," said Crazy Horse. "Would that make him want to serve the bluecoats? When Spotted Tail spoke for peace, we heard Long Rider argue against him. Are those the words of a man who wants us to be afraid?"

There was another chorus of agreement, louder than before.

"Iron Hawk is the one who holds us back," said Crazy Horse. "It has been four days since we honored Long Rider with a feast. We have filled those days with talk, and yet we have come no closer to the planning of a summer campaign. We fill our days with words that already have been said. We know we are united and strong. Now it is time to decide *how* we will drive out the whites."

Crazy Horse thought for a moment, then nodded with finality and sat down. Long Rider stood up, grateful for the intercession and encouraged by the murmur of excitement among the chiefs and warriors. He squinted at them through the dim, smoky air inside the lodge, deciding it was time to speak his thoughts.

"When I first returned," he said, "I was pleased to see so many of the People gathered here. I am even more pleased by the talk I have heard these past four days, because I see that the People are thinking with one mind. They are strong for going to war. I am pleased because I believe war is our only hope for keeping the whites out of our country. We are strong, as Crazy Horse says—*but only as long as we fight together*. Otherwise our enemies will defeat us, because *they* fight together."

Long Rider held up his left hand, pointing one finger in the air.

"When we fight in the old way," he said, "a Lakota warrior is like this. He battles an individual bluecoat while other battles go on around him."

Long Rider opened his hand so that all five fingers were extended.

"Each finger is strong enough to do certain things," he said, "but even five fingers are still not as strong as the same five fingers closed together."

He made a fist and hit his chest hard enough to make a thumping sound that carried through the lodge. Then he held up the fist again.

"I say the bluecoats have learned this. They know how to fight together with great discipline, and their chiefs do not let them quit when they get tired of fighting."

This was the part that made Long Rider nervous. It was something he'd been thinking about for a long time, and he wasn't surprised when he saw that many of the warriors and chiefs had dark scowls on their faces. He took a deep breath and kept going.

"My ears have been open these past four days," he said. "I have heard the stories of our victories. I have also heard you ridicule the soldiers. I know you don't wish to hear them praised. But that is not what I mean to do. I do not say they are good fighters, taken one at a time."

Long Rider had to pause for another chorus of fervent "Hows!" and a few shrill war whoops.

"But I do say that they fight in a different manner," he continued, "and we cannot ignore it. Think of us here, talking and talking for four days, and still we have agreed on nothing. The soldiers do not do this. A soldier-chief would decide what to do, and everyone would have to do it."

There was a rumble of angry voices and a few harsh looks, and again he understood why. Indian men were used to obeying only those orders they'd already agreed to accept, and they were always free to pull out whenever they felt like it. There was no man more free than an Indian warrior.

"I do not say we must make ourselves slaves, like white men," Long Rider said quickly, showing his contempt. "But the kinds of victories we have won in the past will not be enough. The white man does not *see* them as victories, so he will not feel defeated. He will not be driven away. Our only hope is to go to war as a people, because otherwise we fight for different *reasons* than the white man. Now we must go to war to protect the country we live in, and not for the sake of any single man's reward."

Long Rider hesitated, praying to Wakan-tanka for the power to make his words clear.

"Think of the raiding parties that are going out against the whites who use the road on the Platte River," he said. "These skirmishes bring glory and plunder for the warriors—scalps and women and fresh horses—*but they don't stop the white man from using the road*. The whites will only travel in larger numbers for protection. The only way to stop them is to act together in a strong way."

Now there was a profound silence in the lodge, broken only by the crackling of the fire in its pit. The councilors and chiefs and warriors frowned at each other or stared thoughtfully at the ground, struggling with the meaning of Long Rider's words.

Crazy Horse stood again, his voice soft in the silence but a sharp clarity in his eyes. "I believe we have just heard something important," he said. "It is not the old way. It is not the way we have known. But it could be the way to push the whites out of our country. I say we halt the raiding parties and rest our ponies while we make plans to break the white man's road." He closed his hand into a fist, just as Long Rider had done. "I say we move together as the white man's army does, until we have rubbed them out."

There were more animal screams and wild cries of derision, while Crazy Horse looked at Long Rider in a way in which he seldom looked at other people. An understanding passed between them. Long Rider had seen the warrior pay attention to young children in camp, but usually he went around without noticing anyone else. He always seemed to be looking through things, as if he were thinking deep thoughts.

Perhaps it has to do with his vision, Long Rider thought with pride. *Perhaps he sees things that most men don't see, and he believes I see them in the same way.*

A sudden quiet fell over the council lodge, and Long Rider looked up to see that Red Cloud was standing before the fire. Long Rider shivered a little in spite of himself, seeing the old man's wide mouth with its cruel-looking downward twist at the corners. The great warrior's narrow face was dominated by that wide mouth and a beaklike nose that seemed as long and sharp as a knife blade.

"Sometimes it is hard to hear wisdom in the words of men who are so young," he said. "But I believe Crazy Horse speaks the truth and Long Rider speaks with great vision."

Long Rider kept his head down, trying to maintain at the least the appearance of humility, but his heart seemed to fill his chest.

"I propose this to the councilors and the warrior societies," Red Cloud was saying. "Let us put a stop to the raiding parties, just as Crazy Horse has suggested. Let there be a severe penalty for warriors who disobey. Then let us move together against the white man's road." He looked from man to man. "We have talked about this, and already we have agreed that our best chance is to attack the bridge where the road crosses the river. I propose we do it now."

Red Cloud's voice grew more forceful and commanding, while the listeners nodded vigorously and repeated their "Hows!"

"Now is the time to pass the war pipe among the People," said the great warrior chief. "Let us move our village to Crazy Woman Creek before the next moon. We will strike from there. We will rub out the tiny soldier fort and destroy the bridge, so that no whites may travel the road."

Red Cloud looked down at Long Rider and noticed his look of concern.

"I do not know about these bluecoats that Long Rider speaks of," he said. "I am one of those who cannot believe they would be so foolish. But I say, let them come." There was a sharp glitter in the old chief's eyes. "I say, let them march around our country if they like. We will not be here. We will be closing the road they came to protect.''

Long Rider laughed, and so did many of the chiefs and warriors. It was a natural thing among the People to make jokes and see the funny side of things.

The laughter died suddenly, however, as Spotted Tail rose to his feet. He had come in just the day before, leading a band of Brule who were fleeing from the bluecoats along with a band of Oglala under Man Afraid of His Horses. There were maybe fifteen hundred Brule and Oglala altogether, and they had been living in a camp of tame Indians near Fort Laramie. The wild northerners looked upon them with little respect, calling them ''hangs-around-the-fort'' people.

It wasn't even a change in heart that had brought them to the Powder River.

The newcomers said the Army had suddenly decided that the friendly Indians should go east to live around Fort Kearney, keeping them away from the influence of their hostile relatives. But the Lakota had no desire to live among their traditional enemies, the Pawnee, so they ran away from the soldiers who were guarding them on the road. The soldier-chief, Moonlight, had come after them, they said, but they had run off most of his horses and forced the bluecoats to walk back to Fort Laramie.

Long Rider had listened to this story with bitter amusement.

Even so, Man Afraid of His Horses and Spotted Tail were still speaking for peace with the whites. Spotted Tail's voice was very grave.

''Crazy Horse talked of blindness when he scoffed at Iron Hawk. But I fear you *are* blind.'' The leader of the Brule ignored a murmur of angry voices. ''The orators have told and retold the terrible stories of Sand Creek around the council fire, and you say that this is a reason to fight. You speak of a desire for vengeance among the People. But if you go to war against the whites, you will only make sure that the orators have many more such stories to tell. Many more women and children will die. Many others will become widows and orphans. There will be much keening in our villages.''

Spotted Tail looked at Iron Hawk with grave disdain.

''Some say I am a weak chief. But I was eager to go to war against the Pawnee and the Crow, and the People know I have killed many enemies. I say the whites are not our enemies—not all of them. There are bad whites just as there are bad Indians, but their leaders wish to make treaties with us and live in peace.''

Spotted Tail pulled his white man's blanket tightly around his shoulders.

"I will not smoke the war pipe with you," he said. "In the morning I will lead the Brule away from here and we will make our own camp."

Spotted Tail walked stiffly out of the council lodge, and the warriors turned their attention to Man Afraid of His Horses.

"I would like to follow Spotted Tail," said the chief of one of the Oglala bands. "I believe what he says is the truth. But my young men would not follow me. I believe we are walking a path that will lead to much sorrow and destruction. But the Oglala are strong for war, and so am I."

"Then let us begin to make plans," said Red Cloud, the corners of his broad mouth turning down in a fierce look of triumph. "Let us pass the war pipe among all the People and bring them together in this war." He glanced at Long Rider, and the small twinkle returned to his eyes. "I propose we send Long Rider as our messenger to Black Bear's camp on the Tongue, so the Arapaho may make preparations to join us."

Long Rider showed his surprise as Crazy Horse clapped him on the back with a rare grin of pleasure. Long Rider saw that many others were also smiling, or laughing, knowing that his mother was a visitor in the Arapaho camp. He saw also that the chiefs and warriors—except for Iron Hawk—were looking at him with respect, and it made his heart swell with a powerful feeling of pleasure that seemed oddly familiar.

He wondered about this feeling and found himself remembering his childhood. He remembered the way he would often stray far from camp, playing with other boys in the snow and cold, and then the pleasure of returning home to the warmth of his mother's lodge.

It is the same now, he thought. *I have come home.*

Crazy Horse followed Long Rider from the council lodge when the day's deliberations had come to an end, his expression once again distant and thoughtful. Long Rider had been a guest in the young warrior's lodge, and now they walked in a comfortable silence, following the grassy riverbank toward the Oglala village. The smell of wood smoke was everywhere, as well as the happy sounds of children playing among the lodges.

"If you need assistance against Iron Hawk," Crazy Horse said, "I will stand with you."

Long Rider turned sharply to stare at him, and Crazy Horse laughed.

"Do not worry, my friend. I cannot hear your thoughts. I only know what I would do in your place."

"Be thankful you are not."

"I wish I was," Crazy Horse said. "But I am not as lucky as you."

Long Rider turned again, seeing a wistful look in the warrior's strange, faraway eyes. But Crazy Horse did not speak of himself.

"The People know Yellow Buckskin Girl wishes to be your woman," he said. "And custom says she may fly away from Iron Hawk as long as you can keep and protect her. What happens now will be determined only by your power, Long Rider. Why else do you think Iron Hawk tried so hard to make the People distrust you? He was hoping to force you from the village."

"I understood," Long Rider said. "That is why I haven't spoken to Yellow Buckskin Girl. I believed I could defeat Iron Hawk in an equal fight, but I feared there might be other problems."

"You were wise," said Crazy Horse, a dark look in his eyes. "No one can know what Iron Hawk might do. But it is better now. The People will look kindly on your efforts and turn away from Iron Hawk if he acts badly. And if he does—if he seeks allies against you—then you will have an ally also."

Long Rider stopped walking long enough to face Crazy Horse, gripping his shoulder in silent gratitude. "I hope you are right about the People," he said. "It will make me very happy if I can take Yellow Buckskin Girl as my woman."

"I understand," said Crazy Horse. "I have also wanted a woman I knew in my childhood. She was called Black Buffalo Girl, and I believed she would look upon me with favor." The warrior started walking again, turning his eyes toward the setting sun. "But she took another husband," he said, "and she does not appear to regret it."

Long Rider made a sound of sympathy. "At least your present woman is a good one," he said hopefully. "She is comely and keeps a fine lodge.''

Crazy Horse only nodded, still looking blindly toward the west, as if he weren't seeing the smoky orange haze that merged with the grassy slopes in the distance. Long Rider let out a long breath and said, ''Yes, I can see that I am more fortunate.''

''Tell me your plans, then, so I may help when the time comes to claim Yellow Buckskin Girl.''

''I am not sure, Crazy Horse. I hope to take her with me when I go to Black Bear's camp on the Tongue. But first there is something else I must do.''

''You desire to seek a vision,'' said High Backbone. ''This is a solemn matter. You should not undertake it from curiosity only.''

Long Rider dipped his head to indicate that he understood, closing his eyes for a moment against the searing steam heat in the purification lodge. A steady stream of sweat was pouring from his chin.

''Then you must do this according to the forms we will teach you,'' High Backbone continued in a ritual tone. ''You must find a high place where no one will interrupt you. You must prepare it in the sacred manner. After you have entered upon it to seek a vision, you must not step beyond its boundaries, nor speak to any man, woman, or child until you have seen a vision. Or until you know that you will not see one.''

Long Rider prayed that this would not happen to him.

''When you have entered on this place, Long Rider, you should meditate only on seeing a vision. You may invoke the spirits in words or song, and you must always address them in a reverent manner. The vision may come to you as a man, a beast, a bird, or as some form that is not known. Or it may come to you as a voice only. It may speak to you so that you understand its meaning, or it may be that you will not understand.''

Long Rider nodded, his eyes stinging from the sweat that was running into them.

''If you know you have done something the spirits do not like, you better not attempt to seek a vision, for you will not see one.''

Long Rider nodded again, taking pleasure in his purity. This had been his reason for avoiding Yellow Buckskin Girl. He had feared that he might give in to his desire to lie with her while she was still Iron Hawk's woman, and he did not want to displease the spirits.

"Do not be discouraged," High Backbone said, "for the spirits may wait a long time before they bring a vision to you. When you have seen a vision, do not call upon the spirits anymore but return to me and I will advise you about its meaning. You should be sincere in this matter and truthful to me. If you lie and say you have seen a vision when you have not, then I may advise you to do those things the spirits do not want you to do, and so bring harm upon you."

When High Backbone had finished the instructions, his deputies opened the purification lodge and gave Long Rider four small wands of plum wood with medicine bags tied to the ends. Long Rider took these with him to the top of a grassy hill far away from the village, wearing only his breechclout and carrying only the pipe he had received from Two Face. At the top of the hill he selected a place that was big enough for him to lie down, scraping away all the grass and every other living thing he found. Then he pushed the four medicine wands into the earth, one on each side of the square, and finally he was ready to enter the place he had prepared. He sat down on the bare dirt and began to sing.

He smoked and meditated and sang aloud and prayed in silence for four days, waiting for his vision.

CHAPTER TWELVE

"The sun went away and returned four times," said Long Rider, "and the spirits remained silent. I offered my smoke to the four directions, but there was no response. On the fourth day I bowed my head and vowed to look upon nothing else until I had received my vision."

High Backbone nodded with approval, reaching down between his crossed legs to pluck a stem of grass, which he put between his teeth. Long Rider had found the shaman in his lodge, just finishing his noon meal. Now they were sitting on a slope above the village.

"Almost immediately," Long Rider continued, "I heard a voice telling me to look up. I believed it was someone from the village and replied that I had made a vow. The voice said, 'We have heard your vow and we are pleased.' Still, I did not look up, thinking that someone was playing a trick on me. Then the same voice said, 'There is no need to worry, Long Rider. High Backbone's medicine guards you against the tricks of Iktomi.'"

High Backbone smiled at that, nodding his head. He had remained silent since Long Rider came to him, offering guidance only with looks and gestures.

"So I raised my head," said Long Rider, "and the village had disappeared from the valley. The river was still there, winding peacefully through the grass, but there were no lodges on its banks. There were no children playing, no horses grazing in the grass, no columns of smoke rising to the sky. I rubbed my eyes and looked again, but it was as if the Lakota had never existed. They had all gone away somewhere. It filled me with sadness and despair.

"I begged the spirits to tell me the meaning of what I saw, but they were silent now. I felt only a rumbling in the earth, and then the place I had prepared for my vision quest began sinking into the top of the hill. Walls of dirt rose up around me until I could not see over them. I wanted to scramble out of the hole, but I could not move my arms or legs. The sky seemed far away, and the hole was very dark, although I could see a layer of fine, golden strands on its floor. I thought it was like the grass of the prairie that feeds our game."

High Backbone pulled the stem of grass from his mouth and looked at it with a somber expression.

"Then the voice said, 'Behold,' and when I turned, there was an opening in the wall of earth that faced to the west. It was black and empty. I floated into the opening against my will, going downward into the earth. I saw the bones of old animals and the broken roots of trees. Then the tunnel entered into the stone that lies beneath the dirt.

"I floated for quite a while through the stone, as if I had entered a long cave in a cliff. It became very cold, and I wanted to return for the buffalo robe I had left on the hilltop. But when I turned, I saw that the tunnel was disappearing behind me. I knew I could never return. I could only go forward, no matter where the tunnel would lead me.

"I was in the ground a long time, and it became so cold that I thought death was near. Then I felt that I was moving upward again. The tunnel came to an opening in a bluff beside the river. The river sparkled under brilliant sunlight, dazzling my eyes. Then I heard a great beating of wings and saw a shadow growing over the sun. The shadow took the form of Wakinyan."

Long Rider used the Lakota word for the Winged One, or the Winged God, which the whites called Thunderbird. High Backbone frowned at the appearance of the Winged One in Long Rider's vision and nodded for him to continue.

"Wakinyan came at me from the sun, blotting it out and looking very big. But just when I wanted to run, the Winged God folded its wings over my shoulders and said, 'Behold.'

When I turned, I saw that the tunnel in the bluff by the river had disappeared. In its place there was a path made of crushed stone. The path was white, winding in curves like the river. I began to walk up the path with Wakinyan still clinging to my shoulders. As I came away from the sounds of the river, I could hear again the barking of dogs and the laughter of children. It came from all around me, and yet there was no one there. There was only the wind blowing in the yellow grass.

"Then I understood that the curves in the white stone path were winding among the lodges of the People, even though I could not see them. No one called my name, so I believed they could not see me, either. I wanted to stop and listen to the happy sounds of the village, but I was propelled forward as before, and soon the sounds faded from my ear. The path returned me to the place on the hilltop where I started, and everything there was just as it had been before. I slept a while, and then I came to find you."

High Backbone closed his eyes. Long Rider watched the afternoon breeze ruffling his hair. After a long time the old man stirred a little and said, "On some parts of your vision I will have to meditate further, Long Rider, for they are unclear to me. But I believe your medicine will be very powerful."

"What type will it be, Grandfather?"

"First there is the yellow color, representing the rock through which you traveled with such ease. Rock has the greatest power of all our spirits, and it made the path on which you walked." High Backbone frowned. "It troubles me that the color of this path was white, and that the village was invisible to you. It is possible you will not always remain among the Lakota."

A cold hand gripped Long Rider's heart. He tried to keep his face composed, but his adviser was watching him closely.

"Do not be alarmed," High Backbone said gently. "There are good people among the whites, and perhaps one day we will live in peace. I believe it was a good sign that your ears were open to the sounds of the Lakota, even if you could not see them. They were all around you, even as you walked the white road."

"I would fight to the death before I lived among the whites."

High Backbone shook his head with a disturbed frown. "Do not be so quick to speak of death," he said. "I am worried by this tunnel of no return. I fear there is a bad time coming. It is good that you will be sustained by the Rock Spirit, and in the end you will be blessed by Wakinyan. He will protect you, just as he cloaked you with his wings in the dream. I will meditate further on your vision, Long Rider, and consult with the other medicine men, but I am pleased that you saw the patron of desperate courage.''

High Backbone nodded with satisfaction, not seeing the change that came into Long Rider's face.

"I will make a cutting of horsehair," the shaman announced, "and I will paint it red, to show that you dreamed of the Winged One. As long as you wear it, you will benefit from Wakinyan's great power, no matter what road you travel. He will sustain the courage you require to perform deeds of valor, and Long Rider's name will be remembered with honor and respect.''

Long Rider was staring toward the village in a way that made High Backbone turn to follow the direction of his gaze.

"What is wrong?" asked the shaman. "Did you recall something else from your vision?"

"No, Grandfather, but there is something about it that frightens me. When you spoke of death and the white man's road, it made me think of the graves I saw at the soldier town. They looked like my vision place after the ground began to sink. I feel as if I were in my own grave, lying on a bed of golden—'' Long Rider stopped suddenly, a stricken look on his face. "It was golden!" he said. "Not yellow. The bottom of the grave was the color of my mother's hair!"

High Backbone placed his roughened hand on Long Rider's arm. "I do not think you have cause for worry," he said. "When the spirits bring us visions, there are certain forms that are known to us. Only the shamans can interpret them, with the help of the spirits.''

Long Rider studied the old adviser, his sun-bleached brows drawn together above his eyes. "You don't believe my vision to be an omen?"

"Not in the way you see it," High Backbone said in a kindly way. "I will tell you if there is a change in my opinion, but I believe there are other meanings to your vision.''

Long Rider nodded, but in his mind he still saw the square vision place sinking into the cold earth, and the golden color on the floor. "I am grateful for your counsel," he said, "but I must go now. I want to leave for Black Bear's camp as soon as possible."

Yellow Buckskin Girl jumped up when she saw him coming along the shallow wash, but she made no move in his direction. Instead she looked quickly toward the ridge that lay between them and the village.

Perhaps I am not wanted here, Long Rider thought, feeling a sudden emptiness in his belly. *Perhaps she has decided to stay with Iron Hawk.* But Yellow Buckskin Girl was smiling when she turned his way again. It was such a happy smile that he could see the brilliant flash of her teeth from fifty yards away. He quickened his pace, the tall yellow grass sweeping against his bare legs.

"I began to think I had only dreamed of your return," said Yellow Buckskin Girl. She tried to laugh, but the sound caught in her throat. "What a cruel dream it would have been."

Long Rider saw the shine of tears in her eyes as he came closer. He reached for her, and she dropped the wild turnips she had been digging, her arms going around him with a powerful hunger.

"I wanted to wait until the time was right," he said against her hair. "But now I can ask it. Will you leave Iron Hawk and become my woman?"

She squeezed him even harder, clinging to him for a moment before she pulled away. She held him at arm's length while she looked into his eyes. "You know there will be trouble," she said.

Long Rider brushed away the tears that glistened on her cheeks. "You have no reason for worry."

"But you have seen the way he is."

Long Rider nodded, a look coming into his pale eyes that made Yellow Buckskin Girl a little frightened. "I know Iron Hawk will make a fight," he said, "but I would not ask you to be my woman if I could not protect you."

She lowered her gaze to the black army holster hanging from Long Rider's belt. "I do not doubt you," she said. "I beg you to believe me. But I am worried that Iron Hawk will not permit an equal match between you."

"You think I have failed to consider that?" Long Rider said

stiffly. "If Iron Hawk is afraid to face me alone, then I will also have an ally."

The woman's expression came alive with hope. "Then you truly think we can succeed?"

"I told you, I would not have come if—"

She squeezed his hand and said, "Forgive me, Long Rider. I should not have questioned you. Tell me what you want me to do."

Long Rider touched her cheek, looking down into her eyes.

"I will do anything you say," she told him. "I know I will be safe under your protection."

Long Rider's chin lifted an inch or two. "Will you leave with me tonight, then? Will you go with me to Black Bear's camp?"

"Of course!"

He nodded sharply and said, "Good. Go and prepare to pack your lodge while I find Crazy Horse."

Yellow Buckskin Girl had started to turn away, but now she faced him again. "Is he the ally you spoke of?"

Long Rider nodded again. "He offered me his help before I was even able to ask for it."

Yellow Buckskin Girl tilted her head a little, looking at him in a new way. "He is said to be a great warrior."

Long Rider smiled. "You are thinking that he is a strange man who spends little time with other people. But I have been a guest in his lodge, and we have much to talk about. I feel we are like brothers who share the same thoughts."

"I have heard about the council," said Yellow Buckskin Girl. "My friends said that you and Crazy Horse spoke as one, and Red Cloud listened." She gave him a sudden shining smile and pressed herself against him. "I will be honored to be your woman, as long as you will have me."

"The honor is mine," said Long Rider, putting his arms around her again and resting his chin on top of her head. "I have dreamed of this so often that now I'm afraid to let you go. Is it really possible that tonight we will lie together?"

There was a giggle against his throat, but when Yellow Buckskin Girl pulled away, he could see a hunger in her eyes that matched his own.

"Let us move fast," he said.

"The faster the better."

"We will leave here as soon as we can."

"I only need to gather my things and strike the lodge. When you come, I will be ready."

"Gather your belongings," said Long Rider. "But don't take down your lodge. If Iron Hawk sees you, he will know our plans before I'm ready."

Yellow Buckskin Girl nodded gravely.

"I am sure he will be watching for you," Long Rider went on, bending to pick up the wild turnips she had dropped. "Take these and go back the way you came. I will follow in a while."

She stood on her toes to press the soft skin of her cheek against his, then started walking toward the ridge. Her hips rolled smoothly beneath her soft leather dress, and Long Rider's breath became a little shallow as he watched. After a while he couldn't see the sway of her body, but still he continued to watch. He almost began to fear that she had been a part of his vision, in danger of disappearing if he took his eyes away from her.

The thought disturbed him. Yellow Buckskin Girl looked small and unprotected on the open hillside. Long Rider began to follow her, keeping his eyes fixed on her as he walked with increasing urgency.

Yellow Buckskin Girl stopped near the top of the ridge and turned back to look at him, as if to make sure he were still there. She raised her arm to wave, and again he saw the flash of her smile. It gleamed briefly, and then it was gone as she turned suddenly to look toward the crest. In the next instant she was running back down the slope.

Long Rider was already running toward her, pumping his legs even more frantically when two figures appeared over the crest of the ridge. He had known they were coming, just as he knew that one of them was Iron Hawk. A wave of bitter hopelessness washed over Long Rider when he saw that they would catch Yellow Buckskin Girl long before he could reach her.

Iron Hawk was in the lead and gaining fast, and already he was reaching for the woman's arm. Long Rider yearned for the old Sharps carbine that was still in Crazy Horse's lodge. Yellow Buckskin Girl had trusted him with her safety, and now she was screaming as she tried to avoid the grasping hands of her husband. He caught her by the shoulder and slammed her to the ground, dropping instantly to his knees to straddle her waist.

The second man stopped behind the chief, his deep-shadowed

eyes intent on Long Rider's approach. He was an Oglala warrior named Kills Enemy, and he was reaching over his shoulder for an arrow to fit the bow in his hand.

Yellow Buckskin Girl lashed out at Iron Hawk, but he caught her wrists and pinned them under his legs. She continued to writhe beneath him, screaming again when Iron Hawk twisted his fingers in her hair. He yanked down hard to hold her head against the ground while he drew a knife from his belt.

Long Rider ran still more desperately, pulling the Remington from his own belt as Yellow Buckskin Girl stopped struggling. He saw that she had turned her chin up a little to stare defiantly at the blade of the knife that glittered only a hand's width in front of her eyes.

"Don't do it," Long Rider cried out, pointing the revolver. "Harm her and you will die, Iron Hawk."

The chief glanced at him, and the familiar blind rage was in his eyes. There was no question about Iron Hawk's intent, and no hope of stopping him. Long Rider came to a sudden halt, cocking the revolver and bringing it up to eye level at the same time that he was weighing the mutilation of Yellow Buckskin Girl against the danger of harming her with a badly aimed shot.

Long Rider made his decision in the time it took to aim, as Kills Enemy was drawing his bow. Iron Hawk had already returned his attention to the helpless woman beneath him when Long Rider squeezed the trigger.

The Remington bucked in Long Rider's hand. In the same movement he was leaping and twisting to the side as an arrow hissed past his shoulder. Long Rider barely noticed. His eyes were fixed on Iron Hawk, who seemed frozen in place. Kills Enemy was reaching for another arrow. Long Rider aimed and squeezed the trigger just as the bow came up. The warrior staggered backward, his second arrow arcing high into the air as Long Rider fired again. The warrior stumbled and dropped his bow.

Iron Hawk was still holding Yellow Buckskin Girl's head against the ground. Now he lowered his knife slowly toward her face, his movements stiff and awkward. Long Rider had an extra moment to swing his revolver away from the toppling warrior. He felt as if he lined up his sights and pulled the trigger in the same instant, just as Iron Hawk touched the woman's nose with the edge of his knife.

Long Rider thought the chief's body shuddered a little with the impact of the bullet, but he wasn't really looking at anything besides the knife blade. He was cocking the revolver again, but he knew the outcome had already been decided. It would only take a short flick of Iron Hawk's wrist to slice off the tip of Yellow Buckskin Girl's nose.

Long Rider could imagine the quick slicing motion, and then her scream as the blood pulsed and flowed down over her face. He had seen other women who were mutilated in the same way, and he believed it to be an even more terrible punishment than the loss of an ear. It would not be easy for other men to ignore the wound. Long Rider had wondered whether he himself ever could enjoy lying beside a woman who had been so marked.

But Iron Hawk's hand remained still, his glassy eyes fixed on some point in the distance. He seemed frozen again. Then his body began to sag, falling slowly off to the side. Yellow Buckskin Girl arched her back suddenly and threw him off, scrambling to her feet. She ran toward Long Rider and wrapped her arms around him, pressing her face against his chest.

Long Rider held her while he looked across the top of her head at the two bodies crumpled in the grass. The tall stalks of yellow grass blew in the breeze, and for a long time they were the only thing that moved on the hillside.

CHAPTER THIRTEEN

The strands of horsehair felt rough against Long Rider's skin. He rubbed them between his thumb and fingers, brooding over them in silence.

This was the roach that High Backbone had promised to prepare, given as a parting gift when Long Rider and Yellow Buckskin Girl were ready to leave the Lakota camp on the Powder River. The horsehair roach was dyed red to show that Long Rider had dreamed of the Winged God, but it looked black in the light from the fire burning in the pit before him.

Long Rider and Yellow Buckskin Girl had traveled late into the night, putting as much distance as possible between themselves and the camp. There had been few words between them as they rode, and no words at all when they finally stopped to eat a small meal of pemmican. The mixture of dried meat and buffalo fat had had no flavor for Long Rider, and now there was no pleasure in the warmth from the flames.

He studied the roach as he rolled it beneath his thumb, then he threw it into the blackness beyond the ring of firelight.

He heard a sharp breath at his side, but he did not look at Yellow Buckskin Girl as she leaned toward him on her knees. He was vaguely aware of her face hovering near his shoulder, glowing warmly as it came closer to the fire, but Long Rider still did not meet her eyes directly. He kept looking into the flames while she looked at him.

When she knew her husband was not going to speak, she said, "I am confused. Why do you throw away your medicine?"

Long Rider only grunted in disgust.

"It represents the power of Wakinyan, does it not?"

"Where was the power of the Thunderbird today? Did I show myself worthy of his protection?"

Yellow Buckskin Girl looked puzzled. "I believe so," she said.

"You believe so," Long Rider echoed, still staring into the fire. "Then why did Iron Hawk nearly succeed in slicing off your nose?"

"But he did not succeed. You prevented it."

Long Rider finally looked at Yellow Buckskin Girl and saw the tender concern in her eyes. It made him want to touch the dark line across the bridge of her nose. Iron Hawk's blade had cut into her skin there, drawing blood just before Long Rider shot the chief a second time. It was not a serious cut, but feeling the sharp ridge of crusted blood brought a deeper frown to Long Rider's features.

"You might still be suffering tonight," he said. "The blood might still be flowing. If either of my bullets had missed, or if my gun had not been working, your beauty would have been ruined forever."

Yellow Buckskin Girl smiled and took his fingers in her hand, pressing them against her cheek. "But the gun did work," she said. "Nor did you miss, even though Kills Enemy was aiming an arrow at your heart."

Long Rider shrugged and said, "I had no choice."

"That is what I mean. You could only show the courage of a man who has dreamed of the Winged God."

Long Rider frowned, and Yellow Buckskin Girl squeezed his hand.

"It was just as you said, my husband. I was safe under your protection."

"That is what I said. But then I sent you up the hill, never thinking that Iron Hawk might be watching us even then."

"You must have thought of it. I saw you following me."

"Something made me uneasy," Long Rider admitted. "Even so, I was almost too late."

"Have you forgotten that you endured without sleep for four days and four nights? You were dulled by the ordeal, and yet you still heard Wakinyan's warning. It was he who made you uneasy, Long Rider. He directed your bullets while Kills Enemy was drawing his bow.''

Long Rider shook his head, as if he couldn't find words for the thoughts that tortured him. ''I should have been more careful with my plans. I was successful because nothing else went wrong, but it came too close.''

''But you did protect me, did you not?'' Yellow Buckskin Girl sounded almost angry now. ''That is the only thing that matters. Why do you judge yourself so hard?''

''Because I made mistakes.'' He pulled his hand roughly away from hers. ''Look at this broken finger,'' he said. ''Look at the hole where the pitchfork went through my hand. These are the results of my foolishness. If I am the one who suffers, that is all right. But you might have been disfigured today because of my mistakes.''

Yellow Buckskin Girl seemed to understand better now. ''All men make mistakes,'' she said with a soft smile. ''Should you hope to be different? But your spirit and power are strong, Long Rider. You were able to protect me, just as you protected Hump and Crazy Horse and Runs Alone from the Crow. The People have honored your courage in a great feast, and now they speak of your wisdom in the council. I also know that you will continue to serve them well.''

Long Rider had been watching her closely as she spoke. ''That was the vision of Two Face,'' he said thoughtfully. ''He told me I would return to the People and save many lives.''

''His vision has already been achieved,'' said Yellow Buckskin Girl. ''But I did not need a vision. I can see your spirit with my own eyes and heart. I saw it even when we were children.''

Long Rider tried to remember himself as a young boy, and soon he was thinking about the powers of understanding possessed by a young girl. Perhaps that is the way it is, he thought. Perhaps women are able to see things more clearly than men do. He began to wonder why women didn't speak more often in the council lodges. The People might be guided with even greater wisdom. But then he thought of his mother's decision to send him away with Jim Bridger, which he thought had been a mistake.

Now he was less sure.

The sudden doubts brought a troubled look into his eyes,

which Yellow Buckskin Girl misunderstood. She reached again for his injured hand, holding it against the deerhide gown that covered her breasts.

"You must believe what I say," she told him. "I often remembered the way your hands made me feel, Long Rider. But it was not just your hands, it was the greatness of your power."

Long Rider had been wishing he could talk to his new wife about his mother and his duties as a son, but the feel of her breasts and the sound of her voice drove everything else from his mind. There was a pounding roar in his ears and a sudden pressure between his legs. He shifted position a little to make room for his growing erection, and had to move again when he heard the music of Yellow Buckskin Girl's playful laugh.

"That is another kind of power I remember," she said, looking directly at his breechclout.

"You mean the power that you have over me," Long Rider said. He was pleased to hear her laugh as he reached to touch her breasts. They were firm and heavy in his hands. He rolled them between his fingers, feeling the way they shifted under the deerskin gown. He hadn't touched a woman in more than five winters, and his desire nearly overwhelmed him. He began stroking the soft-tanned leather, his hands moving in wider circles over her body until he touched her bare shoulders and then the smooth flesh of her thighs.

Yellow Buckskin Girl moaned softly, her head rolling back to expose the long, delicate curve of her throat. She spread her legs farther apart as Long Rider's hand disappeared between them, moving slowly along her thigh. He was teasing her a little and also savoring the softness of her skin. But she squirmed closer to him, still on her knees, clutching and pulling his arm until his hand was covering the patch of hair between her legs.

"Let me feel them," she pleaded. "I ached for the touch of your fingers, Long Rider."

He didn't need encouragement. He had dreamed of this with equal hunger, longing for the hot wetness that greeted his fingers. They slipped inside her body while the broken finger tucked perfectly out of the way. It came to him that for this one thing he might be grateful to Captain Price. His lips twisted into a sour smile, but Yellow Buckskin Girl didn't see it. Her eyes were closed and she was holding his arm as she rolled her hips against his hand. Long Rider moved his fingers inside her, squeezing her leather-covered breasts with his other hand, lifting them in turn to feel their weight.

Yellow Buckskin Girl let go of Long Rider's arm, looking down again as she stroked the length of him beneath his breechclout. Then she began to fumble with the leather flap, pulling it free from the belt so Long Rider's shaft could spring up, standing straight and free. Her eyes went wide as she stared at it. She took it gently in her hands, holding it with a kind of awe, her mouth falling open while her hips continued to writhe against his hand, and her chest rose and fell with the labor of her breathing.

Long Rider found that his own hips were moving, pushing his shaft through the soft hands that held it. Yellow Buckskin Girl began to stroke him, never taking her eyes away from him, and slowly she began to lower her head. Long Rider had to pull his fingers out of her as she folded over him on her knees, and then he had to wait. Yellow Buckskin Girl moved so slowly that Long Rider thought he would never feel the touch of her hungry mouth. The agony of waiting almost seemed greater than all his dreams of Yellow Buckskin Girl, when he'd thought he would never see her again. But then he felt her lips, as hot and wet against him as her secret place had been for his fingers.

He watched himself disappear inside her mouth, her lips sliding down to meet her hand. Her tongue circled his shaft, her lips and fingers moving up and down together while the firelight played softly against her skin. Her breath began to sound louder as her hands and mouth moved with more urgency, and Long Rider was forced to hold her still for a moment.

"Not yet," he pleaded.

Yellow Buckskin Girl still tried to stroke him, and it required all his will to stop her. Long Rider wanted more than anything else to release himself, to feel the flooding pleasure he had been denied for so long, but he knew that the pleasure would then be over for a while. Slowly he lifted her head, stirred by the way her dark eyes and wet lips gleamed in the firelight. She smiled slyly at him, and a moment later she was pushing him onto his back as she lifted her knee across to straddle his hips.

"You are the only man I ever wanted," she whispered. "My life would have been without fire if you had not returned, Long Rider."

She still held his shaft in her hands, and now she was guiding it home. Long Rider had pushed her gown up around her waist and was starting to unlace the leather leggings that covered her calves when he felt her engulfing him. He closed his eyes to concentrate on the waves of pleasure that poured over him.

When he opened his eyes again, Yellow Buckskin Girl was pulling her dress over her head, her breasts hanging loose and swaying heavily from side to side. They glowed a dusky red, and Long Rider was sure he could feel a smoldering fire within them. Yellow Buckskin Girl arched her back, pushing her breasts into his hands as she tossed her dress aside and plunged herself down against his manhood.

She was groaning louder and louder, and Long Rider watched her throat moving with the sound, rippling in the light from the flames. He squeezed her breasts hard between his fingers and thrust himself up to meet her plunging thighs, and this time he had no will to stop. In a moment he was clutching her hips to hold her still while he exploded into her depths. He could feel himself being gripped inside her, and then she was crying out, her face lifted to the heavens, their bodies shuddering together. Long Rider settled slowly back against the grass while Yellow Buckskin Girl stroked his chest, looking down at him with eyes that were dark and suddenly moist.

"It is a cruel thing that kept us apart," she said, her breasts still rising and falling as she struggled to control her breathing.

Long Rider nodded sadly, brushing his hands softly over her skin. "This is the way it always should have been."

Their eyes locked together, and for a time there was only the powerful feeling that passed between them. He remained inside her, but the sound of their breathing became softer while the crackling of the fire seemed louder. Then the distant howl of a coyote drifted toward them across the prairie, and Yellow Buckskin Girl smiled.

"Iktomi is laughing over the trick he played on us," she said. The howl died away, and the mournful sound was reflected in her smile. "Why did it happen, Long Rider? You told me you were taken away against your will, but you did not tell me why."

"It was a white man," he said. "A great warrior named Jim Bridger. He bound me and took me from my mother's lodge during the night."

Yellow Buckskin Girl looked troubled, and Long Rider knew he had told her too much. "From your mother's lodge?" she said. "How could that have happened?"

Long Rider turned his head, trying to think of a way to avoid telling her the truth, but she had already seen it in his eyes.

"It was your mother's will," she said. "Is that it? She wanted you to escape to your own people?"

"The Oglala are my people," Long Rider snapped. "And you cannot call it escape when someone is already free and happy. That is why Bridger tied my hands." The impatience faded from his tone, replaced by an edge of bitterness. "But you are right about my mother," he said. "Bridger was only doing what she wanted him to do."

"And now you are angry at her."

"*She* is the one who kept us apart, Yellow Buckskin Girl. She drove me away from my people and sent me to live among strangers. It is because of her that I spent three winters in a white man's jail and you were left to Iron Hawk."

Yellow Buckskin Girl was gazing into the flames. "But I also remember Yellow Hair's grief," she said. "I believe she suffered a terrible loneliness when she gave up her only son. There must have been a good reason for her to do it."

Long Rider's heart swelled with tenderness for his woman, and an even greater respect for her wisdom and understanding. "You have always shown kindness and tolerance toward other people," he said, the tenderness giving way to a thoughtful frown. "But I don't know whether my mother's reasons were good. I wish I did know. Bridger said she feared for my safety. He said he believed there were bad times coming for the People."

"Do you know why she believed it?"

"The whites," Long Rider said, his tone turning bitter again. "She saw that the Wasichus were pressing in on us, and she heard that they were discovering the yellow metal in places near our country."

Yellow Buckskin Girl looked out into the darkness, as if she could see the sweeping grasslands that lay beyond their little ring of firelight. "It is true they have already driven us away from certain places," she said. "But the warriors will never allow them here." She looked down at Long Rider again. "Will they?"

"I believe we are strong," he said. "I believe we can fight them off."

Yellow Buckskin Girl bent closer, studying his face in the dying light of the fire. "I see something else in your eyes," she said.

"I also remember Bridger's words," he said. "He is sure the People will not be able to live in the old way much longer."

"But those are a *white man's* words."

"He has lived sixty-one winters," said Long Rider, "and he has seen many things. His concern was great enough that he sent me here."

"He sent you?"

"Only to take my mother to safety," Long Rider said quickly. "Not to spy for the Army. He freed me from the prison and gave me the weapons I used to rub out the Crow war party."

Yellow Buckskin Girl's dark eyes were filled with confusion. "Is that why you have come, then? To take your mother away? I thought that you and I—"

Long Rider touched her lips with his fingers. "You and I are man and woman," he assured her. "That will never change as long as we live. I told Bridger only that I would think about his words, but even if they are true, they will not change the thing I told you when I first saw you again. Do you remember what it was?"

"I can still hear it, Long Rider. 'I have come back to stay with the Lakota,' you said. I remember the words because they gave me so much joy."

Long Rider's smile was full of happiness. "I already knew I would rather die among the People than live in safety among the whites," he said. "But then I returned to find the People strong, and also to find that the woman of my dreams had not forgotten me."

Yellow Buckskin Girl sighed, staring down at him with great affection. Then her hips began to move with the first stirrings of renewed desire, and Long Rider felt his shaft swelling inside her.

"Did you think of this while you were in the white man's prison?" said Yellow Buckskin Girl.

Long Rider nodded, closing his eyes and moving his hands around her hips to grasp the firm flesh behind. He pulled himself farther inside her, growing harder and harder as Yellow Buckskin Girl began to moan softly again, stroking his chest.

And again Long Rider felt himself soaring like an eagle far above the earth, except that this time he stayed aloft for a long while.

Long Rider came awake very slowly, feeling the hot sun against his face as he struggled to remember where he was. He knew without looking that the sun had already climbed high above the horizon, and this was also puzzling. He wondered why he had slept so late, and why he was not inside a lodge. Then the memories began to return, driving away the mists that tried to shroud them. He saw again the killing of Iron Hawk, and the things that had come to him in his vision before that.

Long Rider frowned, remembering that he had thrown away the horsehair roach supplied by High Backbone. It worried him that Wakinyan would be displeased and perhaps withdraw his protection. But Yellow Buckskin Girl had reminded him of his own power, and he smiled when he thought of the honors given to him by his People. He had returned to them as a warrior, and he might be able to beg forgiveness from the Winged God, as well as any of the other spirits he had offended. His smile grew wider when he thought of the way Yellow Buckskin Girl's body had looked in the light from the fire, and he reached out for her. His arms felt heavy after so much sleep, but his eyes snapped open quickly when he could not find his woman beside him.

He saw her as soon as he sat up, far out in the tall yellow grass beyond the fire pit. She was bent over at the waist as if she were examining something on the ground. Long Rider was about to call out when she took a step forward, and then another. He thought he knew what she was doing, and decided to watch.

Yellow Buckskin Girl moved a step at a time, always bent over and staring toward her feet, and there was something in her manner that suggested she'd been doing the same thing for a long time. Long Rider looked at the grass between them, seeing where a large patch had been trampled as she walked through it, back and forth. Long Rider watched her with a growing spark of passion in his pale gray eyes. He knew there could be no other woman like this one. He gave thanks to Wakan-tanka that she had been sent to him, and prayed for their happiness together.

Yellow Buckskin Girl reached down suddenly, and when she straightened again, she looked toward the fire, laughing with delight when she saw that he had been watching her.

"I told you your power was great," she said, holding her hand high above her head. "But I never believed you could have thrown it so far."

She hurried toward the fire, the tall grass whispering against her bare legs. The sun glistened on her oiled hair and on the softness of her breasts. He touched her lightly as she kneeled down beside him, making no protest when she began to tie the shaman's roach into the hair behind his ear.

"They say this is where Crazy Horse ties the stone that gives him his power," she said. "Is that true, Long Rider?"

"I have seen it there myself," he said.

"I believe you are brothers in spirit, my husband, and it makes me proud."

Long Rider laughed. "Just as there is pride for me in having such a good and devoted wife," he said, suddenly turning serious. "But now there is something I must ask of you."

Yellow Buckskin Girl sat back on her haunches, watching him expectantly.

"No one else can hear what I told you last night," said Long Rider. "My mother would be dishonored if the People knew she sent me away."

"They will not know," she promised. "Yellow Hair should not have to suffer more than she already has." Yellow Buckskin Girl looked closely at her husband. "You feel the same, do you not?"

He looked at her in surprise. "I want to," he said slowly. "Two Face also told me of her suffering, and Bridger thought her reasons were good for sending me away."

"But you believe she made a mistake," Yellow Buckskin Girl suggested.

Long Rider looked closely at her again, studying her face. He didn't know whether to laugh or be angry. "You are reminding me that I made mistakes as well," he said.

Yellow Buckskin Girl gave him a gentle smile. "I am seeing that you find it difficult to forgive your mother," she said. "Just as you find it difficult to forgive yourself."

Long Rider stared out toward the snow-crested peaks of the Big Horn Mountains, hanging like ghosts above the far horizon. Then he felt his new wife's hand on his arm.

"This will not be an easy time for either of you," she said. "Your mother will be happy to see you, but perhaps she will be unhappy that you have returned from the white man's world. She may also fear that you hate her, or that you will reveal her secret. This is a time that will require all of your wisdom and power, my husband."

Long Rider covered her hand with his, smiling a little as he looked out toward the distant mountains. "It is good that I also have the wisdom of a woman who is not afraid to tell me what she feels."

"There is still something else you should consider," Yellow Buckskin Girl said slowly.

Long Rider waited, and when she didn't say anything, he turned to meet her eyes again. There was a look of sorrow in them.

"Perhaps you have already thought of this," she finally said, "but I hope you are not expecting to find the same woman you left as a boy."

"I did not leave her," he said curtly.

Yellow Buckskin Girl gazed at him a moment longer. "I hope you can put away this anger," she said. "But I also hope you will remember that she has suffered much. Five hard winters have gone by."

Long Rider looked puzzled, wondering whether he had understood her meaning. "Can she have changed so much?" he said.

Yellow Buckskin Girl nodded slowly, her eyes dark with sadness. "She has become an old woman, my husband. She is not the same. I tell you this because I do not want you to be distressed when you see her. And also because I do not want her to see the changes in the way you look at her."

CHAPTER FOURTEEN

Long Rider and Yellow Buckskin Girl made three more camps on the trail to the Tongue River, joining their bodies by the fire at night and joining them again as the rising sun warmed their flesh. Afterward they would watch the snow on the Big Horn peaks turn from pink to glaring white as the sun climbed higher. Then they would pack up and move on toward the peaks, which shimmered through the day like a vision on the horizon.

The sun was still high above them on the fifth day when they reached Black Bear's camp of more than two hundred lodges, clustered on a low mesa where Wolf Creek empties into the Tongue. Children were playing among the tepees while their mothers made clothing or dried meat for the winter. Surrounding the camp was a rich herd of perhaps three thousand ponies grazing in the tall grass on the mesa.

It was a scene of peaceful abundance, but Long Rider took no pleasure in it. He was brooding as he rode through the pony herd toward the camp. Yellow Buckskin Girl watched her husband with concern, determined to keep her silence, but the words she had already spoken came back to him while he was seeking out his mother's lodge.

As soon as he saw her, Long Rider was grateful for the warning he'd received from Yellow Buckskin Girl.

His mother was scraping a buffalo hide in front of her tepee,

bent over on her knees so that her face was hidden at first. But
Long Rider could see that the golden hair he remembered was
now the color and texture of the straw he'd fed to the army
horses. Then she looked up to see who was coming, and Long
Rider felt an even greater sorrow. The sparkling blue eyes he'd
known had turned pale and lifeless, looking out from an empty
and weathered face that made him want to turn away.

The emptiness in her eyes disturbed him even more. Long
Rider had not expected his mother to show surprise. He was
sure that the news of his return had already arrived with other
travelers between the two camps, during the days of the war
council and his vision quest. But he had hoped she would be
pleased to see him. Even with his wife's warning, he was not
prepared to see the way his mother stood before him without
saying or doing anything.

Yellow Buckskin Girl brought her horse close to Long Rider's
and touched his arm. "I will find a place for our lodge," she
said softly. "Then I will turn the ponies out to graze."

Long Rider thanked her—with a deep feeling she understood
—and slid to the ground. He watched her leading the mounts
away, delaying the passions he still thought were coming, but
when he looked at his mother, he saw that her eyes remained
empty of love or warmth. His sorrow disappeared in an instant,
swept away by a burning rage that frightened and confused him.
Without wanting to, he was remembering his exile among the
soldiers, and his long, empty days in the Fort Laramie jail.

"It was not your place to do what you did," he said stiffly,
still trying to control the feelings he had wanted to hide. "It was
not your decision to make. I was ready to become a warrior
when you tore me away from my people."

Yellow Hair seemed to shrink away from him. "Oh, Gabe,"
she said.

"Do not use that name!" he shouted. "Do not use any of the
white man's words in my hearing. The whites are greedy and
evil, and they make me ashamed for the color of my skin. They
make me ashamed of *you*."

Long Rider was leaning over his mother. She stumbled
backward, her pale blue eyes filling with tears.

"You robbed me of five winters among the Lakota," Long
Rider yelled. The fire of his rage was growing smaller beneath
his mother's tears, but he tried to resist them. "You robbed me

of Yellow Buckskin Girl and the joy we could have had together. Instead of living free among my people, I spent three winters in a white man's jail. I could only dream of freedom while I looked at the sky through a small hole covered by metal bars.''

"Oh, my son," Yellow Hair cried out. "What made you come back?"

Long Rider stepped back in surprise. "You don't want to see me even now?" he said. "This is where I belong."

"No, this is where you will die," said his mother. She wiped at the tears that were pouring down over the leathery flesh of her face. "I sent you away so you might have a long life, but now you've come back."

"It was not your decision to make," Long Rider said again. But the anger was gone from his voice, replaced by a pleading tone, as if he wanted Yellow Hair to acknowledge the terrible wrong she had done to him. He fought the stinging in his own eyes and said, "Only the rocks live forever, my mother. Surely you have been a Lakota long enough to know that much. What does the time of my death matter, as long as I live in a way that pleases the spirits and brings me happiness?"

Yellow Hair only shook her head, crying brokenly and unable to speak. Long Rider lost the final part of his rage and took her into his arms. He had been able to see her as his enemy when the cold emptiness was still in her eyes. He had been able to imagine that she wanted to hurt him, and to hate her for destroying his life.

But now he knew that Two Face and Yellow Buckskin Girl had both been right. Yellow Hair had proved her love by sacrificing her happiness for what she thought would be good for him. He believed his only remaining anger was for the evil spirits that try to rule the world. He raged silently against the spirits for causing his mother to believe the wrong thing, making them both so unhappy.

"I truly believed you wanted to be rid of me," he said as he held his mother, all the sadness of his exile coming back to overwhelm him. "I truly believed I was not wanted among the People."

Yellow Hair cried harder, clutching at his waist with rough, bony hands. "I know you can never forgive me," she said. "But I only wanted you to *live*."

Long Rider was angry with himself for the thing he had just

said, and also confused. He saw that he still wanted his mother to pay a price for what she had done, as if it would help the sadness that still lived inside him. At the same time he wanted to take away her anguish.

"I have already forgiven you," he said, gently squeezing her shoulders. "I heard of your grief after you sent me away, and your reasons have been explained to me. Yellow Buckskin Girl said you have suffered enough already. She is a wise woman."

Yellow Hair pulled back far enough to give him a worried look. "Where is Iron Hawk?" she said, her voice still rough with sobbing. "Will he come here to take her back?"

Long Rider shook his head. "I had to kill him," he said. "Yellow Buckskin Girl is my woman now."

He told her what had happened, and for the first time there was something like pleasure or hope in her expression, even if it was mingled with many other things. "I'm glad you have been able to come together again," she said, "but it's bad that you were forced to kill Iron Hawk. I know that if I hadn't sent you away—"

Long Rider touched her cracked and swollen lips. "It is done," he said. "I went to the white man's jail because of my own mistakes, not yours, and I learned an important lesson there. We must not worry about the things that cannot be changed. Only unhappiness lies that way. We must put those thoughts away and look forward."

Yellow Hair blinked rapidly, gazing up at her son as if she were seeing him for the first time. "You have come back a stronger man, and much wiser," she said, her eyes shining with pride as well as sorrow. "I have already heard of your bravery against the Crow, from visitors who praised the great deeds of the white Oglala. They even say that Red Cloud listened to your advice in the council lodge."

Long Rider nodded. "The Lakota are joining together to drive the whites out of our country, my mother. Soon we will be roaming our old hunting grounds again."

Yellow Hair touched his cheek, and fresh tears welled up in her eyes. "No, my son, that is not what will happen. That is why the news of your return caused me so much grief."

Long Rider shifted his balance, looking impatient. "I know you believe the whites will defeat us," he said sharply. "Jim Bridger already told me the same thing. Perhaps you heard that

he sent me here with a warning for the Lakota''—Yellow Hair
nodded to show that she had—''but there was another reason he
freed me from the prison. He sent me to carry you away. He said
the whites will also take the Powder River country—''

"He is right," said Yellow Hair. "Someday it will happen."

"No! The People are strong for war. They are united behind
Red Cloud, and now they will learn to fight like the white
man."

Long Rider's mother was shaking her head with a sad,
faraway look. "No they won't," she said. "I wish it were true,
my son, but I have observed their ways for many years, and I see
things in a way you cannot see them. The Lakota will not change
so completely. In the end they will be defeated."

Her tone was so confident, and so resigned, that it made Long
Rider uneasy. "I have just come from the fort," he said. "I
have seen the puny soldier forces. They are nothing compared to
the forces gathered on the Powder River."

"Which, in turn, are nothing," insisted Yellow Hair, "compared to the number of whites who will be coming."

Long Rider scowled and said, "Bridger told me the same
thing."

"Don't forget that we come from the land of the whites. We
have seen them there, just as you saw the soldiers at the fort. We
also know how they are, and how they will behave when they
hear that the yellow metal has been discovered here. It is
something you cannot imagine."

"If that is true," Long Rider said in a challenging tone,
"then perhaps I should take you away as Bridger wanted. He
said the whites will find you among the Oglala. He said they will
force you to live in shame among them."

Yellow Hair looked puzzled. "Why would I want to go and
live in shame any sooner than is necessary?"

"You might not have to. Bridger also said there will be plenty
of new villages, where the people wouldn't know where you
came from."

"Of course they'd know," she snapped. "Just look at my
ruined face! Everyone would know immediately where I had
been." She sighed deeply and shook her head. "No, Long
Rider, my fate lies here."

"And so does mine, my mother."

Yellow Hair looked thoughtfully at her son, then she seemed

to change her mind. "It is not the same," she said decisively. "You are still young. You have a chance to—"

"No," Long Rider said, breaking in. "It is decided."

"But the fighting will be terrible," Yellow Hair pleaded. "The dangers will be great."

"I am not afraid. Two Face saw in a dream that I would take care of my people. I have also seen Wakinyan in a vision of my own. The Thunderbird flew down and wrapped his wings about my shoulders, cloaking me with his power." Long Rider fingered the red horsehair cutting that was tied into his own hair behind his ear. "High Backbone made this to show that I am protected by the Winged God."

Yellow Hair seemed proud that he had received such a powerful vision, but she was also wistful. "I don't know, my son. Many winters ago I would have thought of your vision as nothing but foolishness. Whites don't believe in such magic. But I have seen the power that comes from believing, and perhaps that is the power of Wakinyan. Even so, it frightens me to think of you on the battlefield, fighting in the terrible fights that I know are coming."

"Only the rocks live forever," Long Rider repeated, smiling easily as he looked at the lodges surrounding them. "It is not important. It matters only that I am here with my mother and my wife, where the game is plentiful and the ponies find good grass, and the children laugh as they run free over the prairie. I am truly happy for the first time in many winters."

His mother was looking up at him with the same combination of pleasure and sadness she had shown before, but he saw that her eyes had a new life in them. She began to nod, slowly at first and then with greater certainty.

"I am also happy," she finally said. "It makes me sad that you returned in these bad times, and I fear the things that will come tomorrow, but it fills me with joy to see you here before me. Welcome home, my son."

A Cheyenne warrior named Little Horse tried to warn the camp that same afternoon, but Long Rider never heard of it until a long time after.

Almost no one did.

Little Horse and his Arapaho wife came galloping in from the south, telling those who met them that there were soldiers approaching the Tongue River. But the Arapaho didn't believe their story. "The bluecoats would never come into our country," they said.

Little Horse's wife tried to convince the village crier to go among the lodges and alert her people, but he refused.

"Little Horse has made a mistake," the crier told her. "He just saw some Indians coming over the trail, and nothing more."

Little Horse gave up and took his wife in search of her relatives, finding her brother, Panther, as he rested in front of his tepee. They told him to pack whatever he owned so they could leave the village that night. But Panther also refused to believe that the soldiers could be anywhere nearby.

"It is true," Little Horse told him. "Your sister saw them before I did. She got down to tie a pack that had become loose on our travois. That's when she glanced back over the ridge and saw them: a straight line of soldiers coming along the trail far behind us."

"We waited until we were over the next hill," his wife said. "Then we cut the travois loose and ran our horses straight for the camp."

Panther scoffed at his Cheyenne brother-in-law. "You're always getting frightened and making mistakes about things," he said. "You saw nothing but some buffalo."

"Very well," said Little Horse. "You need not go unless you want to, but we will leave tonight."

Little Horse and his wife had better luck persuading some of her other relatives to pack up and go along. They left before sunset, moving their lodges farther up the Tongue.

Long Rider thought later that he might have noticed a disturbance on the other side of the village, about the time that Little Horse and his wife first galloped in. He was never sure whether he'd really been aware of it, or whether his imagination had simply added it to his memory. But for a long time he tortured himself over his failure to find out what had caused it, until he finally admitted to himself that there had been no reason to do so. Hunting parties often returned in the midst of such excitement, which also might have been caused by a horse race or some other social event.

In any case, he had been absorbed in conversation with his mother, who begged him for every piece of news he could remember from the outside world.

She had heard about the war among the white people, for example, but she could not understand why they would fight each other. It had troubled her for many winters. Long Rider thought back to the things he'd overheard, which had something to do with slaves.

"I think the"—he frowned, using the white word—"the *states* in the north wanted to steal the slaves from the *states* in the south."

Yellow Hair laughed. "No," she said, "I think I understand now. They wanted to set the slaves free. You say the war is over now?"

"That is what Bridger told me. I think it is over because the whites killed their Great Father. A man named Lincoln."

Yellow Hair frowned again, repeating the name. "I don't know who that is," she said.

It turned out that Long Rider's mother understood what Bridger had meant by little houses on wheels, rolling on steel bars. She called them *railroads* and said she had seen them in the land of her childhood. But it surprised her that they were coming in this direction. "That is not a good sign," she said. "Bridger was right. The whites will be arriving in great numbers."

That made Long Rider think with more urgency about the other reason for his trip to the Arapaho camp. He went with his mother to find Chief Black Bear, so he could arrange to speak before the village council the next day. Black Bear said he welcomed the news that Red Cloud was sending the war pipe to his people, but he never mentioned Little Horse's warning about the soldiers. For his part, Long Rider did not mention, during this first meeting with Black Bear, the army plans for a summer campaign. He thought there would be time the next day.

Long Rider wondered later whether his visit to Black Bear came before Little Horse had entered the camp, or whether the chief had simply believed that the Cheyenne warrior's message wasn't important enough to discuss. Long Rider never knew the answer, but sometimes he was tormented by thoughts of the way things might have been.

If he had heard about the soldiers, he could have assured the Arapaho that they were real. He could have told them about his meeting with Colonel Moonlight, and the invasion force under General Patrick Connor. He could have explained that Moonlight had revealed the Army's plans when he thought Long Rider might act as a scout, and Jim Bridger had confirmed the colonel's words. The moon had completed almost a full cycle between the time when Gabe Conrad heard of these Army plans and the time Long Rider arrived in the Arapaho camp. That would have been plenty of time for Star Chief Connor to assemble his forces and bring them north to the Tongue River.

But no matter how many times Long Rider imagined a happier outcome, he could never escape the fact that his knowledge of the Army's plans, and Little Horse's warning, did not come together in time.

Yellow Buckskin Girl was waiting for Long Rider and his mother when they returned from the meeting with Black Bear, and she smiled broadly when she saw the happiness in their faces. She joined them in making plans for the summer.

Yellow Hair's husband came to the lodge a short time later to greet the son he had raised as his own. Little Wound was a tall, lean warrior with a hawk's nose and close-set eyes that were, at first, full of suspicion.

The suspicion seemed to fade as he listened to the story of Long Rider's abduction by the white scout named Bridger. Long Rider told it in a way that made Bridger sound like a very brave and clever man. Only such a man, after all, could have stolen the boy from his own lodge in the middle of the camp without alerting anyone else. Long Rider could not explain why the scout would do what he had done, except to say that Bridger might have believed it was the right thing for a young boy with white skin.

"It is hard to understand the whites," Long Rider said with a shrug.

His mother only smiled and said she did not care about understanding what had happened. Her son, who she thought was dead, had been returned to her. That was the only thing that mattered.

Little Wound studied her face carefully, then turned to look at his stepson. Long Rider bore up beneath his hard gaze, wondering what else he might say if Little Wound began to ask more probing questions. Then he saw a gleam of warmth appear in the dark eyes of his stepfather, just before Little Wound clamped his hand on Long Rider's arm.

"It is a good thing you have returned," he said with gruff

affection. "It makes my heart full to see Yellow Hair's pleasure."

Yellow Hair and Yellow Buckskin Girl began to prepare a meal while Long Rider told Little Wound about his fight with the Crow and his return to Red Cloud's camp on the Powder. Little Wound asked many questions about the council and about the fight with Iron Hawk, his eyes glittering with a fierce pride in his stepson's wisdom and courage. Later they sat around the fire, laughing and joking with the women as they feasted on the sweet meat of the buffalo hump.

Long Rider often thought about that time in later years. He remembered the red sun drifting down behind the Big Horn Mountains, and the sounds of dogs barking and children laughing nearby. Most of all he remembered the fond looks he received from his mother and his wife and his father. He never knew such joy as he felt that night. His heart felt as if it might burst. After five winters in exile he was back among the people who loved him.

He didn't see Little Horse and his wife riding away from the camp.

CHAPTER FIFTEEN

"Who was my father?" said Long Rider.

Yellow Hair turned away from the design she was painting on the side of her tepee and gave him a puzzled look. "I have already told you about him," she said. "Do you not remember the time I spoke of Adam Conrad? The trader of goods who became my husband in St. Louis?"

The name stirred a familiar bitterness in Long Rider's heart. "Yes," he said, "I remember the man who came into this country without permission from the Lakota, exposing his wife and the other travelers to great danger—"

"Oh, my son," said Yellow Hair. "I beg of you—"

"You told me of the man who was your husband. But was he my father?"

Long Rider's mother looked hard into his face, her blue eyes gleaming in the light from the fire in front of her tepee. The feast had ended long before, and they were alone now. Yellow Buckskin Girl had made an excuse to return to her lodge when Little Wound announced that he was going to visit the relatives of his other wife.

Mother and son had continued talking near the fire, until Yellow Hair asked to hear more about Long Rider's vision. When he finished telling her about it, she had decided to add a Thunderbird to the other images on the walls of her tepee. She said it would be a sign to everyone that her son had received the special attention of the Winged God.

She had gone inside her lodge for a small bag of powder that she'd ground from yellow clay, mixed with fat rendered from bone marrow, and Long Rider had watched in silence as she worked the pigment into the buffalo hide with a tool made from the porous part of a stag horn. He had gathered his courage for a long time before he could ask about his father. And still, it was not exactly the question he had meant to ask. His mother seemed to understand, for she was still watching his expression.

"Could it be that Jim Bridger was my father?" he finally said.

His mother's eyes and mouth opened wide, showing such surprise that Long Rider knew it could not be true. He turned away, but not before Yellow Hair saw her son's disappointment.

"You have a great respect for Bridger," she said tenderly, "is that not so? You hoped I would say yes?"

Long Rider nodded. "He is a great fighter, and a man of wisdom."

"That is true," Yellow Hair said wistfully, her eyes shining more brightly than before. "But you would feel the same about your true father if he was alive."

"No!" said Long Rider. "He was a foolish man, full of greed for the yellow metal."

"So was I, my son. We made the decision to come here together."

"I don't believe that. You would not willingly violate the sacred hunting grounds of the Lakota."

"We didn't understand those things," Yellow Hair said sadly. "That is what you must remember. We didn't think much about Indians at all, except as a bunch of strange savages to be feared. We only wanted excitement and a chance to gather wealth."

"You ask me to believe that you were greedy, like the other whites?"

Yellow Hair looked at her son with pain in her eyes. "We did not think of it that way, Long Rider. I know you will find this hard to understand. You have been taught to share your food and shelter with those who are less fortunate. The Lakota teach their children right away that those who horde their wealth are selfish and maybe evil. But the whites are taught differently from the time they are children. Great wealth is considered a mark of honor, just as horses are a mark of honor for a warrior. Or poverty for a chief.''

Yellow Hair saw that her son was struggling with this new way of seeing things. She put down the paint and the horn tool so she could place her hands on his shoulders. Then she waited until he met her gaze.

"You must not hate your father," she said. "He was a good man. He was generous with his friends. And his spirit was strong. Otherwise I would not have become his wife.''

Long Rider continued to look into her eyes, but she was no longer seeing him. She began to smile.

"I was wooed by many young men," she said in a soft voice. "But they were all so dull that they put me to sleep. It was your father who won me, because he had a great vision of what he wanted to do. He was strong and restless.'' She came back from her memories and looked at him again. "I think you have the same wild streak," she said. "I don't believe you will ever stay long in one place. You will always yearn to be somewhere else doing something different.''

"I thought that was the way of the Lakota," Long Rider said with a laugh.

Yellow Hair laughed too. "Perhaps it was not an accident that placed your father and me in the Black Hills country. Perhaps this is the place for a certain kind of people.''

"People like Jim Bridger?" said Long Rider, turning serious again. He was staring into the darkness. "Did you know that Bridger called me 'son' when we traveled together?''

"That is something a white man says to show a good heart," his mother said gently. "It doesn't mean you truly are his son.''

Long Rider looked at her again. "He also told me he loved you.''

His mother's hand went to her hair, and she smiled quickly, fighting to control her expression. But she looked closely at her son as if to make sure he was telling the truth. "He did?" she said. "He told you that?''

"That wasn't the reason he sent me here," Long Rider said quickly. "He did tell me he had always loved you, but he said he already had a woman and children waiting for him somewhere else.''

"Well, of course," said Yellow Hair. She bent to pick up the horn tool and the pigment and began to work on the Thunderbird. Her movements were quick and nervous, and the bright look of excitement was still dancing in her eyes.

"Did you love Bridger?" Long Rider asked.

"Of course not!" said Yellow Hair, continuing to spread the pigment on the buffalo hide. "I was your father's woman."

Long Rider didn't say anything, and after a while his mother's strokes came slower and slower. Then it seemed she had forgotten completely about the Thunderbird.

"I wish you could have seen him when he came to St. Louis," she said. "He had not visited a village in seventeen winters, and the way people looked at him when he went down the—"

Yellow Hair broke off and looked up at her son from beneath her eyelashes. "*—streets,*" she said, using the white word. "I guess you know what they are."

Long Rider nodded, a mischievous glint in his eye.

"I don't suppose I'm fooling you," his mother said with a laugh. "I forget you are a grown man now, who knows that sometimes a woman can love more than one man. But I was always true to your father, Long Rider, and I always loved him. I know you would like to believe otherwise, but nothing ever happened that would make it possible for Jim Bridger to be your father."

Long Rider touched his mother's cheek. "It also gives me pleasure to hear that my mother was an honorable woman," he said.

"Thank you, my son. I wish you had known your father. I don't believe you would feel as you do." She fell silent for a moment, once again staring at him without seeing him. "It happens that I know exactly when you came into existence, Long Rider, because it was the same morning that your father died. Almost in the shadow of the Black Hills."

Her eyes filled with tears.

"It seemed to us that all our dreams lay before us that morning," she said. "We were a day's travel from the hills, and we thought they would contain everything we wanted. We lay in the wagon and talked about the things that might happen, and we were excited. Soon it turned into another kind of excitement." She looked at Long Rider with a shy grin. "Your father always gave me great pleasure, and that morning it was sweeter than ever before."

Yellow Hair sighed deeply, looking toward the fire.

"Or maybe that was just a trick of memory. We heard the first war cries just as we finished, and in a moment there was shooting all through the camp. Adam grabbed his musket and jumped out of the wagon. I wasn't far behind, but the fight was almost over already. I saw my husband's body on the ground, full of arrows. I picked up his musket, but he had fired it already. Then I saw a warrior coming toward me, so I took the powder horn from my husband's body and began to reload the musket. The Indian stopped to watch what I was doing, and he was smiling." Yellow Hair smiled now at the memory. "I started screaming at him, and he just kept watching me and smiling, until I rolled a ball into the muzzle. I was pushing it down with the ramrod when the warrior—"

"Little Wound?" said Long Rider.

Yellow Hair nodded and said, "Yes, that was Little Wound. He took the rifle out of my hands and laughed when I tried to beat him. He still laughs when he thinks of that day, but I know he also feels bad now that my husband was killed."

"He spared your life because of your courage?"

Yellow Hair lowered her head in modesty and laughed lightly. "I ran back to the wagon, knowing I was about to die or be taken to live among the Indians. I could think of only one thing. That's when I took the Bible of my family—the black book I used to teach you the white man's language."

"I remember it," said Long Rider.

"Little Wound wanted me to throw it away. He became very angry, but I would not be parted with my Bible, and in the end he let me keep it." Yellow Hair gave him a serious look. "You must keep it now," she said. "It will tell you things you must know about yourself, in case anything happens to me."

"This is not the time—"

"Promise me!" She gripped his arms with a sudden force that surprised him. "Keep the black book with you all your life, Long Rider, and someday you will understand the reason I ask this of you."

"Very well," he said.

"You make a vow?"

Long Rider nodded.

"And promise me that you will try to think well of your father?"

Long Rider nodded again, more stiffly this time.

"He was a good man, my son. Remember that it was my decision as much as his to come in search of the yellow metal."

Long Rider looked down.

"I see you are troubled by what I say," said Yellow Hair. "But I was a white woman then, and that is the way the whites are. It doesn't hurt me that you turn your eyes away from me, because I know that someday you will understand this as well."

Long Rider nodded, still staring at the ground. He looked up again when his mother laughed.

"I was thinking that I came to this country for the yellow metal, but also for excitement. I did not want to be like all the other white women."

Long Rider frowned.

"You do not see?" said Yellow Hair. She laughed again, and there was something in the sound of it that made Long Rider look at her closely.

"It's a joke!" she said. "The Great Spirit played a joke on your mother. He granted my wish."

Long Rider raised himself up on his elbows and looked at the lean, firm body of Yellow Buckskin Girl lying beneath him. It seemed to shine in the early-morning light that filtered down from the smoke hole of their tepee. His shaft was beginning to dwindle inside her, but even so, he felt a stir when he saw the swelling of her breasts. Yellow Buckskin Girl watched the movement of her husband's eyes and felt his new arousal, and she laughed with a musical sound that stirred him even further.

"Is it possible we could always be so happy?" she said.

A dark feeling touched Long Rider but he brushed it away. "Is there a reason to believe otherwise?" he said.

Yellow Buckskin Girl smiled and said, "I hope you know how much you please me, my husband."

The dark feeling persisted. Long Rider thought of his mother's story about her final morning with his father, and the great pleasure she said Adam Conrad had given her. Perhaps it was this story—and the echo in his wife's words—that had caused the dark cloud.

"What troubles you?" asked Yellow Buckskin Girl.

"There is nothing." But Long Rider saw the way his wife looked at him and knew he couldn't hide the uneasiness that had overtaken him. "I was remembering something my mother told me, about a bad time."

As he spoke, however, Long Rider was suddenly thinking of Colonel Moonlight and the soldiers who were coming under Star Chief Connor. He could almost see the soldiers, as if in a dream. Long Rider felt himself shrinking rapidly. He eased out of Yellow Buckskin Girl and rolled onto his side.

"I must go down to the river," he said.

Yellow Buckskin Girl frowned, guessing his intentions and knowing what they meant. "Are you expecting trouble, my husband?"

Long Rider shook his head, but again he saw she was not convinced. "It will be good to remain vigilant," he said. "Perhaps you should go to my mother's lodge. I can come and find you there."

Yellow Buckskin Girl watched her husband gathering up his revolvers and the big Sharps carbine, frowning when he slipped the Army-issue cartridge case onto his belt and made sure it was full.

"There is no need to look so worried," Long Rider said from the entrance. "Remember that the People are strong and that Wakinyan protects us."

Yellow Buckskin Girl nodded, and Long Rider ducked out of the tepee, squinting against the brilliant morning sunshine. He had staked his best horse in front of the lodge, and now he decided to take it to the river. He had hoped that riding through the peaceful camp would ease the dark feeling, but his uneasiness continued to grow—just as it had when he'd watched Yellow Buckskin Girl walking up the hill toward the village on the Powder River.

Long Rider searched the land and sky around the camp for any sign of intruders, urging more speed from his pony as he passed into the herd on the mesa. At the far edge he went down a steep clay bank to the river, where he set aside his weapons and removed his breechclout.

Soon he would make a scout of the country around the village, but first it was important to wash. He would have been very frightened if he got into a fight after he had been lying with a woman unless he had cleansed himself first. This was the thing Yellow Buckskin Girl knew about male customs that had made her worried. When Long Rider said he was going to the river,

she had understood that he foresaw the chance of a fight that
day.

He was neck-deep in the icy water and rubbing his genitals
when he heard a sound that didn't belong in a land of unshod
ponies. It echoed very faintly up between the high river walls,
but Long Rider knew it immediately as the ring of an iron
horseshoe striking a rock. He ran out of the river and dressed
himself, then mounted his pony and raced it back up the bank
and through the herd toward the village.

There was an instant when he hesitated, seeing the children at
play among the tepees and the women tending their fires. It
seemed hard to believe that trouble could be anywhere nearby,
and the sound of the horseshoe had been so faint that Long
Rider was able to wonder if he had truly heard it.

But he knew the answer, and in another instant he was among
the tepees crying out his warning that soldiers were about to
attack. Mothers rushed to gather up their children while warriors
dashed out of their lodges. Many of the Arapaho had horses
staked in the village, and they put their women and children on
them, sending them up Wolf Creek to begin the retreat.

Other warriors ran toward the pony herd, which sent up a
sudden chorus of whinnying. Long Rider glanced back through
the roiling dust and saw a column of bluecoats coming up over
the riverbank, wheeling into line to face the village. The
Arapaho horses, frightened by the appearance and smell of the
white men, were racing toward their owners.

A group of enemy riders veered off toward the herd, and Long
Rider identified them as Pawnee scouts intent on plunder. The
sight of the Pawnee filled him with rage, and he started yelling
out his warning again. Then the crackle of rifle fire drifted up
from the river beneath the sound of a bugle blowing the charge,
and Long Rider knew there was no more need for him to alert
the People.

He was turning back toward his mother's lodge when he
heard a whistling sound above him and a boom from the river.
In the next instant the world around him blew up with a crash of
noise and pieces of metal slashing through the tepees. Long
Rider's horse shuddered and rolled out from under him, blood
spouting from a hole torn in its side. Long Rider jumped,
staying on his feet while the echoes of the explosion rolled away.
Only then did he hear the children screaming and their mothers

crying while a thousand dogs barked and the warriors shrieked their war whoops.

A cloud of smoke and dust billowed from the explosion, and out of it ran a woman who was clutching half of her baby. The baby whimpered even though its hips and legs had been blown away by the shell, spilling entrails that dragged along in the dirt. The baby had died by the time Long Rider could wrench it from the woman's arms. He led her away, catching up a horse that was running through the village. He calmed the terrified animal and guided it toward the creek with the woman on its back.

There were more women and children streaming out of the camp toward the creek, but Long Rider didn't see his mother or wife among them. He strained to see his mother's yellow hair through the smoke as he listened to the rifle fire approaching the village. Then he could hear the thunder of the cavalry charge, and Long Rider started racing toward her lodge, which lay directly in the path of the soldiers.

A runaway pony came between the tepees carrying an Arapaho who was clutching his belly and singing his death chant. The warrior fell, and Long Rider caught the horse, galloping back toward the bluecoats with other warriors who were trying to shield the fleeing women and children. Bullets whipped through the tepees and a second shell from the gun-that-shoots-twice slammed into the village. People were falling everywhere, screaming in agony or fear. Dogs ran in frantic circles, and the air was choked with dust and smoke.

Long Rider had almost reached his mother's lodge when the main body of soldiers poured in among the tepees. Long Rider emptied two saddles with one of his revolvers, but then he couldn't see anything clearly in the smoke from all the shooting. He saw that the force of the charge had carried the soldiers through the thin line of warriors who'd been ready to meet them. The bluecoats ran deep into the village before they could turn their horses to face the Arapaho again.

But now there were women and children caught between the two lines, overtaken by the soldiers in their headlong rush. Cut off from their escape, some of the women took lances and clubs from fallen warriors and ran through the smoke and bullets to stand with their defenders.

The warriors were rushing to meet them when Long Rider noticed one young mother trying to scramble out of the way with two baby boys in her arms. She had only gone a few steps when she screamed and threw up her hands. A thick stream of blood spurted from her neck. She clutched her throat as she fell, but the blood poured out between her fingers. It arched high into the air and rained down over her sons, who sat where they had fallen and began to cry.

Long Rider jammed his revolver back into its holster and tied the flap down. Then he kicked his horse into a gallop and folded himself over its neck, running straight for the fallen babies and also toward the soldiers who were charging back to fight the Arapaho. Silently he implored the Winged God to grant his protection, picturing the Thunderbird of his vision to give him power. He could almost feel its wings wrapped around his shoulders. Then he was plucking the boys off the ground by their arms while the bluecoats swept by him again. No bullets had touched him.

Long Rider whooped in triumph and took a better grip on the boys, whose bodies were slippery with their mother's blood. He tucked one baby under each arm and glanced back toward the desperate hand-to-hand fight behind him.

The yell of triumph caught in his throat when he saw his mother through a gap in the smoke and dust. She was seventy or eighty yards back and was trying to get around behind a tepee, carrying a lance in one hand while she supported Yellow Buckskin Girl with the other.

Long Rider saw instantly that his wife had been wounded—perhaps in the first volley of rifle fire—and that this is what had delayed their escape. He turned his pony toward them with a nudge of his knee, thinking he could give them the mount and the orphaned babies, leaving him free to fight.

He had kicked the horse into a run when he saw that a soldier was chasing the women behind the tepee. Long Rider's heart leapt with fear, and he started to shift both babies under one arm, opening his mouth to cry out a warning.

But the soldier was already raising a revolver from his side. Long Rider's cry became a shrill scream of rage that tore through all the other sounds of battle.

Yellow Hair must have heard it. She spun on her heel, swinging Yellow Buckskin Girl around in time to see the gun being aimed—the gun that kept coming up no matter what Long Rider could do or how fast the horse could run. He would see the gun coming up all his life, and it would always seem to take forever even though it was hardly the time it takes to draw a breath. Certainly much less time than it would take to drop two baby boys from the back of a horse—even if he could have brought himself to do it—and draw his revolver from a holster that had the flap tied down.

All his life he would see that gun coming up and hear himself screaming and see his mother and his wife spinning around to meet the bullet that hit Yellow Buckskin Girl just above her right eye. He would see the sudden hole in her brow and the way her head jerked back, knowing that she was dead even as the soldier turned to find the source of the scream.

That's when he saw that the soldier was Captain Stanley Price. Their eyes met, and an evil look of knowledge came over the captain's face—knowledge of the yellow-haired woman's identity, and also the power he held over his enemy. It was only a fleeting look because Price sensed danger and turned back in time to fend off the lance that Yellow Hair was thrusting toward his belly.

The captain knocked the lance aside with his gun hand while he drew his saber with the other. He glanced back once more as the blade came free, his black eyes gleaming with wild hatred through the smoke and dust. Long Rider was transfixed by the look, and by the horror of the long blade flashing in the sun. His gun hand was free and he was still running the pony, but Long Rider knew he was far too late. His fingers had only closed around the butt of his revolver when the flashing blade disappeared in his mother's breast.

All his life Long Rider would see his mother's body impaled on the piece of steel through her heart. He was bringing his revolver up over the neck of the pony as it ran, but Yellow Hair's body was already shuddering as Price pulled the saber free.

His mother stood a moment longer, staring up at the captain with pale blue eyes full of pain and disbelief. Then she crumpled slowly, and the captain turned to look at Long Rider again with a grin of savage triumph.

CHAPTER SIXTEEN

Everything else that happened to Long Rider that day felt as if it was happening to someone else. He watched it all from a great distance, even in his memories.

The front sight of his revolver was lined up on Captain Price, and he pulled the trigger while Price was still taking aim. But the cap snapped harmlessly on a bad load, and then he had to face another soldier who was bearing down on him just a few yards away. The next load was good, and Long Rider's ball caught the soldier in the belly, knocking him over. The captain had apparently missed with his own shot in the meantime and was disappearing through the smoke when Long Rider had a chance to look again. Long Rider got off two more rounds before he lost sight of Price among the tepees.

He was still running his pony flat out, and he started to follow the captain, but there was no more time to think about revenge. The bluecoats were pushing the Arapaho back, and Long Rider found himself trying to protect two baby boys in the middle of a bitter hand-to-hand contest.

The Arapaho fought well but they only had a few old smoothbore muskets among them, while the rest were going up against revolvers and carbines with lances, bows and war clubs. Long Rider retreated with the Indians toward the protection of the gullies along Wolf Creek, avoiding direct conflict for the sake of the boys. He put away his empty Remington and reached beneath them to get the other one out of his belt, but with only six shots left, he didn't fire unless he was sure of success. He ran or ducked or slashed out with the gun whenever he could, until he found a woman who was willing to take the babies with her. After that he fought with great ferocity, slowing the progress of the soldiers who pursued the Indians far up the creek.

Long Rider noticed that some of the warriors were casting suspicious glances at his light hair and pale skin. Even the man who had raised him as his own son gave him several hard looks. He knew that Little Wound and the others were disturbed by the coincidence of his sudden reappearance and this unexpected attack by the cavalry. But Long Rider fought harder than ever, if anything, and took more chances, and his Sharps carbine accounted for many dead and wounded bluecoats as the morning wore on.

Many others were forced to quit when their horses gave out, which cut the number of pursuing soldiers even further. By the time the sun was almost straight overhead, they had journeyed far from the Tongue River and there were so few of them remaining that the Arapaho turned on their attackers and drove them back. But the soldier forces grew as they retreated and picked up the stragglers, and the Indians never had a chance to get the best of them. They could only throw a few poorly aimed bullets with their old trade guns and sting the soldiers with arrows.

The Indians were even more helpless when the retreating soldiers got back to the village. Two of the big-talking guns had been set up there to keep them at a distance with the whistling pieces of metal. The Arapaho were forced to watch from the surrounding hills while the soldiers tore down their tepees and stacked the lodge poles into great piles.

Long Rider was among the first to understand what was going to happen. He raged with fresh hatred as the soldiers piled tepee covers and buffalo robes on top of the lodge poles and set them on fire. The bluecoats worked throughout the afternoon, hauling blankets and furs and even the camp's entire winter meat supply, all of which was thrown into the flames.

Long Rider led some of the warriors down through the shelter of tree-filled ravines to ambush stragglers and launch scattered attacks, but the guns-that-shoot-twice always drove them back. The Indians failed in all their efforts to stampede the horses taken by the Pawnee, and they couldn't do anything to keep the soldiers from destroying nearly every piece of shelter, food, and clothing the Arapaho owned.

During one of the raids Long Rider sighted down the barrel of the Sharps at a man in buckskins. He was squeezing the trigger when the man turned his graying old face toward the hillside, and Long Rider recognized Jim Bridger. It startled him that Bridger turned when he did, almost as if he could feel the sights of his own rifle on his back. But the old man didn't duck or run, and Long Rider reminded himself that he was hidden in shadow beneath the trees.

He held the sights on Bridger for a long while, knowing that he owed his freedom and his life to Bridger. In the end he shot a bluecoat who had shown himself behind one of the howitzers.

It was late in the afternoon when the soldiers finally released the women and children they had captured. Then they mounted up and rode away, leaving the Arapaho to come down and take care of their dead.

Long Rider wandered among the smoldering piles left by the soldiers, coughing in the thick smoke that still hung over the village. He couldn't bring himself to go to the place where his mother and his wife had fallen. Instead he roamed without direction, gazing absently at the other bodies strewn in the grass and listening to the high keening of the mourners who had found their relatives among them. He knew he would soon be joining the mourners, but something in him was trying to put it off.

He looked at the Arapaho kneeling by the bodies, and after a while he began to think about the ways this day might have been different. If only he had not delayed for his vision quest, he thought. If only he and his wife—he couldn't bring himself to think of her name—if only they had traveled faster on the trail. Just one day's difference might have resulted in a scouting party that could have alerted the Arapaho to the presence of soldiers.

He also thought about Bridger's insistence that he carry his mother away—without her consent, if necessary. If Long Rider had already followed the scout's advice, his mother would be alive now, instead of dead.

But Long Rider quickly turned away from all these thoughts, as he had learned to do in the guardhouse at Fort Laramie. He knew they would sometimes return to torment him during his life, but he also knew it was useless to dwell on things that could not be changed.

His eye was caught by a flash of yellow on one of the piles. When he looked closer, he saw the image of the Thunderbird his mother had painted on her tepee cover the night before. The fresh pigment seemed to shine through the smoke hanging above the pile, and Long Rider scrambled toward it over the ashes and glowing embers, closing his nose against the terrible stink of burning meat and hides.

Most of the buffalo skins that formed the tepee cover had crumbled into charred pieces, like almost everything else in the pile, but the fire hadn't touched a large section of the hide that bore the Thunderbird. Long Rider stared at it for a long time with a stirring in his heart that had no name.

Perhaps it was the stirring of many feelings at once, he thought later. There was the ache of remembering his mother's love for him, now lost forever, but also the knowledge that he had brought her happiness in the final hours of her life. There was bitterness that Wakinyan had not protected her, but also a sign of hope in the image that lay at his feet. This is the Thunderbird's power, he told himself, holding his head a little higher. A greater power than the flames that had destroyed the village.

It was easy to separate the undamaged piece of hide from the rest of the tepee cover, which fell away along the edges where the fire had stopped. He dragged it down off the pile, realizing that he felt a little stronger now that he was holding it in his hands. He felt he was ready to go and prepare the bodies of his mother and his wife for burial.

But Little Wound had already found them. He was kneeling beside Yellow Hair's body, which was partially covered by a blanket, and he was making the high, trilling sound called keening. As Long Rider came up behind him Little Wound pulled a knife from his belt and began to slice long, deep cuts in the flesh on his arms. Then he heard the sound of the buffalo hide Long Rider was dragging, and he looked around, leaping to his feet when he recognized his stepson.

"You!" he cried.

Long Rider stopped short, frowning uncertainly while Little Wound stood before him with a wild light flaring in his eyes. Blood was streaming down his arms and dripping from the tips of his fingers. In the next instant he screamed a war whoop and rushed at Long Rider with his knife.

Long Rider saw the blade coming up toward his belly and stepped back, automatically trying to fend it off with the hand that still held the piece of his mother's tepee cover. The thick buffalo hide deflected the thrust of the knife, and Little Wound's momentum carried him past. By the time he'd spun around, Long Rider had drawn one of his Remingtons.

But Little Wound rushed again, as if he didn't see the revolver or didn't care, his eyes still fired with a look that Long Rider had never seen before.

"Wait!" Long Rider cried. He was pointing the gun, but he knew he couldn't pull the triger. Long Rider stepped aside and smashed the revolver down on Little Wound's knife arm as he went by. Then he dropped the weapon and the buffalo hide in the grass and grabbed for the Sharps that was slung across his back. He pulled it around just in time to fend off another attack from his stepfather.

Long Rider was hoping the length of the rifle would be helpful in keeping Little Wound at a distance. "Wait," he pleaded again. "Why are you doing this?"

The old warrior circled him without answering, his eyes still gleaming with hatred, and Long Rider knew he had asked a foolish question.

"I did not bring the bluecoats," Long Rider said. "I would not bring them here to kill my mother and my wife."

His words had no effect on the fire in Little Wound's eyes, and Long Rider decided it was his white skin alone that provoked this fury.

"I beg of you," he said. "We must stop this, my father."

But Little Wound only continued to circle, making tentative thrusts as if to test his stepson's reactions. Long Rider didn't guess his true intentions until the old warrior circled to the place where Long Rider had dropped his revolver. Little Wound suddenly fell to his knees, reaching for the pistol lying in the grass.

"No!" screamed Long Rider.

But he was already bringing down the muzzle of his Sharps and earing back the hammer while Little Wound raised the pistol and cocked it with enough skill to show that he'd used one before. The cold rage was also still in the warrior's eyes, and Long Rider saw he had no choice. He yanked the trigger, firing from the hip.

The ball went through Little Wound's chin and tore a hole in his throat. His arms flopped to his side, his head snapped back, and for a moment he was looking down his nose at Long Rider while blood gushed out of his neck. Then his eyes bulged wide and he rose up on his feet, taking one step before he fell back near the bodies of Yellow Hair and Yellow Buckskin Girl.

Long Rider stood frozen in place, his eyes fixed on the blood pulsing from Little Wound's throat. He watched the flow becoming weaker and weaker until it stopped, and still he didn't move. He heard other Indians running up to investigate the shot, but he knew that several people had witnessed his fight and that they would explain it to the others. There would be no need for immediate action. Later he would be expected to make restitution to the Arapaho woman who was Little Wound's second wife, if she had survived the battle.

Long Rider stared at the remains of his own family, aware of the murmured conversations among the Indians who watched him from a distance. He thought he heard sympathy in their tone and he wondered how many of them knew what he had lost that day. His mother was dead, and so was the childhood love who had become his wife. He'd also been forced to kill the only father he had ever known, who had killed Long Rider's true father long before he was born.

He felt as if he had lost everything it was possible to lose. He moved closer to the bodies of his family and looked down into Yellow Buckskin Girl's wide-open eyes. They had almost popped out of their sockets from the force of the bullet inside her skull. They were as dark as ever, but they didn't have the shine he had seen for the last time that morning—when he told her not to worry. Long Rider remembered his wife's laughter, which he would never hear again, and a sorrow gripped his heart that was more than he could stand.

He turned away and noticed a piece of paper sticking out of Yellow Hair's fingers. It had been torn from a military pocket notebook, and there was a note written on it. "Gabe," it read. "Am heartsick. More than you can know. Bridger."

That explained the blanket that covered her legs, Long Rider thought dully, and the fact that her body was arranged more neatly than he remembered. Bridger had covered it in the white custom Long Rider had seen at the fort. He also might have wanted to keep the soldiers from seeing her, so they wouldn't get ideas about bringing the white woman's body back with them.

Little Wound had thrown the blanket aside when he found her.

Long Rider wadded the notebook paper into a little ball and dropped it in the grass. "You should have stayed in St. Louis," he said to his mother's body. His words came out in a soft, sad tone, but then he looked at Little Wound and Yellow Buckskin Girl and his eyes turned hard.

All the whites should have stayed where they belonged, he thought. It is the soldiers who have done this to us—Captain Stanley Price and the others of his kind. They have invaded our land and killed our people without reason.

"I make a vow to you," he said aloud. "Hear me well, for I tell you that the soldiers will suffer for this. And Price will die."

Long Rider stood over the bodies a while longer, until he began to think again about the assurance he had given to Yellow Buckskin Girl, and about the pleasures of lying with her by the fire. Then he found Little Wound's knife and began to slash his chest and arms while he keened.

Before the sun went down, he found some tepee poles that were only partially burned and used them to build scaffolds for Little Wound and Yellow Buckskin Girl, thinking all the while about what he should do with his mother's body. It was a problem because he knew how much the Indians hated it when their dead were buried in the white custom, without the provisions required for their journey to the spirit world. Long Rider didn't understand the reason for planting bodies in the earth, but he worried that Yellow Hair's spirit might suffer among the white gods if he prepared her in the Lakota way.

It was not an easy thing to dig a white man's grave without a white man's shovel. Long Rider worked through most of the night, grateful for the light of a half-moon. He cut roots and sod with Little Wound's knife and scooped out the dirt beneath them with a buffalo hipbone. Most of the Arapaho came by at one time or another to witness his strange behavior, then went away without speaking to him. He collapsed for a while and slept, curling up inside the piece of buffalo hide with the Thunderbird on it, but his dreams made him glad to be awake again.

By the time the next sun came up, he had dug out a hole that looked like the ones he remembered from the fort. He lowered

Yellow Hair's body into it and then he went back to the place where her lodge had stood, searching for the black talking book she'd used in teaching him the white man's language. He found it wrapped in an elkskin bundle among the backrests and cooking tools that the soldiers hadn't bothered with.

A morning breeze had sprung up by the time Long Rider returned to his grave on the hillside. It blew his long hair around his ears as he read his mother's favorite words from the black book. This was something else he had seen at the fort, although he still didn't understand every word he read. He had never seen any sheep, for example, and he couldn't grasp the idea of moving groups of animals around, the way people called shepherds did.

He was closing the black book when he noticed that there was writing on the inside of the cover. It was small and the lines were crooked, but he thought he could make out most of the words. "Perhaps someone will find this one day," he read, "and they will know what happened to Adam and Amelia Conrad."

The more he read, the more he understood why his mother had begged him to keep this book. It was like a Lakota winter count, except that it was the story of one woman instead of a whole band of people. It also contained many details instead of only one event to mark each winter, and it recorded Yellow Hair's thoughts and feelings.

Long Rider saw that her gift to him was a great treasure, allowing her to speak to him from the spirit world. He looked down at his mother's body and thanked her in silence.

He noticed the way her hair was spread out over the black dirt at the bottom of the hole, and he remembered the golden strands in the grave of his vision. High Backbone had been right in saying that the spirits didn't usually foretell the future in the visions they provide, but Long Rider almost expected a dark opening to appear in one wall of his mother's grave.

He shivered in the bright light of the morning sun.

Then he remembered the Winged God, which had appeared out of the sun. He picked up the piece of buffalo hide that remained from Yellow Hair's tepee and wrapped it around his body, finding comfort in its solid weight.

He wore it so the painted image of the Thunderbird was draped across his shoulders, just as he had seen it in his vision.

CHAPTER SEVENTEEN

Long Rider had to put off killing Captain Price.

He thought about it almost all the time. He read his mother's words in the black book, over and over, thinking of the good feelings he would have when Price was dead.

He shared many fires with Crazy Horse, planning ways of getting close enough to the captain to kill him.

He worked many hours making a long coat from the buffalo hide that had been part of his mother's tepee. It hung from his shoulders almost down to his ankles, with holes in the sides for his bare arms. He cut and sewed the coat so the yellow Thunderbird was centered across his back. He imagined that he would be wearing it when he killed Captain Price.

He worked hardest of all on developing his skills for delivering death. When he was not making the coat—or eating or reading the book or talking to Crazy Horse—Long Rider was shooting the revolvers that he had not been able to use in time at Black Bear's camp on the Tongue River. He loaded them and emptied them a thousand times, until they felt as natural to him as a horse or a bow.

Every bullet he fired was meant for the captain's heart.

But Long Rider's first duty was always to the People. After the Tongue River fight he helped the Arapaho move their sick and wounded to the big Lakota camp on the Powder, where the Indians opened up their lodges and gave away everything they could to resupply the stricken Indians.

Then, before Long Rider could go looking for vengeance, Red Cloud asked him to be his personal adviser.

The chief had gained even more respect for Long Rider during his absence, after the Oglala stopped a wagon train of white gold hunters. The bluecoats who guarded them said they were looking for a fort that other bluecoats were planning to build on a new road going to the place called Montana. This confirmed everything Long Rider had said about soldiers coming into the Powder River country. It also confirmed his story of a trail they planned to build through the Lakota's best hunting grounds—the trail Long Rider had called the Bozeman Road.

Then came word of the other soldier columns that Long Rider had predicted, joining together near the Black Hills and moving toward the Powder. The columns were being followed and harassed by warriors from the northern Lakota tribes, the Hunkpapa and Minneconjou. Many of the Oglala wanted to go and join them, but Long Rider convinced Red Cloud to stick with the original plan for attacking the bridge across the Platte River.

Long Rider insisted that capturing the fort and destroying the bridge would choke off the hated road, bringing travel to a complete stop. Then the whites would see that the Indians could keep control of their own country, and they would have to abandon their plans for the Bozeman Road.

The entire village of Lakota, Arapaho, and Dull Knife's Cheyenne moved south to Crazy Woman Creek in the Moon of Red Cherries, which the whites call July. When Long Rider rode out with two thousand warriors a few days later, he felt sure the bluecoats would soon be made to suffer as he had vowed before the bodies of his family.

His hopes for revenge rose even higher when he looked down from a hill near the Platte Bridge and saw the soldier named Tuttle, the one who had used his rifle butt on the Oglala chief Two Face in the guardhouse. Private Tuttle was coming to the post with several other bluecoats who appeared to be bringing mail from Fort Laramie.

The Indians decided not to attack the mail escort, which would have ruined the grand strategy that Long Rider and Crazy Horse had helped prepare. The strategy called for hiding warriors near the river, then luring the soldiers out of the fort with decoys. Once the soldiers had crossed the river, the Indians would capture the bridge and cut off their retreat.

But the soldiers didn't take the bait. On the first day they either stopped short of the bridge or sent out such small parties that the Indians continued to hold off on springing their trap, believing the prize was still too small.

The Indians were setting their trap again on the second day when a group of twenty-five soldiers suddenly came out of the fort and headed west. Long Rider and hundreds of other surprised warriors stormed out of the canyons to surround the soldiers.

The small detachment still managed to fight its way back to the bridge, which was being held by another group of soldiers who had come out of the fort. These bluecoats had the new rifles that shoot many times without reloading, and they were able to exact a heavy toll on the Sioux and Arapaho warriors pouring out from their hiding places behind the riverbank. The Sioux also suffered losses from Cheyenne rifle fire aimed at the retreating party of soldiers. They fell back without capturing the bridge, while the main body of Sioux and Cheyenne were forced to give up their attack.

Long Rider fought savagely in this battle, knowing that he was protected by the red horsehair cutting behind his ear and the buffalo-hide coat with the Thunderbird across his shoulders. He rode into the heavy fire of the soldiers with such bravery that his name would be heard for many winters around the Lakota council fires, even if he himself did not think of his actions as bravery. He was sure no bullets could touch him as long as he wore the Thunderbird coat in battle, but he also knew that it didn't matter to him whether he lived or died, now that everything he cared about had been lost to him.

He was at the height of his fighting frenzy when he saw Private Tuttle among the ambushed soldiers, his horse shot from under him in the headlong retreat. Tuttle was trying to crawl to the bridge through the tall grass, but Long Rider followed and shot him through the chest. Tuttle fell back, terror coming into his eyes when he recognized the light-haired warrior who stood over him with a knife. Long Rider knelt and began to slice the flesh of Tuttle's scalp away from his skull while the dying soldier tried to fight, screaming in agony.

Long Rider was unmoved by the screams. "Do you still wish to attack helpless prisoners?" he said harshly, using the white man's words.

Bullets were flying all around, but Long Rider ignored them also, working quickly with Little Wound's knife. He wanted Tuttle to feel as much pain and fear as possible before he died. When Long Rider had torn away the soldier's scalp, he pulled Tuttle's saber from its sheath and slashed at the soldier's bulging eyes. The blinded soldier screamed louder than before, maddened in the terror of his helplessness and thrashing wildly when he felt Long Rider hacking at his body with the saber. Long Rider cut off Tuttle's private parts and then both of his arms. The private parts he stuffed in the soldier's gaping mouth.

But by then Tuttle wasn't moving or screaming anymore, and the blood had stopped flowing from his wounds. Long Rider squatted over Tuttle's mutilated body and felt his fury beginning to leak away. Instead there was a feeling of sickness that slowly filled his belly. He tried to think about the fate of his mother and his wife, and the suffering endured in the guardhouse by Two Face, but the sickness was still in Long Rider's belly as he joined the other warriors leaving the battlefield.

He was further disheartened by a bitter fight that broke out between the Lakota and Cheyenne, who blamed each other for losing the fight. The Lakota warriors were angry that they'd been fired on, while the Cheyenne called them cowards for failing to capture the bridge. Some of the Cheyenne vowed never to fight beside the Lakota again.

The warriors still tried to lure the soldiers from the fort, however, showing themselves and taunting the bluecoats, but the soldiers had already seen how badly they were outnumbered and stayed behind the log walls of their fort.

Army supply wagons appeared on the road later in the afternoon, which explained why the first group of soldiers had left the fort and headed in the direction from which the wagons were coming. But now the bluecoats refused to come out of the fort again, even when the Indians laid siege to the wagons.

The Indians killed all the soldiers guarding the supply train, then turned their attention back to the fort. But they did not attack. They knew they would suffer heavy losses in a direct assault, and they had no stomach for that kind of sacrifice—even if it would close the trail.

Long Rider raged with anger and frustration. He guessed that fewer than a hundred bluecoats remained inside, but the fort's log walls and its howitzers—the guns-that-shoot-twice—protected them from two thousand warriors.

Defiance was all that remained to the Indians. They gathered in front of the post the next morning and passed by in something like a soldier review. They marched slowly away along the river until its banks were empty and silent.

Long Rider rode north with a heavy heart. The fight had given him a chance to take revenge on the soldier named Tuttle, and he had found plenty of powder and lead in the army supply wagons, but these things meant nothing compared to the failure of the Indian plan. The biggest gathering of warriors he'd ever seen had not been able to dislodge a few soldiers from a small fort on the white man's road.

He knew that superior weapons were part of the reason for the Indians' defeat, but he also believed they had given up too easily. They had developed a powerful strategy, and yet they had grown tired of it when something went wrong. Soon, he guessed, they would return to the old ways. Small raiding parties would go out to harass travelers using the road. The warriors would return with tales of glory and plenty of plunder, but they wouldn't stop more whites from passing through the country and driving away the game.

Long Rider pondered the failure of the Indian attack and remembered some of the words in his mother's Bible. She had written them long before, when he had seen only ten winters.

Near Black Hills with tribes from all over. Furious about more whites using the Platte road. Gold found in Calif(?), I guess. (Glad *someone* gets some.) Indians agree to fight to keep whites out of this country. Wish they knew how silly. They're born to fight, but no organization, no long view, no ability to make plans and carry through. If whites ever really set their sights here . . . But maybe they'll ignore us a while longer and son and I can be safe.

Long Rider was troubled by words like these, but after the fight at the bridge he spent more time than ever with the black book. He lost interest in talking with anyone besides Crazy Horse, and often he walked through the camp without noticing other people. The Oglala respected his privacy and left him alone, saying his thoughts were someplace else—perhaps with his dead wife and mother. Long Rider continued to fulfill his immediate duties as a warrior, rejecting raids against the whites in favor of hunting buffalo for the winter food supply. But when he wasn't hunting, he would go off by himself, carrying his mother's book.

She had written wherever she could find space around the printed words, so Long Rider would have to turn the book in all directions as he read, struggling to follow her meaning. When he came to the end of what she had written, he would start over on the first page inside the cover. He believed he could hear his mother's voice when he read her words.

June (I think) 1845: My son is born! But how my heart aches. If only Adam could see. Has his proud chin. And your pale, piercing eyes, my own father. Oh, Daddy, it tears at my heart that you might never know my fate. To think of you grieving for me. Terrible thing to do to you. But given up on escape. Always found and brought back. Such a big country and I am so alone. Hope this will be solace, putting down words with a turkey feather and some juice squeezed from chokecherries. Maybe they will be read someday and someone will know. Maybe returned to my father? Oh, please! I beg of you, whoever reads these words, forward them to Mr. Thomas Reid, who is an attorney in Boston.

"There he is. The strange young man of the Oglala."

Long Rider looked up from the black book and smiled when he saw Crazy Horse coming toward him through the trees along the river. "I thought that was what the People said about you."

Crazy Horse laughed. "Now they say I have an equal. They don't know what to think about a warrior who stares at a white man's book all day and never speaks to anyone. They say you might be more strange than I am."

"I'm honored if I'm considered an equal of my friend, whose medicine is so powerful."

"Not powerful enough," Crazy Horse said with a sudden scowl. "I've just heard that our scouts have found the new fort on the Powder, and now my heart is filled with dread. I don't think we can stop the whites from using this new road, Long Rider. Not if we couldn't destroy the bridge in the south. I fear our country will soon be overrun.''

These same thoughts had been occurring to Long Rider as well, but he found it hard to admit they might be true. ''Red Cloud has said it won't happen, Crazy Horse. He promises to fight the soldiers until the whites stop using the road.''

''I hope he does as he says. But I don't believe he has enough hatred for the whites.''

''You've heard him speak in the council, haven't you?''

''I know he speaks strong for war, but there was a time when I heard Spotted Tail speak just as strong. Now he counsels peace. The whites have tricked our people before, Long Rider. They will offer to make peace, and I believe Red Cloud will listen to them.''

Long Rider started to protest, but Crazy Horse touched his chest, his light brown eyes turning sharp with anger.

''This is something I feel here,'' he said. ''It is hard to tell you more, except that no one hates the whites as much as I do. I will never talk peace with them, and I will never stop fighting them. They will have to kill me before there is peace.''

Long Rider looked closely at the warrior, a little frightened by the cold, glowing light in his eyes. They had talked often since his return, but Long Rider had never before seen this look. Gradually it went away, and Crazy Horse seemed to be peering at something that lay beyond the present world.

''One day the whites will know my name,'' he said softly. ''They will be frightened when they hear it, and they will want to know more about me. You must make a vow, Long Rider, that you will tell them nothing.''

''It's an easy vow to make. I won't talk to the whites before you do.''

Crazy Horse focused on Long Rider again, gazing at him a long time. ''If you say so,'' he finally said. ''But you still must promise not to tell the whites anything about me.''

''You have your promise,'' Long Rider said stiffly.

''Good,'' said Crazy Horse. He gripped Long Rider's arm as if he hadn't noticed his anger. ''We have become like brothers, and it pleases me to know my words will not be repeated.''

Long Rider only nodded.

Crazy Horse looked down at Long Rider's holster, which was

missing the big flap that normally covered the butt of the
revolver. "You have made a change," he said. "Is this another
part of the white man's medicine?"

"It's my own idea," said Long Rider, eyeing the warrior.
"Would you like me to show you the reason?"

"Yes."

"Then reach for your knife as if you intend to kill me."

Crazy Horse looked into Long Rider's eyes and once again
held his gaze, as if he were considering the white Oglala's
intentions. Then his hand flashed suddenly toward his side.

Long Rider's hand dipped with even greater speed, and there
was a dry click as it came up again, holding the big Remington
revolver, already cocked. Crazy Horse froze with his fingers
around the handle of his knife, still at his side. He had seen only
a movement, and now he was looking with awe at the barrel of
the revolver pointed at his chest.

He looked up into Long Rider's face, and neither man moved
until Long Rider sighed and returned the revolver to its holster.
Then Crazy Horse took his hand away from his knife.

"I have observed that the snake that rattles is a dangerous
enemy because he strikes so quickly," said Long Rider. "I have
tried to learn a lesson from my brother the snake."

"You have learned it well," said Crazy Horse.

"I have also tried to make the white man's gun like part of my
hand, so I may hit the thing I strike at."

Long Rider turned with another sudden blurring of his hand.
Crazy Horse started to reach for his knife again, but it was only
because he was startled, and he simply touched its handle. The
Remington had already exploded in a cloud of smoke, and
Crazy Horse looked in the direction in which it was pointing. He
saw a yellow leaf fluttering down from a tree. Then he turned
back as Long Rider was putting the gun away again, and saw the
torment in his eyes.

"Your powers are greater than ever before," Crazy Horse
said carefully. "Your medicine has become very strong. But you
know it could not have changed the way things happened in
Black Bear's camp on the Tongue River."

Long Rider drew and fired a second time, clipping another
yellow leaf. "I don't know that," he said.

"It is what all the people say. You were carrying an infant
beneath each arm when you saw a weapon already in the

soldier's hand. They say there was nothing you could have
done.''

Long Rider drew and fired a third time, his pale eyes staring
blindly as a third yellow leaf fluttered to the ground. Then he
used his left hand to take the other revolver from his belt, pulling
its trigger twice more. The leaf danced in the air. Long Rider
walked over to pick it up, holding it toward the sky as he came
back so Crazy Horse could see the two holes that were side by
side.

"I don't know that, either,'' he said.

The winter that followed the soldier invasion was the hardest
winter anyone could remember. The snow and cold came early
and the People were not prepared. Too many warriors had been
killing white travelers instead of hunting for food. The buffalo
were also more scarce than ever, driven away by the whites
coming through the country. Villages had to move farther in
search of buffalo herds, while many women and children died of
cold and starvation.

Red Cloud's Oglala tried to make the winter even harder for
the soldiers who had been left behind in the new fort on the
Powder River. Long Rider argued many times in the councils
that the fort was a foothold for the whites and should be
destroyed, no matter what the cost. He said the costs would be
even greater if the Indians waited for more whites to come. But
Red Cloud had looked down on the log walls of the stockade and
decided once again that the losses would be too great. Seeing
that the chief had no heart for a direct attack, Long Rider
convinced him to lay siege to the fort. Red Cloud agreed,
directing several bands to camp nearby and cut off all supplies
being sent there.

But the winter was still hard, and messengers began traveling
north from Fort Laramie, carrying talk of peace. They said the
whites offered food and blankets to those who would go in and
sign a treaty. Spotted Tail and some of the more peaceful Lakota
chiefs took their people in during the worst part of the snow and
cold.

Red Cloud sent word that he would also go in to talk. Long
Rider and Crazy Horse urged him to ignore the whites, but Red
Cloud said he could fool them. He said the whites would give
him presents for talking, but he had not promised to agree to

anything. Instead he would try to convince the whites that they should abandon their plans for the Bozeman Road.

"Perhaps he is right," Long Rider said later, when he and Crazy Horse were walking alone near the river. "Perhaps the whites will see they cannot win."

"There is nothing but trouble in talking with the whites," Crazy Horse said harshly. "When Red Cloud goes to Fort Laramie, I will keep going south, to the land where the buffalo are still many."

"Perhaps I will go with you, then."

Crazy Horse gave him a close look, then smiled. "I will be glad to see you there when the time is right," he said. "But I believe you have reasons for going in with Red Cloud that I don't have."

Long Rider nodded slowly, his lips pulling back over his teeth in a fierce grin that made even Crazy Horse a little uneasy. "Yes," he said. "Yes, perhaps it is time I return to the fort."

CHAPTER EIGHTEEN

Red Cloud led his Oglala to the Platte River in the Moon When the Ponies Shed, which the whites call May.

Almost a year had passed since Long Rider's escape with Jim Bridger, but the memories of his exile flooded back in all their bitterness as soon as he saw Fort Laramie. A warm breeze was blowing through the grass and the sun was shining down on the post buildings, but Long Rider remembered only his repeated fights with the other boys his age, the loneliness, the taunts and insults from the soldiers, and finally the endless days of guardhouse confinement. He stopped his pony on a low ridge and frowned at the fort, wondering if it was a wise thing he was doing.

The bitterness of those years was so fresh that Long Rider felt as if he'd only been gone from the fort for a day or two. At the same time it seemed that his year in the north had been only a dream, a period when he was trying not to feel anything at all. He had floated through those days the way he floated through the dark tunnel of his vision.

Then Long Rider remembered the man who had sent him to the guardhouse, the same man who was responsible for the emptiness in his heart, and the look of doubt disappeared from his expression. He turned to see the other Oglala warriors going down toward the river, knowing he would be safe among them, and his pale gray eyes began to shine in the light from the dying sun.

The doubt came back later in the evening when Long Rider glanced up from his cook fire and saw Jim Bridger winding toward him through the tepees. Walking beside the scout was the leather-faced sergeant who had tried to prevent his escape the year before. Long Rider jumped to his feet, his hand going to the butt of the Remington in his belt.

The sergeant and the scout both raised their hands to show their empty palms.

"No need to gun me down," Bridger called out, still advancing with confidence. "I ain't dumb enough to try an' take yuh outa here."

"We're here to talk," said the sergeant. "That's all we want."

Long Rider kept his fingers wrapped around the butt of his revolver as he watched the men coming toward him. They stopped on the other side of the fire, eyeing him with neutral expressions.

Then Bridger nodded tentatively and said, "Howdy, Gabe."

"The People don't call me by the white man's name," Long Rider said coldly. Bridger frowned, and Long Rider felt a touch of regret, remembering the good feelings between them the last time they had talked. "What is it you want here?"

"We're just trying to keep things peaceful," said the sergeant. "That's why Red Cloud came in, ain't it? To make peace? So I'm hoping we can head off anything that might cause problems for the peace talks."

Long Rider studied the sergeant's face, making himself look confused. "Why do you tell me this?" he asked.

The sergeant glanced at Bridger, who sighed and gave Long Rider a sorrowful look. "Don't forget I know what happened to your maw—"

"I received your message," Long Rider said, his tone a little less harsh. "Thank you for your words, Bridger. I am glad I did not shoot you when I had the chance."

"I was kinda happy about that myself," drawled the scout.

Long Rider stared in surprise. "You saw me?"

"Up in the draw? With a shaft o' sunlight fallin' on that purty hair? I figgered it'd be a helluva joke on me, son, gettin' shot with my own rifle."

"But if . . . why didn't you run, Bridger?"

"Didn' really think I'd have ta."

The two men studied each other in silence for a moment, and Long Rider understood that there was still a bond between them. It was a good thing. It touched his heart and made him feel stronger. Bridger nodded suddenly, as if he understood Long Rider's thoughts and meant to confirm them.

"Anyway," said the scout, "what I started out to say was . . . I know who kilt your maw, an' I also know yuh seen it done with your own eyes."

Long Rider didn't say anything to that.

"Some o' the men seen things," Bridger explained, "an' word gets around. It ain't like yuh was hard to spot out there. But if I was in your moccasins, I'd feel jes' like I think you do. I wouldn't rest till the damn son of a bitch was dead." He looked off toward the horizon. "I had half a mind to take care o' him myself, the way I felt about your maw."

"I know it was your loss too," said Long Rider. "But did you see the woman lying beside her, the one who was shot through the belly and again through the head? That was Yellow Buckskin Girl. My wife."

"Jesus Christ, son, I'm sorry to hear it. I truly am."

"You still haven't heard it all," said Long Rider. "After the fight I found my mother's husband kneeling over her body. He was so mad with grief that he tried to stab me. I had to kill this man who raised me as his son."

"Damn!" said Bridger, shaking his head. "I know you're feelin' a lot o' hate. An' don't hardly blame yuh. But what we come to tell yuh is, the critter you're lookin' for ain't here no more."

Long Rider looked from one man to the other.

"He's tellin' the truth," said the sergeant. "Captain Price left the Army. He's been gone since a little after Christmas."

"Colonel Moonlight's been gone even longer'n that," Bridger put in. "He was so dumb, even the Army could figger it out. So the point is, Long Rider . . . well, there ain't no point in lookin' for revenge aroun' here."

Long Rider didn't admit that that was his purpose, but he looked hard into the scout's eyes. They were still a clear blue color after all the winters he had seen, and they didn't falter or look away.

"I'm talkin' straight," Bridger assured him. "Yuh can ask anyone. Yuh can even come to the post an' look aroun'."

Long Rider drew himself erect with a wary look. "You expect me to come in alone, is that it? So you can arrest me again?"

"Hell no," said the sergeant. "That ain't it at all. I found the bundle of clothes where you dropped them. I found the marks of a scuffle by the bathhouse, the pistols in the bucket of water, the blood in the dirt in the stable. Everything I saw backed up Bridger's story. Sure, I was pissed off for a while. But then I figured I couldn't blame you much, at least not for runnin' away."

"Then you don't plan to arrest me?"

"That's what I'm trying to tell you. It's old business as far as the Army is concerned." The sergeant looked around at the lodges scattered along the river, his eyes turning hard. "There might be some other things we ain't too happy about," he said. "I won't lie to you. But we also ain't about to try arresting every warrior who's killed a U.S. soldier."

"Because you want peace," Long Rider said, his tone full of contempt.

The sergeant frowned at him, looking a little surprised. "That's right."

"Then why do you send the soldiers to attack peaceful villages? Why do the whites come through our hunting grounds and kill the animals that give us food and shelter?"

"Now look here!" the sergeant said, flaring. But Bridger was putting a hand on his arm, stepping between him and Long Rider.

"There ain't much sense in debatin' things," the scout said calmly. "It might even be that we don't agree with what the Army done." He glanced toward the sergeant, who scowled and looked at the ground. "The point is, we're tryin' to stop the killin' by makin' a treaty, an' we don't want anything causin' bad feelin's while the talks is goin' on."

"I understand," Long Rider said. "Then tell me where Price has gone."

This time the scout did look away. He glanced at the sergeant again, and Long Rider thought there was regret in his eyes. "I can't do that," Bridger said.

"Anyway, he's gone back East," the sergeant said in a sullen tone. "He's a long way from here—way out of your reach. He ain't even in the Army anymore.''

"You say he quit?'' said Long Rider. "You expect me to believe he gave up his career?''

The sergeant nodded.

"Actually I think he lost his nerve,'' Bridger said. "They say he started gettin' nervous when he heard what yuh done to Private Tuttle.''

The scout's tone was mild, but his eyes were cool, like the sergeant's. Both men were watching for his reaction, but Long Rider knew by their expressions that there was no point in denying what he had done. Instead he lifted his chin and glared at them in defiance. "Tuttle did not deserve to go into the spirit world as a whole man,'' he said.

The two men kept watching him, and he realized suddenly that they weren't judging him by the Indian ways he was used to. His mother had used the black book to try to teach him the white way of thinking, telling him about things like mercy and kindness. They had sounded like weakness to him, but during his exile he had begun to see that the whites at least claimed to believe in such things—even if some of them acted like Private Tuttle. Long Rider gave the sergeant a scornful look.

"You were there in the guardhouse,'' he said. "You know that what I did to Tuttle was nothing more than the things he did to Two Face.''

The sergeant met Long Rider's gaze. "It was also nothing less,'' he said.

Long Rider didn't know how to answer that. He maintained his pose of arrogant defiance, but the two men only continued to watch him as if they were waiting for something else. Their eyes bored into his, but Long Rider saw that there was no hatred in their expressions, and perhaps even a hint of kindness in the way Bridger looked at him. Long Rider let his gaze drift downward.

"I took no pleasure in it,'' he admitted in a soft voice. "I was angry and thought it would be good to make Tuttle suffer as he died. But it didn't feel good after he was dead.''

The scout and the sergeant glanced at each other, and Bridger allowed himself a deep sigh.

"Kinda glad to hear it,'' he said. "Tell yuh the truth, son, at first I didn't even believe them stories. Didn't seem like the man I knew, even if'n yuh was provoked.'' Bridger glanced down at Long Rider's hand. "Everythin' heal up okay?''

Long Rider held out the hand as if he'd forgotten all about it. There was a puckered white circle on either side of his palm where the pitchfork had gone through, and his trigger finger was still bent over at the top knuckle.

"It's healed," he said with a shrug. "And I've learned to use the finger as it is. But the wounds of the flesh are not so hard to overcome."

"I know," said the scout. "It's the other kind that gives yuh trouble. But its gets easier, I can promise yuh that much."

Long Rider nodded, and another look passed between them, making Long Rider think of the night and the day they had spent together a year before. He had felt that this man could teach him a great deal. He had even hoped his mother would tell him that they were father and son.

Long Rider turned his thoughts away from his mother, wishing for a moment that he and Bridger weren't separated by their duties. He thought it would be a fine adventure to serve under him as a scout. . . .

Long Rider frowned, feeling suddenly troubled.

"Why are you here?" he asked Bridger. "I mean, why are you here at the fort?"

Bridger looked surprised. "I'm an Army scout, son."

"But what do they need a scout for if this is a time of peace?"

"Now I get it," said Bridger. "But it ain't so hard a question. The gov'ment's sendin' out a peace commissioner who knows how to talk fer peace, but he don't know a hell of a lot about Injuns. They figger I got a little experience he can use."

The scout's old blue eyes were still clear and steady, but later on Long Rider thought he'd noticed a small flicker that should have warned him.

Or maybe he just made it up.

The peace commissioner came in early June, When the Green Grass Is Up, and started bargaining right away for permission to build a road through the Powder River country. He said the Great Father in Washington only wanted a trail for the whites who were going to the western mining districts, and he offered presents to the Indians who would sign the treaty.

But then a column of seven hundred soldiers marched into the fort while the talks were still going on. When a Brule chief asked their leader where he was taking them, the bluecoat colonel answered that he was going to build two more forts along the Bozeman Road.

The colonel's answer spread quickly among the Indians gathered for the treaty talks, and it was enough—with the help of Long Rider's counsel—to drive away any thoughts of peace that Red Cloud might have entertained.

The Oglala chief stood up during the next day's deliberations and scolded the white colonel for treating the Indians like children. "Great Father sends us presents and wants a new road," he shouted. "But white chief goes with soldiers to steal the road, before Indian says yes or no."

Red Cloud stalked away from the meeting, and by the time the sun rose again the next morning, he had led his Oglala north toward the Powder River country.

Long Rider went south, eager to find Crazy Horse and talk about the new developments. He was happy to see that Red Cloud's resolve was so great, and he was sure there would be war now. But he couldn't help wondering whether it was a war the Indians had any hope of winning.

CHAPTER NINETEEN

Long Rider grunted in unison with the other Indians and pushed up against the log across his shoulder. His legs began to shake under the strain, but he kept pushing, blinking his eyes to keep out the stinging sweat that poured off his forehead.

Nothing seemed to happen, and the Indians let up on the pressure, dropping the log to gather around the stubborn iron rail.

"I think it's looser than before," said Long Rider. He touched one of the spikes that held the rail to a crosstie. "The Big Nail has come out of the wood a little farther, I think."

Some of the other Indians—mostly Oglala, joined by a few Cheyenne—gave Long Rider a dark look. At first they had been excited by the idea of lifting one of the rails, but now they were getting tired of it. Long Rider saw their expressions and it made him angry. *You always give up too soon*, he wanted to yell at them.

Crazy Horse glanced at his friend's face and turned to the warriors. "Let's try it again," he said. "We've already cut the tree and dragged it here. Maybe it will work the way Long Rider said."

The Indians nodded in silence and went back to their places by the log, lifting it and fitting it once more beneath the rail where they had scooped out some of the gravel in the roadbed.

They were members of a hunting party who had crossed and recrossed these tracks all through the summer as they searched the southern prairie for buffalo. Their first look at the white man's Iron Horse had made them angry because it scared away the animals with all its noise. It had also made them curious about the wooden houses on wheels that were pulled along the tracks at great speed. The Indians had watched the new intruder and tried to guess what might be inside the wooden houses, until their curiosity was so aroused that a Cheyenne warrior decided to throw a rope on one of the Iron Horses and pull it off the tracks.

The warrior had been yanked off his pony instead and dragged along at the end of the rope until he could free himself. The other Indians had laughed until their ribs hurt. Then Sleeping Rabbit had suggested that they spread the rails apart.

"Maybe the Iron Horse will fall off," he said, "and we could see what is inside the wooden houses on wheels."

When the Indians discovered they couldn't lift the iron rails by themselves, Long Rider had suggested bringing the trunk of a small tree that might be strong enough to pry up one of the tracks. It took a long time to find a tree on the open prairie, but the Indians had been sustained for a while by their curiosity.

Now they were less eager as they lifted the heavy log and wedged it in place under the rail.

"This time we'll push even harder than before," Crazy Horse said, "and soon we'll have a chance to break open the little houses!"

There were only a few halfhearted nods and a little grudging enthusiasm among the warriors.

"Don't forget that this is also for the People," Long Rider said. His tone was sharp because he was remembering the things Jim Bridger had told him about the railroad, confirmed by his mother. "The Iron Horse will bring more whites into our country than ever before," he told the Oglala and Cheyenne. "We must learn how to stop it before they destroy us."

Long Rider threw back his head and screamed like an eagle, the other warriors joining in as they strained against the weight of the log. The sun beat down on their bare backs, and for a while there was nothing but the grunt of their effort and the creaking of the log. Then they heard a crunch of gravel and felt the iron rail giving way. It didn't rise far, and it fell back in place almost immediately, but some of the spikes had been pulled free.

"Now we know it can be done!" cried Long Rider. "We can keep the Iron Horse from bringing whites to scare away the buffalo and take our land."

The warriors filled the air with war whoops and put their shoulders to the log. With some of the spikes missing, the rail rose higher than before and slipped a little to one side. The log was moved and lifted once more, spreading the tracks by another hand's width. Then the warriors rested while Long Rider and Sleeping Rabbit sighted down the rail, agreeing that the wheels of the Iron Horse could not stay on both tracks at the same time.

The Indians grinned at each other and laughed, moving off to conceal themselves behind a grassy mound near the tracks. They made camp on the other side and settled down to wait.

It was Long Rider who saw the first smoke of a coming train from the lookout place on the mound. The Oglala and Cheyenne had taken turns keeping watch through the night, and Long Rider's time had come when the sky was just beginning to turn light. Now he stared thoughtfully at the little stream of white-gray smoke on the far horizon, hesitating before he called the other warriors.

There was no hurry. Long Rider could see a far distance over the rolling grassland, and he knew there was plenty of time before the Iron Horse arrived. He wanted to use that time to struggle with the thoughts that had been running around inside his head in great confusion. He still hoped to find an answer that might give him peace.

The confusion came because Long Rider was feeling himself drawn toward the rising sun. Every time he had seen the tracks of the Iron Horse, he had been troubled by the knowledge that somewhere at the other end of them—beyond the horizon, in the unknown land called the East—Captain Price was living as a free man. Long Rider couldn't stand the very thought of it. He had begun to understand that he would never be free to make plans or find pleasure in his life until he had killed the captain, because he would always feel the weight of a job left undone. His hatred would continue to burn deep inside his heart and leave no room for anything else.

The sun was fully visible now, and it was casting a blood-red glow on the tracks. Long Rider's gaze followed the shining rails toward the horizon, knowing they could lead him in the direction he yearned to go.

But he was also troubled by the approaching Iron Horse. It made him fearful and angry at the same time, as a man will feel when he doesn't want to admit something that he knows in his heart to be true. It was something he'd felt every other time the hunters had seen the noisy beast, but now Long Rider faced the thing he had not wanted to face before. He admitted to himself that even if the Indians could topple it this time, they could not stand up forever to the strong medicine of the whites that permitted them to build such things.

The superiority of white rifles over Indian bows and arrows had not bothered him so much, because eventually the Indians would have been able to steal or buy their own weapons. But the same could not be said for the guns-that-shoot-twice, or this terrible Iron Horse that Bridger had warned him about. Long Rider was being forced to consider Bridger's other warning, that Indian medicine was no match for these things. Until now there had been some advantage in the Indians' superior numbers, but now Long Rider watched the coming of the Iron Horse and knew it could not be stopped from bringing many more whites with many more weapons.

Nor could he deny any longer that their discipline made them even more powerful. It was something he had known since the Platte Bridge fight, since the final Indian march of retreat along the riverbank. He knew a white army would not have given up after a couple of days. They would have attacked the fort if it was considered important enough, or they might have surrounded it until it fell. In any case, the soldiers would have had to obey their orders under the threat of death, while Indian warriors were always free to drift away when they got bored.

Long Rider turned toward the north with an aching heart, trying to tell himself that none of these things should matter. Even if he knew that the Indian way of life was doomed, all his training since childhood told him that he should fight with the People until the end. Their situation was more desperate than ever now, and his duty was to defend the sick and the helpless, to make sure that the women and children had enough to eat. He should go and fight, saying before each battle, "It is a good day to die."

But the thought of his own death made him look back toward the East, tormented by the possibility that Captain Price—or Stanley Price, if he truly had resigned—might go unpunished. Long Rider squinted against the sun and felt himself torn by the decision he had to make. To the east was the necessity of revenge. To the north was the threat against his People.

Long Rider sighed and got to his feet, knowing he would not find an answer that morning. He decided only that he would seek another vision when he had a chance, asking the spirits to show him what he should do. This was enough to give him some hope as he walked down the hill toward the camp, calling out to wake the warriors who were still sleeping.

They quickly stripped down to their breechclouts and painted themselves for battle while Long Rider slipped the heavy buffalo-hide coat over his shoulders, with the yellow Thunderbird centered across his back. Then the warriors caught up their horses and followed him toward the hill, concealing themselves just behind the crest and whooping with excitement when they saw the Iron Horse speeding toward them across the prairie. It was dragging four of the wooden houses on wheels, one of them with windows in its side.

Long Rider did not join in the war cries of the other warriors. There was a fury rising in his breast that was already greater than theirs, a fury mixed with sadness when he looked upon the Indians who did not know that their way of life was doomed. Long Rider felt burdened by his knowledge of the future. The warriors were working themselves up for a good show, and maybe a good fight, but for Long Rider the train coming toward them represented all the whites who were coming to destroy the Indians. This was not just another fight for him but a confrontation with all that was evil. He watched the Iron Horse with a sharp glitter of rage in his eyes, his heart pounding and his blood running hot for the spilling of more blood.

Suddenly there was a loud whistle, and then a terrifying squeal from the direction of the train. The ponies pranced nervously and the warriors looked worried.

"Don't be afraid," said Long Rider. "That is the sound of metal rubbing metal. I think they have seen the danger."

The wheels of the Iron Horse had stopped rolling, but still it moved toward the place where the tracks had been spread apart, dropping onto the cross ties and then jumping up over the rails to hurtle down the steep bank of the roadbed. The warriors stared like wide-eyed children, shouting their war cries again when the Iron Horse toppled slowly onto its side. They saw a man leap from the back end, flailing his arms and running frantically as soon as his feet hit the ground. But the man disappeared beneath the wooden houses that followed the Iron Horse down the embankment, tipping over one by one.

Long Rider would always remember the squealing and crunching of the Iron Horse as it came to rest in great, boiling clouds of smoke and steam and dust. It was a fine show, and all was still for the space of a breath while the Indians watched in awe. Then they heard a scream and saw people struggling out of the wooden house with the windows. The people scrambled away through the smoke and dust, and the warriors ran their horses down the hill, screaming in victory as they spread out to chase the people across the prairie.

One man turned suddenly with a breech-loading rifle and shot a Cheyenne warrior off his horse. Long Rider rode down on the man while he was trying to reload, felling him with a bullet in the stomach. The man rolled in the grass, clutching his wound and crying out in agony. He screamed when he saw the fierce-looking warrior with the light brown hair staring down at him from the back of a horse. The man saw hatred and death in the empty gray eyes sighting over the barrel of the Remington revolver, until his screams were cut short by a bullet that punched through his eyeball and tore off the back of his head.

For Long Rider it was an act of mercy. Even in his raging hatred he had no more desire to see a white man suffer. But his taste for blood was stronger than ever. He rode his horse up onto the railroad embankment, stopping to look for more whites to kill on the other side of the train.

Most of them had already been ridden down. Their bodies lay scattered across the prairie while the Indians chased the fastest survivors in the distance. Long Rider saw an Oglala named White Wing nearby, off to one side at the head of the train. He was shooting arrows down into two bodies that lay in a little heap, one on top of the other, even though the bodies already bristled with arrows. Long Rider nodded in understanding when he saw Turkey Leg and Standing Bear lying dead not far away. One or both of the whites had killed the Oglala, and White Wing was venting his rage. As Long Rider watched, the warrior suddenly turned his horse and galloped off with a shrill animal cry.

Long Rider was about to follow when he saw a movement from the corner of his eye. He looked down the length of the train, staring hard into the deep shadow in front of the Iron Horse. Unsure of what he'd seen, he put his pony into an easy walk along the tracks.

A black-haired man burst out of the shadows, knowing he'd been discovered. He ran across the short distance between the Iron Horse and the two whites whose bodies had been filled with arrows. Long Rider gave chase, angling down off the embankment just as another warrior came across the tracks behind him. Long Rider looked back and recognized Crazy Horse. They exchanged glances and yipped like coyotes as they raced to cut off the black-haired man.

He reached the bodies ahead of them and snatched up a revolver that had been lying in the grass. That would account for the dead Oglalas, Long Rider thought. Then the man was facing them and aiming with a steady hand while Long Rider and Crazy Horse came toward him, shouting their war cries. It was a brave thing for any man to do, but now it was possible to see that he was only a boy of no more than fourteen or fifteen winters.

Long Rider looked at the boy and saw a fleeting picture of himself at the same age, being stolen away from his mother.

Then he was shaking off the picture as the warriors bent low, protecting themselves behind the necks of their galloping ponies. But nothing happened when the boy pulled the trigger. Long Rider saw the hammer rise and fall two times and guessed that the dead man had emptied the chambers of the revolver before he died.

The boy's face was shining with tears, but he calmly turned the revolver around to examine the cylinder. When he saw it was empty, he tossed it aside and fell to his knees beside the bodies that lay across each other, tugging desperately at the clothing of the man on top.

Long Rider frowned, seeing many things all at once. He saw that the second arrow-filled body belonged to a woman, and she was lying beneath the man as if he'd been trying to protect her. Long Rider also noticed that the dead man had the same gleaming black hair as the boy who was kneeling beside him. The boy seemed to be shouting something as he tugged at the

man's clothing, the tears still flowing down his cheeks. Long
Rider saw all this in the time it takes to blink an eye, knowing in
the same instant that the dead man was the boy's father, and the
woman his mother.

The boy looked up at the warriors as Crazy Horse was fitting
an arrow to his bow. The Indians bore down on him, and still he
struggled with something twisted inside his father's coat, tilting
his face up a little more to face his death with unblinking eyes.

Long Rider swerved suddenly to grab Crazy Horse's arm,
spoiling his aim so the arrow flew wild. The warrior grunted in
surprise and turned with a harsh glare while Long Rider swerved
again to put himself between the boy and two other Oglala who
were converging on him. Long Rider brought his excited pony to
a prancing halt in front of the boy and challenged all three
warriors with his eyes, holding his revolver down by his side but
showing them he would use it if he had to.

"What are you doing?" demanded the Oglala named White
Wing. "Why do you protect a white man?"

"I'm defending a white *boy*," said Long Rider, trying to hide
the confusion he was feeling. "A boy who has shown great
courage."

"He is white and he must die," said White Wing.

"I am also white," Long Rider said. "Do you wish to try to
kill me?"

The warrior blinked, still showing arrogance but unable to say
anything. Long Rider's skill with the revolver had become
well-known among the Lakota, and White Wing had no wish to
challenge him. Long Rider glanced quickly at the black-haired
boy, who was wiping the tears from his cheeks as he watched the
scene intently. He had brilliant green eyes that shone with sharp
intelligence.

"But why do you do this?" insisted Crazy Horse, his anger
slowly giving way to confusion. "We have been like brothers,
Long Rider, and I know your heart is bad against the whites.
Why do you spare this one's life?"

Long Rider hesitated, fearing that he would not be able to
explain himself. He had a vague idea that he'd acted out of
sympathy, although it was not for this unknown boy who stood
beside him. It was for any boy or all boys who had seen their
parents killed. Only much later did he begin to feel as if he had

been trying to save himself that day, trying to change something that had already happened and could never really be changed. At the moment, however, he was only aware of a feeling that he could not have tolerated the boy's death. Sympathy was the only name he could have used for that feeling, and sympathy was a weakness that the warriors would not have understood.

Long Rider had also been impressed by the boy's courage, but that was not a good excuse, either. It would only have meant more honor for the warrior who killed such a fearless opponent and counted first coup.

The silence grew as more Indians came up to see what was happening. The boy watched without visible fear as they surrounded him, and Long Rider tried to look equally sure of himself. He met their eyes while he searched for words to tell them, almost giving up before a perfect explanation came into his mind. It was a little frightening because it meant an instant decision that would change his life completely, but the idea seemed so good that he began to wonder if it secretly had been one of his true reasons for saving the boy.

"I need him to serve me," Long Rider announced. "I have decided to go to the land where the sun rises, to find and kill the man who killed my woman and my mother. This boy will show me the way to travel. He will teach me how to live in the white man's villages. Without him I would fail."

Crazy Horse glanced at the boy, his eyes narrowed in suspicion. "I don't think you should go among the whites," he told Long Rider. "There is danger that way. You might never return to the People."

The words made Long Rider uneasy, reminding him of the white stone road that he had traveled in his vision. "The Lakota will always be my people," he said, a little too harshly. "I will come back to protect them and provide them with food. But my thoughts will not be clear enough to serve them well until I have killed Stanley Price."

"I know it is a thing you feel you must do," said Crazy Horse. He stared toward the eastern horizon, but he didn't speak the thoughts that moved behind his eyes. The other warriors took his silence as a sign that they should not interfere. Gradually they began to drift back toward the train.

Long Rider put away his revolver and slipped off his horse,

tying the boy's wrists with a short length of horsehair rope.
Crazy Horse watched in silence, his eyes full of doubt and
something like sadness.

"I wish you would not do this," he said after a while. "It
gives me a bad feeling."

Long Rider frowned as he tugged at the knots to make sure
they were tight. "I know you have been to the real world behind
this one," he said, "and perhaps I should listen harder to the
things you tell me. But I have thought on this a great deal, Crazy
Horse, and the deaths of my wife and my mother weigh heavy
on my heart. I have seen them being killed again and again, and
I fear I will not stop seeing it until I have removed the cause."

Crazy Horse nodded once. "May you be successful, Long
Rider. And may the hand of Wakan-tanka guide your return."

"There is no need for such a long face, Crazy Horse. We will
meet again soon and share a fire."

The young Oglala shook his head, moving it sadly from side
to side. "I do not believe we will. I hope I am wrong.
Good-bye, my friend."

The warrior turned his pony toward the train, and Long Rider
watched him go, feeling a heavy weight beneath his heart. But
he believed the things he had said about the need for finding
Captain Price, and he knew that the boy was his best chance for
traveling east. So he remained silent as his closest friend and
ally rode away beneath the great blue sky. Crazy Horse looked
smaller and smaller against the endless sky and the endless land
of grass that surrounded them.

CHAPTER TWENTY

Long Rider's reverie was interrupted by a soft, drawn-out sigh that made him look at the black-haired boy by his side. The boy was watching him with steady eyes that held a measure of hope and curiosity, until he was distracted by a flurry of excited shouts that drifted across the prairie from the train. Some of the warriors were dragging trunks and cartons from the wreckage, while others were passing among the bodies of the passengers. Long Rider frowned, knowing that soon they would be coming for the man and woman who lay at the boy's feet. The warriors would take whatever spoils and plunder they wanted, then mutilate the flesh. The enemies of the Lakota would not be allowed to go into the spirit world with their bodies intact, even if they had sons who were still alive.

Long Rider brought his pony closer to the boy and held out his hand. The boy fell back for a moment before he grasped the warrior's hand and let himself be pulled up onto the horse. Long Rider tried to place the boy's arm underneath his own, but the boy resisted.

"Hold on," Long Rider commanded.

"I knew it!" said the boy, grabbing hold as Long Rider urged his pony into a gentle lope. "Goddamn if I didn't know it all along. Where are we going?"

Long Rider pointed across his pony's neck. "Our camp is

near that hill," he called back. "My things are there."

"But it's true, ain't it?" the boy yelled against the wind. "I mean, you *are* a white man?"

"My parents had white skin," the warrior said stiffly, "but I was born an Oglala. I am called Long Rider by my people."

"An Oglala Sioux?" said the boy. "You mean, I been saved from a real-life Injun attack by a white man who's been *raised* by Injuns? Goddamn, wait till the guys hear about this!"

"Does that mean you would like to go back? To the place you came from?"

"Are you kidding? Shit, yes!"

"Good. I will help you get there in safety. But you must take me with you and show me how to live among the whites."

"Whatever you say." The boy shrugged. Long Rider could feel the lifting of the arms that grasped his midsection. Then he felt them twisting and straining, and guessed that the boy was looking back toward the bodies that lay in the grass.

"Did you know those people?" Long Rider asked. "The man and the woman?"

"Yeah," said the boy. "They were *my* folks."

Long Rider turned around to stare at the boy. "I hear no grief in your voice."

"For those two? Shit, the only reason we were out here in the first place was because they were tryin' to take me away from my friends."

Long Rider peered at the boy a moment longer, trying to guess why his parents might want to do such a thing, but he quickly gave it up. He expected that many things about the whites would remain a mystery to him, and it wasn't important, anyway. He only needed the boy to act as a guide. "Even so," he said, "it will be best not to look back at them. Oglala custom requires harsh treatment for dead enemies."

"So I see," said the boy, his voice dry and flat. Then he shrugged again. "But what the hell, they can't feel anything, anyway."

Gabe frowned but said nothing more. He guided his pony up and over the tracks in front of the fallen Iron Horse, which made a sharp hissing sound and filled the air with a strange white smoke. Through the smoke Long Rider saw some of the Oglala tipping brown bottles over their upturned faces.

"Whiskey!" said the boy. He smacked his lips behind Long

Rider's shoulders. "A little of that would sure go over big right now."

Long Rider shook his head in disgust and kept riding toward the low hill on the other side of the tracks, gathering two more of his horses along the way. He led them into the camp and began to pack one of them while the boy looked on.

Long Rider took off his Thunderbird coat and laid it out in the grass. On top of the coat he arranged the sacred pipe he had received from Two Face, and a hide-wrapped bundle that held his mother's Bible. He also added some powder and lead, some dried meat, and a few wild turnips. Finally he rolled up the coat and tied it across the back of his pony. He kept the Sharps carbine slung behind his back, and the Remington revolvers were thrust in his belt. When he had finished, Long Rider stood and looked at the camp one last time. A steady breeze made gentle waves in the grass and ruffled Long Rider's hair. He pushed the hair out of his eyes and wished he could just as easily push aside the sadness that made a hollow place in his belly.

Long Rider thought of the boy watching him and turned around, but the boy was staring across the prairie toward the place where the bodies of his mother and father lay. Long Rider went to stand beside him, leading the three horses.

"We can wait until the warriors have left," he said. "Then you may bury them in the white man's way."

The boy shrugged. "They wouldn't know the difference."

"But how will their spirits travel to the—"

"Who believes in spirits! Besides, they ain't no loss to me."

"Didn't I see tears?"

"I was pretty scared, I guess. I thought sure you was about to kill me." The boy turned to face Long Rider. "What made em' lay off, anyway? What did you tell 'em?"

"The same thing I told you. That I needed someone to help me travel in the land of the whites."

The boy frowned. "You really serious about that?"

Long Rider nodded.

"What is it you're after?"

Long Rider only stared at him and didn't answer.

"Does it have something to do with this Stanley Price?" said the boy. Long Rider gave him a fierce look and took a step back. "You said his name before, remember? It was the only thing I understood in all that mumbo jumbo."

"Your wits are sharp," said Long Rider. "Yes, I am looking for a man named Stanley Price."

"Why?"

"That is not something you need to know."

"Do you know where he is, at least?"

Long Rider shook his head. "I will take you home first. Then I will search."

The boy swept Long Rider with a critical eye. "You ain't gonna get far lookin' like that," he said. "You'll need to cut your hair and—"

"No!" said Long Rider. "A warrior does not cut his hair."

"Suit yourself," the boy said with a shrug. "I'm just tellin' you that it'll cause a lot of trouble. Maybe a hat will . . . say, have you got any money for clothes?"

"Money?" Long Rider said with a frown. He remembered the metal and paper that the whites had used in trading at the fort. "You think I will need money?"

The boy laughed. "How the hell do you expect to eat? Where would you sleep?"

"I will have my guns for hunting," Long Rider suggested. "And I could bring my lodge."

The boy laughed again. "I can just see that in New York. Chief Long Rider shooting pigeons in Central Park."

Long Rider frowned. "Perhaps I should use the white name my mother gave me."

"That would be a start. What is it?"

"Gabe Conrad."

The boy repeated the name, then offered his right hand. "Well, I'm Rory Cavanaugh," he said, "and I'm glad as hell you were here today. Do you know how to shake like a white man?"

Gabe nodded, gripping the hand. "I lived among the soldiers at Fort Laramie for a time."

"Yeah, I thought there was something like that," said the boy. "The way you talk the lingo an' all. It'll sure make things easier."

Rory looked toward the train, his green eyes shining with excitement as he lost himself in the challenge and adventure of his job. Gabe saw the boy's eyes stop once as he surveyed the prairie, losing their shine for a moment before he forced himself to look at other things.

"I bet we could find you some clothes out there," he told Gabe. "Would there be any trouble if we looked?"

"No one will trouble us."

Gabe meant to say it only as a matter of fact, but something in his tone made the boy give him a closer look.

"I guess not," Rory said. "So let's see what we can find."

They set out on foot, leading the horses, and the first thing they came across was a black slouch hat blowing through the grass near the hill. The hat was barely large enough to hold Gabe's hair out of sight. "Maybe you could cut it just a little?" Rory said hopefully. "Down to your shoulders, anyway? Then you could claim to be a scout or a mountain man."

Gabe said he would consider it, and moved on toward the things that had been scattered from boxes and bags along the length of the train.

"Just look at this stuff!" Rory kept saying. "What a haul it could've been!"

The Lakota and Cheyenne warriors were paying them little attention. One brave had found a bugle and was learning how to use it, the sour notes floating through the air while the brass glinted in the sun. Other braves were trying on tall black hats or cavorting about with parasols above their heads, showing off for each other and roaring with laughter. A few Indians ignored the fun and continued loading their travois with sacks of flour and coffee and sugar, and any trinkets that might amuse their women.

Rory grinned and said, "I bet I can tell which ones drank the whiskey."

"The ones who act like fools," said Gabe.

"They're sure havin' a great time, though."

Gabe made a sound of disgust. "It makes my heart bad," he said. "Wakan-tanka did not make the Indian for drinking whiskey."

"Then thank the Lord you're a white man, right?"

"What do you mean? I would never touch it."

Rory rolled his eyes. "How can you say that if you don't know what you're missing?"

Gabe fell to studying the boy, his anger fading slowly and the hint of a smile forming on his lips. "How many years have you lived?" he finally asked.

"Sixteen, almost. I'll be sixteen in a couple months." He

laughed. "Or maybe I should say moons."

"Are all white boys like you?"

"Not hardly," said Rory. He laughed again, but now there was a bitter edge to the sound. "Most of 'em go to school and do what their folks tell 'em and act all nice and proper. About the worst thing they do is maybe sneak a little tobacco."

"But you are different?"

"Yeah," said Rory, lifting his chin a little. "Me and my friends in New York, we don't fall for that stuff. We do what we want."

"You don't respect the elders?"

"What's to respect?" Rory sneered. "Hey, look at that!"

Some of the warriors had found a shipment of cloth wrapped in bolts, and they were tying the ends onto the tails of their ponies. Then the Indians went racing away with the cloth unfurling behind them and blowing in long streamers over the prairie.

"See, we're like that," Rory said with pride. "We have fun."

"You and your friends."

"Yeah. It's a gang, actually. That's what we call it back there."

"A gang?"

"It's sort of like a tribe, I bet. Like Indian braves! We fight the other gangs to keep 'em out of our territory."

Gabe was wearing a perplexed frown. He was getting used to it. "But don't you have any relatives?" he asked. "Who will take you in now that your mother and father are dead?"

"Maybe I'll stay with my friends. A lot of 'em just stay in boxes or under loading docks."

"But a young man needs the wisdom of the old ones if he wants to grow strong."

"Wisdom," Rory spat out. "Hell, everything I need to learn I can get from the Tough Boys."

Gabe looked thoughtful, feeling more sympathy for Rory's dead parents as he and the boy continued their search through the things that had been left behind by the warriors. Rory thought one trunk looked more promising than the others. It had burst at the seams when it fell, spilling a jumble of black and white clothing into the tall yellow grass. He pulled a white linen shirt out of the pile.

"Must've been that preacher," Rory said. "He was even bigger than you, I think." He held the shirt up against Gabe's chest and said, "Good. Try it on."

When he saw the way the shirt looked, he nodded and bent over the pile again, extracting a pair of black broadcloth trousers. Gabe pulled them over his breechclout, but there was so much room to spare that they fell back down around his knees. Rory laughed so hard he couldn't speak for a moment. Then he said, "Maybe this fellow was a little *too* big."

"I could hold them up with this," said Gabe, touching the deerhide belt that supported his holster.

Rory shook his head. "They won't let you carry guns in the city. At least not showing like that. You'll have to put 'em away."

"How could I go among the whites without a gun?"

"They figure the police will protect you if anything goes wrong."

Gabe asked what police were, and Rory explained until Gabe understood that they were like the *akicita*, the marshals in a Lakota village. "But a warrior must still defend himself," said Gabe. "Even if there are *akicita*."

"I'll go along with that," Rory said with feeling. "The police ain't much use, anyway. I could show you what some folks do to get around it."

Rory told Gabe to untie his belt and loop it up over one shoulder so the holster would hang under his arm. Then he handed up a black coat from the pile of clothing. "Here's where the guy's size'll come in handy," he said.

The coat slipped easily over Gabe's shoulders, with plenty of room for the holstered Remington.

"See?" said Rory. "You can't tell the gun is there, even when the coat is buttoned. A lot of people are doin' it." He looked back down at Gabe's knees and smiled. "But we're still gonna have to buy you some decent pants when we get to a town. And some boots."

The humor died from Rory's eyes, and he looked out across the prairie. "Actually," he said, "I know where we can get all the money we need. My father carried it in a special belt underneath his clothes."

Gabe followed the direction of the boy's gaze, thinking about the condition in which they would find his father's body. "Do we really need it?'' he said. "I could trade my ponies for some of this money.''

Rory was shaking his head. "Not nearly enough, Gabe. Not for the things you got in mind.''

"Then I will go,'' said Gabe. "It would not be a good thing for you to see.''

"I keep tellin' you, it ain't no big deal. We might as well just get it over with.'' Rory helped Gabe tie his new clothes behind the Thunderbird coat on the packhorse, laughing once again with that edge of bitterness. "Maybe somebody'll ask you to preach,'' he said as they led their ponies away from the train. "What the hell would you say then?''

"Preach?'' said Gabe, glancing at the boy with a puzzled frown. But Rory was staring toward the thicket of arrows that marked the location of his father's body. A rigid line of muscle stood out along his jaw. "It's high time I got a little of the old man's money, anyway,'' he said. "The bastard sure made enough of it, sellin' coats an' stuff to the Army. Makin' profits off all them poor suckers that fought in the war. But did he ever give me any of it? Hell, no. Said he didn't like the way I'd spend it with my friends. What the hell did *he* know about anything?''

The boy talked without stopping, even when they came to the bodies and saw the terrible mess. His mother's fiery red hair seemed untouched, but there was only a pulpy mass of blood and flesh where his father's hair had been. The man's arms and legs had been hacked off. His entrails had been scooped out and piled on his chest. Flies swarmed over everything, but Rory ignored them, still talking while he kneeled down to untangle a wide belt from bloody pieces of flesh.

"Believed in cash, he did. Plenty of cash so he could buy whatever he wanted. But the bastard couldn't buy off my friends. No, sir. Couldn't get 'em to kick *me* out of the gang. Figured he'd have it easy, just the way he always had it, but they surprised him. He didn't know we all stick together no matter what. Probably didn't even know what loyalty *was*.''

The boy's voice was getting louder, and Gabe watched him with a worried frown, wondering what he should do.

"So he brings me out to this godforsaken place instead,'' Rory was saying, "and gets my mother killed in the bargain. The bastard. She tried to talk him out of it, but no, *he* knew what was best. Well, I'd say the bastard got what he deserved, wouldn't you?''

Rory stood up and kicked his father's body in the side. There was a dull thud and the sharp sound of a rib cracking, and then Rory was swinging his foot back for another kick before Gabe could grab him and pull him away.

"Well, wouldn't you?" screamed the boy, still staring at his father as he struggled against Gabe's hold. "Wouldn't you?"

"Perhaps he tried to do what he thought was best," Gabe said.

"No, he didn't. It wasn't my fault! It was *his* idea. Why did he have to do it?'' Rory sagged suddenly in Gabe's arms, sobbing brokenly while Gabe remembered the way he felt after he'd killed his stepfather. It was the only thing that kept him from feeling disgusted with the boy's display of weakness— that, and reminding himself that children might be taught in a different way among the whites.

But Rory stopped crying just as suddenly and pulled away from Gabe, avoiding his eyes. He walked to his pony and climbed on, then sat quietly and stared off toward the low hills. For a while there was only the buzzing of flies over the bodies, and no sound from the Indians near the train. Gabe looked that way and saw that the warriors had stopped what they were doing to watch them. Then Rory cleared his throat, still gazing into the distance.

"Well, did you enjoy the show?" he said.

"The show?" said Gabe.

"You know what I mean."

Gabe scratched his hair and stared at Rory's back. "I think you have become a man today."

Rory turned around with a suspicious look. Gabe met his gaze, and gradually the suspicion faded. Rory turned back toward the hills and kicked at his pony.

"We might as well get going," he said in a weary tone.

Gabe looked down at the bodies of the boy's parents. A warm breeze ruffled the feathers sprouting from their bodies, and Gabe frowned over another example of behavior he could not understand. "Are you sure you don't want to take care of them?" he said.

"You know it won't be long," Rory called back over his

shoulder. "The Army'll come when the train doesn't show up on time. Do you really wanna try explaining what you were doing out here? Looking like that?"

"But how can you ride off and leave them here?"

The boy kept riding, turning his head slightly to make his words better understood. "As far as I'm concerned," he said, "they left me."

CHAPTER TWENTY-ONE

Gabe and Rory followed the railroad tracks toward the rising sun, dodging Army patrols and making wide circles around the smaller towns where strangers might be noticed. Their route took them through a sweeping landscape of rolling yellow grass and hard blue sky, but the boy never seemed to notice. He brooded silently for hours at a time, then talked endlessly about the friends he longed to see again in New York. Gabe sometimes had to keep himself from smiling when Rory boasted of their adventures.

"We're at war," Rory said more than once. "That's what it really is, Gabe. We're at war with everyone else. Suppose they get one of us alone and knock him down? Maybe even steal his coat that shows the gang he belongs to? Well, then we get our knives and pipes and attack 'em right in their own territory." Rory would sit up a little straighter in the hard Lakota saddle. "I'll tell you one thing, Gabe. Ain't nobody ever beat us head to head. They're all afraid of the Tough Boys."

Then the two riders came to North Platte, slipping into town after dark on the third day, and Rory was caught up in the job of introducing Gabe to the ways of white civilians. The warrior had never seen anything beyond a frontier Army post. Now he worked hard to understand the idea behind restaurants and hotels and hid his fear when he entered one of the strange houses-on-wheels the next afternoon. By that time he and Rory were carrying new luggage and wearing store-bought clothes, all financed by the sale of the horses, and they still had more than two thousand dollars from the bloody leather money belt that the boy had taken from his father's body.

On the train it was Rory who watched Gabe, trying to keep the warrior from making mistakes that might reveal his origins to the other passengers, and it was Gabe who began to brood. He stared out through the soot-streaked window as the train rolled east, his face impassive while he met the boy's questions with nods or one-word answers.

"Is something wrong?" Rory finally asked as they neared Chicago. "I mean, are you just seeing the sights, or is there something I should know about?"

Gabe looked at Rory for a moment before he spoke, as if he hadn't heard the question. "Are we close to New York?"

Rory laughed. "Hell, no. We still have—"

"And you say New York is larger than Omaha?"

"Lots! So is Chicago and Philadelphia and Boston and—"

Gabe was shaking his head. He went back to staring out the window with a bleak and empty look in his pale gray eyes. "There are so many of you," he said. "Even when we gathered along the Powder, more Lakota coming together than ever before, I think there were still more whites in Omaha." He lifted his chin, pointing it toward the landscape. "And still it goes on. The small villages in between, the farms . . ."

"This ain't nothin', Gabe. It gets really crowded past Chicago."

Rory was waiting for the warrior to look impressed. Instead he saw a worried frown. "What's the problem?" he asked.

"There are so many," Gabe repeated. "My People will fight for their hunting grounds and many of them will die, and now I think it will all be for nothing. I talked strong for war, but I never believed there could be so many whites."

"I don't get this stuff about 'your people,' Gabe. *You're* a white man."

"The Lakota raised me and taught me their ways," said Gabe, fixing his eyes on the boy, "and they are good ways. I have seen nothing good about the way of the whites. They kill my People and steal our land."

"Just if you break the rules," Rory said, flaring. "Like the way you stopped our train and—"

"Don't be stupid!" Gabe glanced around at the other passengers, then leaned closer to the boy. "We attacked the train because it brings more whites to plague us."

"But—"

"The Arapaho had nothing to do with the whites," said Gabe, leaning even closer. "They lived peacefully in their own country until the soldiers came to kill them."

Rory was trying not to flinch under Gabe's harsh stare and his even harsher words, but his eyes were troubled. "Didn't they start it?" he asked. "I bet one of the Indians fired the first shot."

Gabe grunted bitterly. "The soldiers attacked a sleeping camp. We tried to stay away from the whites, but they came deep into our country. They would have killed the People in their robes if I hadn't sounded the warning."

Rory's eyes opened wide. "You were there?"

Gabe's chin came down in a sharp nod. "I was washing myself below the bluffs of the Tongue when I heard them coming. I warned the People, but it was very bad that day. The soldiers came among the tepees before we could mount a defense. Some of the women were trapped between us. They fought well beside the men, but the soldiers killed many of us with their rifles."

"Jesus!" Rory breathed. "A real battle!"

Gabe stared out the window without seeing the peaceful Illinois farmhouse on the horizon. "The soldiers chased us into the hills," he said. "Then they turned back to destroy our camp. They burned our lodges and all the food we had prepared for the winter."

Rory frowned, looking even more troubled than before.

"When they were done, the soldiers came to chase us again, trying to kill more of the People. We could only sting them a little with our arrows. They chased us all that day, until their horses grew tired. Then we drove them back and the soldiers went away. But our homes and our food were gone, and more than sixty of us had been killed."

"Sixty people!" Rory shook his head in wonder. "Makes *my* stories seem awful puny. But at least you survived, Gabe."

"There was no joy in that."

"Jesus Christ, why *not*?"

Gabe looked at the wide green eyes that seemed so young,

wondering whether he should burden the boy with his own bitterness. "Because others died," he said simply. "My mother and my new wife were among them."

"Oh, no," said Rory. There was such anguish in his tone that Gabe knew the boy's grief was also for himself. "You mean, your real mother? She was there?"

Gabe nodded. "She had gone to Black Bear's camp to—"

"But wait a minute. Couldn't the soldiers see she was white?"

Gabe's face hardened into a cold mask. "He knew. But he also knew she was my mother and his hatred for me was—"

"You mean, you know who did it?" Rory exploded. "You *saw* it?"

"I saw it. I saw him plunge the steel into her breast. I saw the fear and pain in her—"

"Jesus Christ," Rory said with a shudder, as if he were trying to shake off his own memories. "But how did you know . . . well, sure, you said you'd spent some time at one of the forts."

Gabe nodded.

"And you met him there? The man who—" Rory suddenly broke off and snapped his fingers. "Stanley Price!" he said. "That's why you're lookin' for him, ain't it? Stanley Price is the one who cut your women down, and now you're lookin' to make him pay."

Gabe stared at Rory, impressed by the cleverness of the boy's thoughts and also angry with himself for revealing so much. It could be dangerous if other whites knew he was planning to kill a white soldier.

"Don't fret," said Rory, "your secret is safe with me. I know I'd like to catch the bastard that killed *my* mother."

"That might have been an accident," Gabe said with a frown. "Lakota warriors do not fight women. But our hearts were bad toward the whites and the Iron Horse."

"Hell," said Rory, "my old man shouldn't've brought her out here in the first place." He looked out the window for a moment, then turned back to Gabe. "What happened with Stanley Price? Why did he hate you so much?"

"It is a long story."

"We have all the time in the world," Rory said with a grin.

Gabe studied him for a moment, wondering what had happened to the boy who boasted of childhood games and pretended to feel nothing for his parents. Now Rory looked back at him with sharp green eyes, waiting to understand the things he might hear, and Gabe began to tell him what had happened. He described his abduction by Jim Bridger and his life at Fort Laramie, his fight over the captain's horse followed by the years in the stockade, and finally the fight in the livery barn. Rory listened as if he were in a trance, his mouth hanging open and his eyes fixed on Gabe's face. "The son of a bitch!" he said when Gabe was done. "A pitchfork! The son of a bitch *deserves* to die."

Gabe said nothing. It didn't make him happy to remember.

"At least it'll be easy to find him," said Rory. "The Army'll know."

"Someone told me he left the Army."

Rory shrugged. "They'll know, anyway. They keep track of the officers. You could—no, wait. *I* could go to Washington. Pretend I'm his bastard son or something. That way they'd never make the connection between you and him."

"I am thankful for your offer," Gabe said solemnly. "But you are still a boy, and your heart should live in peace."

"I ain't much younger than you were when you fought the captain."

"But I couldn't prevent it. And this is not your fight."

"You saved my life, didn't you? Besides, I'd feel a lot better knowing Price got what was coming to him."

"What about your friends? All those things you do together?"

"Don't remind me," said Rory, rolling his eyes. "I'm embarrassed I even told you about that kid stuff. The hell with 'em."

"I will meditate on it," Gabe said slowly. "But there is something else I must do first, something my mother wrote in her Bible."

"Bible?" Rory said. "Your mother had a Bible?"

"She kept it when she was captured. She used it to teach me the white man's tongue."

"Do you still have it?" said Rory, sitting forward on his seat.

Gabe nodded. "I kept it because of the words she wrote."

"What words?"

"About the things that happened. Her thoughts . . ."

"Like a diary? That's even better. Let me see it!"

Gabe stared at the boy for a moment, then pulled his new war bag out from between his legs. Gabe had packed away his gunpowder, lead, and buffalo-hide coat in a trunk, but he kept the war bag with him at all times. Now he pulled out the worn deer-hide bundle and extracted the black book, handing it across to Rory.

The boy opened the cover with trembling fingers, holding it up toward the late-afternoon light that filtered through the layer of soot on the window. A grin spread across his face.

"It's her family Bible," he said, "just like I hoped! Everybody's listed in the front. We could track down your mother's relatives!"

Gabe nodded reluctantly. "She also talks of her father," he said, "asking the person who reads her words to—"

"Show me!" said Rory.

Gabe showed him the passage, and Rory became even more excited.

"He's a lawyer," said the boy. "That makes it perfect! I bet he can—"

"What is a lawyer?"

Rory tried to describe law and the courts, but Gabe kept asking why the people who had a problem couldn't solve it among themselves, with the help of their chiefs.

"Never mind," Rory finally said. "All you need to know is that a lawyer has a lot of power among the whites. This one could probably find things out even faster than I could."

Gabe still looked puzzled. "What things?"

"Stanley Price!" said Rory. "We could go up to Boston and tell this Thomas Reid all about your mother's death. Tell him who it was that killed her. Then I bet he'd help us."

Gabe looked doubtful. "What if he doesn't believe that Price should be killed? I don't think white rules permit such things."

"It's worth a try," said Rory. "He might feel the same way you do about a soldier runnin' a helpless white woman through with a saber. An' if he don't, then we just go to Washington like I said."

"Well," said Gabe, "I was planning to see the lawyer, anyway. . . ."

"That's the ticket!"

"But I will go alone, Rory. I'm grateful for your ideas, but you cannot be a part of this thing."

"Aw, come on," Rory said. He pleaded and argued for a long time while the sun disappeared and the sky turned dark, but Gabe held firm. The boy returned the Bible and fell into a sullen silence. Gabe watched the lights of a small town fly past the windows, surprised to feel an ache of sadness in his heart. He thought about letting the boy join him as an ally in the search for Stanley Price, then condemned himself for his selfish thoughts.

The anger faded gradually from Rory's eyes, and after a while he began to look thoughtful. Finally he stirred and said, "Will you listen to me about one thing, at least? Don't go see this lawyer in his office."

"Why not?"

"Suppose he does help you find Price. What if Price dies and you get caught—just supposin', now—and someone remembers you and him havin' a talk?"

Gabe tilted his head to one side and looked at Rory, the rattle of the wheels filling the silence until the boy shifted uncomfortably.

"Well, it's just that he could figure the same thing," Rory said. "And if he did, he wouldn't be so likely to help."

"I understand," Gabe assured him. "I look at you this way because I see a boy, and yet the words that come from your mouth are a man's words. On the first day I said you have sharp wits. Now it pleases me to see I was not wrong."

Rory tried to hide his pleasure with a laugh. "Then take me with you," he said.

Gabe shook his head again, the regret showing in his eyes. "Hatred makes my heart bad, Rory, and I fear it would do the same to yours. Isn't there someone else who could care for you?"

The boy's mouth twisted with distaste. "I got an aunt and uncle in New York. That's my father's sister and her husband. But they're so dumb and boring you wouldn't believe it. They think I should clerk in a store."

"I don't know whether that is bad or good among the whites," Gabe said with a frown. "But I know a boy must have an adviser to show him the right path, just as High Backbone instructed me."

"Why couldn't you be the one?" Rory cried. "You're tougher'n anyone I ever met."

"No," said Gabe. "I know nothing of white ways. Your aunt and uncle would know."

"But that doesn't matter, Gabe. I ain't plannin' to *live* in New York."

"No?"

"No," said Rory, shaking his head with a sense of finality. "All the excitement's out where you come from."

"But maybe it will be good to have a home again," said Gabe. "Let's meet them, at least."

"If that's what you want," Rory said with a shrug. "But I'm going West the first chance I get."

In New York, Gabe discovered that the boy had described his aunt and uncle with accuracy. Diane Leek and her husband, Ed, were tired-looking people who lived on one floor of an old building. They embraced Rory and told him they were sorry for his loss, but Gabe could see no warmth or affection in their eyes. They were only making a show, he thought, acting the way they believed relatives should act. They accepted without questions the tale that Rory and Gabe had met on the train near Chicago, then settled back in a weary silence in their dusty, overstuffed chairs. The woman knitted a scarf while the man stared into the darkness outside the window, occasionally breaking the silence to tell Rory tiresome stories about his childhood. They asked him questions now and then but didn't really listen to his answers.

"See?" Rory said later that night. "They're all the family I got."

Gabe frowned at the closed door of the boy's bedroom and shook his head. "I don't understand these whites," he admitted.

"Then let me come with you. Teach me the things you learned from High Backbone."

Gabe peered into Rory's steady green eyes, remembering the way he had faced three charging mounted warriors with an empty revolver. Gabe considered the boy's courage, and also his quick thoughts, and imagined the man he might become with the proper guidance. "That is truly what you want?" he finally asked.

"You know it is!"

"You would accept the wisdom of what I say?"

"Yes!"

"Even if I said you must wait here until I finish the thing I came to do?"

The boy's eyes filled with disappointment and he looked away for a moment, but then he nodded his head. "If that's the only way," he murmured.

"Good!" said Gabe. "Then tomorrow I will go to Boston."

"Tomorrow?"

"If I leave soon," Gabe said grimly, "then I can also return soon."

Rory glanced around the room as if he were searching for something. "But that's *too* soon," he said. "I—I wanted you to teach me how to shoot before you go."

Gabe frowned.

"Sure!" said Rory. "That way I could practice while you're gone. I'd be ready when we went out West."

"Where could you practice?"

"That's what shooting ranges are for. Please, Gabe? Just a couple days?"

Gabe had to admit to himself that he wasn't anxious to leave. He looked at the boy's eager expression and smiled. "I begin to wonder who will be guiding who," he said.

CHAPTER TWENTY-TWO

The big man with the broad, rugged face strolled into Boston's Public Gardens and sat on a bench in a grove of trees. There was rustling in the red and yellow leaves overhead, and the same cool breeze stirred the man's white hair. He glanced up when Gabe sat down at the other end of the bench, and something about Gabe made him continue to stare. The old man had pale gray eyes that seemed to reveal nothing and see everything.

"Afternoon," said Gabe.

The man's gaze fell briefly to the hide-wrapped bundle in Gabe's hands, then swept slowly around the park.

"Don't worry, Mr. Reid," Gabe said. "I'm alone and I mean you no harm."

"I'll be the judge of that," said the old man. "Who the hell are you and how do you know me?"

Gabe smiled. "There are a lot of people in Boston who know Thomas Reid. You wouldn't have asked that question if I'd approached you in your office."

Reid's clear gray eyes became more intent as the old lawyer studied Gabe, forming a new opinion of this brash young stranger on the park bench.

"Fair enough," said Reid. "I take it that you watched my offices and followed me here, no doubt because you wish to consult me in privacy."

Gabe nodded, partly in appreciation.

"But," said Reid, "you can rest assured I would have asked the first question of any man who didn't have the courtesy to introduce himself."

Gabe nodded again, this time a gesture of agreement. "I'm sorry for that, but you'll find out that I have a good reason. I don't want this to be too disturbing for you."

"It's already disturbing when a stranger accosts me in a public place. Get on with it, man!"

"Well, it concerns your daughter," said Gabe, faltering for a moment when he saw the lawyer's eyes narrow with suspicion. "I'm sorry to have to tell you this, but . . . Amelia Conrad is dead, sir. I wouldn't be so blunt except that I wanted to say it right off, so you wouldn't suffer from any false hopes."

"Hopes!" said Reid. "I haven't had any hopes in twenty years. Nor do I have any reason to believe anything you tell me."

"But I can show—"

"I'll have you know, young man, that I instigated an extensive search after my daughter and her husband disappeared. It cost me thousands, but I was able to discover that they turned off the trail and headed into hostile Indian country. After a year without word I knew she could not have survived."

"But she did, sir. She lived among the Lakota—until she was killed last summer."

"Living with the Indians?" the lawyer said harshly. "I'd rather believe she was dead."

Gabe nodded stiffly. "Maybe. But she wasn't."

"So you say."

Gabe shrugged and opened the deer-hide bundle on his knees, withdrawing his mother's Bible under the lawyer's watchful glare. He slid it carefully along the bench. "This will explain everything. I just wanted you to understand before you read the words."

Reid only glanced at the Bible at first, continuing to stare hard at Gabe. But Gabe bore up under his probing eyes, and gradually the lawyer sagged against the back of the bench, the defiance going out of him as he accepted at least the possibility that Gabe was telling the truth. He picked up the Bible and held it tenderly in his big hands for a long time before he could bring himself to open it. When he did, he looked first for the family history inside the front cover, staring down at it while his eyes filled with tears. "You're right," he said in a rough voice. "This was Amelia's. Could she really have been alive all this time?"

"Have you also noticed the words?" Gabe said uncertainly. "The words she wrote in the book?"

Reid held the Bible closer to his face, blinking quickly and then wiping his eyes with the back of his hand. He squinted at the writing for a moment before looking again at Gabe.

"This appears to be her hand," he said. "But who are *you*, then? How did you come to possess this? And how did my daughter die?"

"Why don't you read the words first, so you can understand—"

"First I want some answers, young man. I have plenty of time for reading."

"I'm sorry," Gabe said firmly, "but I think it would be better to read first. After that I will answer any question you ask."

Reid started to argue, surprised by the young stranger's arrogance, but then he saw a self-assured determination in the boy's eyes that surprised him just as much. It wasn't often that the lawyer met his match in a contest of wills, but now his instincts told him he had. It irritated him, but it also pleased him.

"Very well," he snapped. "I can hardly *force* you to honor the request of an old man."

Gabe only smiled and stood up, offering a short bow before he moved away to wander through the crowds of people enjoying a crisp fall day in the gardens. He admired the few varieties of flowers still blooming and took an even greater delight in the happy faces of the children he saw. Every few minutes he glanced toward the white-haired lawyer on the bench, who seemed a little older each time he looked. Finally he saw that Reid had closed the Bible and was hugging it against his chest as he stared up into the sky. Gabe took his time walking back, and even so, he stood in front of the bench for more than a minute before the lawyer seemed to notice him.

"It sounds as if she were almost content," Reid said softly, still looking off into the distance.

"After she got used to it, anyway. I believe she always tried to make the best of things.''

"That was Amelia," the lawyer said, focusing his attention with difficulty. "You would have to be Gabe, of course. Otherwise known as Long Rider."

Gabe nodded.

"I can see it now," said Reid. "The look and bearing of one who has lived outdoors. The gray eyes your mother talks about. *My* eyes." Tears began streaming down the lawyer's cheeks again. He got to his feet and folded Gabe in a rough embrace. "Can it really be true?" he said, stepping back to hold him at arm's length. "After all these years do I really have a grandson?"

Gabe nodded, looking uncomfortable. "A grandson who has come to ask a favor, I'm afraid."

A new gleam of suspicion flared in the old man's eyes, then died away under Gabe's unfaltering gaze. The lawyer tightened his grip on Gabe's arms and said, "Anything I have is yours, son."

"Please listen before you say so. I must tell you how your daughter died."

A fresh look of pain came into the lawyer's eyes. He nodded and sat on the bench again, bowing his head to listen while Gabe told him about the attack on Black Bear's camp along the Tongue. The lawyer broke in to say that he remembered reading about the battle in the newspapers, so Gabe went backward to tell of his fights with Stanley Price at Fort Laramie. Finally he described the deaths of his wife and mother at the hands of the captain while he fumbled helplessly with the children under his arm. The old man flinched visibly when he heard of the saber entering Amelia Conrad's breast, and Gabe felt a heavy weight on his heart.

"I know you must blame me for your daughter's death," he said at the end, "just as I have blamed myself many times in the last year."

"Why?" said Reid, genuinely surprised.

"Because the captain killed her to avenge my victories in our fights. If I had been able to hold my tongue that first time—"

"—then I'm sure my daughter would still be dead," the lawyer said.

"You believe so?"

"It's obvious from your own account, son. You say Price shot Yellow Buckskin Girl before he knew she was your wife?"

Gabe nodded.

"Then there's no reason to think he would have spared my daughter's life."

"Except that she was white."

"Yes, but living as an Indian."

"But who can say for sure—"

"It doesn't matter!" Reid broke in, his voice booming across the gardens. "You've already suffered too much, son. This man Price is the one who killed Amelia, not you."

The lawyer bowed his head and moved his hands over his daughter's Bible. Gabe watched him, forming his next words with care.

"The problem is," said Gabe, "I don't think Price has suffered at all."

"You're probably right," the lawyer said tonelessly. "But I doubt anything can be done about it. The Army takes care of its own."

"I've been told that Price has resigned, sir."

Reid shrugged, still hunched over the Bible and staring at the ground. "Doesn't matter," he said. "Whatever happened out there is beyond any criminal jurisdiction. And there's no hope at all of recovering civil damages."

"Are you talking about things that happen in a white man's courtroom?"

Reid sat up, raising his eyes to meet Gabe's. "Yes," he said slowly. "Aren't you?"

Gabe shook his head. "I think it's something that's just between me and the captain."

The lawyer carefully placed the Bible on the bench beside him and rested his hands on his knees, turning his head sideways to study Gabe's eyes. "Why are you telling me this?"

"Because I don't know where the captain lives now."

"And what would you do if you did know?"

"Is that a question a lawyer should ask?"

"Hell, yes! This lawyer, anyway."

"In that case," said Gabe, meeting the old man's gaze, "I still think it's something that's between me and the man who plunged a saber into my mother's body."

The lawyer reared back, looking at Gabe a moment longer, then stood up and began to pace around the bench. "No," he said after a while, coming to a stop again in front of Gabe. "No, it's between the three of us. This man killed my only daughter, and I'll be damned if I let the bastard get away with it."

There was a ferocity in the old man's pale eyes that would have made Gabe want to shrink away if it had been directed at him. Then he realized he was looking at a kind of mirror, seeing himself in another man of the same blood, and he began to understand the effect that he himself could have on other people.

"I've always believed in the rule of law," Reid was saying, more to himself than to Gabe. "And it sure isn't easy to change a lifetime of habit. But, by God, the law just doesn't cover every situation."

"I'm only asking for a little help in getting information," Gabe suggested.

"Thanks, son. I know what you're trying to say, but I'll take the responsibility for this, just like anything else I do."

"If that's what you really—"

"I think I'll call on the Pinkerton people," said Reid, moving on to the next point. "They can track the captain down if anyone can."

Gabe didn't say anything at first. He was thinking about something his mother and Jim Bridger and even High Backbone had tried to tell him: that there were good whites as well as bad. He held out his hand and felt it engulfed in the firm grip of the old lawyer.

"I am grateful," he said. "Will a month be enough time, do you think? I can meet you here again and we will talk."

"Not so fast," said Reid, still holding his hand. "Where do you think you're going?"

Gabe frowned uncertainly. "I am staying in a hotel, sir. Did you want the name of it?"

"Hell, no! What I want is for you to move out to Cambridge and stay with me."

"That's very kind of you, Mr. Reid, but—"

"What's this 'Mr. Reid' business? I'm your *grandfather,* son. What's the Sioux word for that?"

"My mother's father would be Tunkansi."

"Then call me that, Gabe. Your Tunkansi rattles around all

alone in a big old house out in Cambridge. I'd welcome your company more than you can begin to imagine.''

"But would it be wise?''

"Ah,'' said the lawyer, "you're still trying to protect me, is that it?''

"Something could go wrong someday.''

Reid squeezed Gabe's hand once more before he let go. "I doubt it,'' he said, "not with the feeling I get about you. But I wouldn't much care, anyway.''

"But, sir . . . I mean, Tunkansi—''

"I'm an old man, Gabe. Things like that aren't so frightening if you only have a few years left, anyway.'' The lawyer grinned for the first time. "When you stop to think about it, what could they really do to me? But I'll tell you what does scare an old man, son, and that's being alone. You'd be doing me a great service if you stayed with me while we waited for the Pinkerton report.''

"I just don't think—''

"Forget about all that! Besides, who do you think the Pinkertons will be reporting to, anyway?'' Reid took a deep breath and let it out slowly. "Look, if you don't want to come, just say so. I know I might be a little hard to get along with these days. But the fact is, Gabe, you're the only family I have left.''

Gabe was sitting cross-legged on the grass near his sweat lodge when his grandfather came through the back door of his house, shivering in the cold winds of December. Reid waved a sheaf of papers at Gabe, who stood up and followed the lawyer inside to the warmth of his study. Gabe took off his Thunderbird coat while Reid sat down and spread the papers across his desk, his gray eyes shining with excitement.

"Price is still in Omaha,'' he said immediately, "and it looks as if he'll be there for a while. The Pinkerton men haven't been able to make friends with him the way we'd hoped—they say he hardly ever comes out of his room—but they heard talk that he's trying to get a start in the livestock business.'' Reid glanced down at the reports in front of him. "There's something else you should be aware of, Gabe. It looks as if he thinks you're coming for him.''

"How would he know?'' Gabe demanded.

"Rumors from Fort Laramie, son. It seems that Price still has a friend there, and he's been hearing stories from"—Reid looked at the report again—"do you know what 'Laramie Loafers' are?"

"Tame Indians," Gabe said with a laugh. "The ones who live near the fort and trade with the whites. They also trade with their relatives from the north and pass on anything they hear."

"Well, it works both ways, I guess. The Loafers have been hearing something about the man they call the White Oglala. The word is getting around that he's disappeared from the Powder River country."

Gabe laughed again. "They're right about that much, anyway."

"I bet you didn't know your fame had spread all the way to Omaha. But it isn't all that funny, you know."

"No, it isn't," Gabe agreed. "But it's good to know that Price is nervous."

"It also means he might be ready for you," Reid warned. "The investigators say he's being very careful. He's always got other men around when he goes somewhere. And he's even paying the hotel clerks to let him know about any new arrivals who fit your description."

"Then I won't stay in a hotel in Omaha."

"I wouldn't take this lightly, Gabe."

"I'm not. I'm glad to know these things. Does he still eat in the same place?"

"It's the only thing he does by himself, apparently. He walks downstairs every night around six-thirty and takes his supper at Stockman's Café, right there in the hotel."

"Then one of them will be his last meal," Gabe said grimly.

Reid pushed the papers aside and stared at Gabe across the desk, a sorrowful look in his eyes. "I guess there's no more reason for you to stay here, is there?"

Gabe shook his head.

"Any chance you'll come back and keep an old man company sometime?"

Gabe looked out the window at the limbs of a bare tree against a cold gray sky.

"No," Reid said before he could answer. "Forget I said

anything. I know better than that. I admit I had hopes once. But I've been watching you around this place. It's like seeing a tiger in a cage, always pacing back and forth. You belong out there, don't you?''

"That is where my spirit lies," said Gabe. "But I'll probably roam about. Perhaps I can come and visit again."

"Only if you want to, son. Hell, if I was a younger man, I'd probably pull up stakes and go see what's happening out there myself. That country's about to boom, Gabe, now that the war is over. Young men can make their fortunes."

Gabe nodded absently, hearing the old man's words but also seeing the sadness he couldn't keep out of his eyes. Gabe began to think of Rory Cavanaugh.

Reid picked a small booklet off his desk and held it across to Gabe. "I want you to have this, in any case," he said. "It's a special bank account I've set up in your name."

"But I can't—"

"Nonsense! You're my only living heir, Gabe. It'll just go to you in the end, right? Hell, you might as well get some of it while it can still do you some good. Just write a draft on that account, anytime, in any amount, and whatever you withdraw will automatically be replenished. It'll be like a bottomless well, son, because you've given me the confidence that you'll use it wisely."

Gabe felt he had to accept the gift with grace, according to the habit of his Lakota custom, but there was still a troubled look in his eyes.

"And then there's this," said the lawyer, handing Amelia Conrad's Bible across the desk. "You'll want your mother's memory out there."

"No," Gabe said firmly. "This I cannot do. I can't take the family Bible that belonged to your only daughter."

"But an old man doesn't need things like this," Reid said scoffingly, pressing the book into Gabe's hands. "I've got all the memories of Amelia I need—and you too. All those wonderful stories about Jim Bridger and Red Cloud and Crazy Horse. What more could I ask for?" He let loose with a sudden hearty laugh. "I mean, besides another lifetime, of course. No, Gabe, you take that book and remember your mother well. There haven't been many women like her."

"Perhaps because there haven't been many men like you," said Gabe.

"You don't have to do that," said Rory Cavanaugh, pushing an envelope across the restaurant table. "I wanted you to have that money as a gift."

Gabe pushed the envelope back. "I would have been honored to accept it, but there is no longer any sense in that. Mr. Reid has given me all the money I can use."

Rory's eyes flared with excitement. "Really?"

Gabe nodded. "He's a wealthy man who has no other family."

"I know about that part," Rory said with feeling.

"Yes, you do. You can understand how lonely the old man is."

"All right, Gabe, what are you getting at?"

Gabe laughed and said, "You're too smart for me. All right, I was thinking that a man like Mr. Reid could teach you more than I can. I also believe you would like him, Rory, and he would take great pleasure in treating you as a son."

"In other words, you're backing out. You don't want me with you anymore."

Gabe looked stricken, remembering the years when he believed his mother had abandoned him. In the same instant he felt he had a perfect understanding of her sorrow in those years. "Believe me," he said, "you're wrong about that."

"Sure I am."

"But what I say is true, Rory. A young man cannot choose his adviser only out of friendship. High Backbone was a man of proven vision, a man of many years experience. But I still have much to learn."

"You've done okay as far as I can tell."

"I have only survived, Rory. You said yourself that a lawyer is important among the whites."

"I don't care. I just want to go with you."

"But look at me now! Could you tell I'd never seen a city three months ago? Look at these clothes, Rory. The best there are."

"I admit I didn't hardly recognize you," said the boy. "I thought you was a regular white man when you came to the house."

"And what about this?" said Gabe, carefully lifting the lapel of his coat to reveal a new shoulder holster. "From the finest craftsman in Boston, Rory. It fits so good, I forget I have it on sometimes. And you should feel the way that Remington slides out of there."

Rory pushed aside an empty dinner plate and put his elbows on the table, leaning closer for a better look. "Beautiful!" he said. "What a piece of work. But what's that hangin' off the end? It looks like a knife handle."

"That was my idea," said Gabe, closing his coat again and smoothing it down. "I had the man sew another piece of leather on the back of the holster to make a sheath. The knife holds firm, but it slips out easy."

Rory shook his head in admiration. "Beautiful," he said again. "And it's exactly what I'm talkin' about. If I go live with that lawyer, I won't learn none of this stuff."

"Don't be stupid. He could hire the best instructors—"

"You're the one that's being stupid, Gabe. I mean how to really *use* it. What could I learn about fighting up in Boston?"

"But why would you *want* to, when you could be an important man like Mr. Reid?"

"Who wants to be important?"

"But look at everything I've learned from him. Think of all the things he knows about the ways of the world."

"*His* world, maybe. He don't know nothing about the West, Gabe, and that's where I'm headed. Whether you take me or not."

Gabe sat back with a heavy sigh. "It's not that I don't want to," he said. "It's just that I saw how lonely the old man was, and I thought if you weren't sure about—"

"I'm sure, Gabe. I bought my own revolver, and I been practicing every day. I read everything I could find about the country out there—which ain't a whole hell of a lot—and I been waiting for you to come back like you said you would."

Gabe lifted his hands off the table and let them drop in a gesture of resignation. "I'm sad for the old man," he said, letting himself smile. "But it makes me glad to think of the time when we will ride together."

"How about right now?"

Gabe shook his head.

"You mean, you still won't let me come to Omaha?"

"You've had trouble enough in your own life, Rory. This is something between Price and me. Between one warrior and another."

"Except that he ain't likely to see it that way."

"No?"

"Jesus, Gabe, I hope you ain't forgot the livery barn! What if Price found himself some more help? What if he's setting a trap?"

"That doesn't change what I must do."

Rory shook his head with disgust, but he was grinning. "You're just as stubborn as I am," he said. "It's a pain in the ass. Are you leaving soon?"

Gabe looked regretful. "There's a train at midnight—"

"—and if you leave soon, you can return soon," Rory finished, echoing Gabe's words.

Gabe laughed. "Or I can send a wire, telling you where to meet me."

"Sure," said Rory. "Anything you say. We have time to stop by my aunt's house first. Then I'll walk you to the station."

CHAPTER
TWENTY-THREE

A wet snow was falling when Gabe stepped off the train in Omaha. He wore a brown wool coat and a brown felt derby, with his hair tucked up inside the hat. He looked like most of the other passengers streaming through the station, except that his skin was still the color of bronze. Anyone who looked a little closer might have seen the crooked trigger finger and the puckered white scar on his right hand. But those were things he could not change.

Low-hanging clouds and heavy snow made Omaha gray and bleak in the middle of the afternoon. The new arrivals pulled their coats tight and bowed their heads against a cold wind. Most of the men carried cloth satchels that looked like Gabe's war bag, and no one paid them any attention.

Gabe wandered through the streets with a vaguely bored expression, memorizing everything he saw. He also walked to the edge of the city and studied the open land beyond, thinking of the hard-eyed men he had seen patrolling the streets with stars on their coats. When he was done, he could look at the city in his mind as if he were looking at a map. He went to a livery stable and bought two horses, a big dun and a smaller chestnut. They both looked fast and durable. He also bought an old saddle and a packing tree. Then he retrieved his trunk from the baggage room at the train station.

It was full dark by the time Gabe led his ponies through a

narrow side street toward the Stockman's Hotel. The wind had died but the snow still fell, muffling the sound of his passage. Gabe had discarded the derby, and the wet snow was clinging to the full length of his hair, down past his shoulders. It also covered the red horsehair roach made for him by High Backbone. Gabe had tied the roach behind his ear after smoking the sacred pipe, given to him by Two Face just before the chief was hung at Fort Laramie. Gabe had smoked the pipe out on the prairie, praying to the Winged God known as Wakinyan, and he had felt the power of the spirit come into his body through the smoke.

The empty trunk was still out on the prairie, getting buried in snow. Its contents were packed on the chestnut, except for the long buffalo-hide coat with the yellow Thunderbird on the back. His mother had painted the symbol of the Winged God when the hide was still part of her tepee. Now Gabe carried the coat over his arm, coming out of the side street and crossing toward the golden glow in the windows of the Stockman's Café. He peered through the glass, then tied the horses to a rail outside. He had seen Stanley Price sitting at a back table, his raven hair shining in the lamplight.

A kind of fire had burned in Gabe's belly all afternoon, but it was gone now. The smoke from the pipe had driven it away. The smoke had cleansed him and brought him the power of his helping spirits. The red horsehair behind his ear was a physical reminder of their presence. It represented the Winged God, the patron of desperate courage.

The coat was another reminder. When he put it on, the painted Thunderbird rode high across his shoulders and reminded him of the Winged God that came to protect him in his vision. Gabe went up onto the boardwalk and stepped through the door of the café with no hurry or strain in his movements. No sign of fear. He knew his preparations had pleased the spirits and that nothing could withstand the power of his vision.

There were only five other customers on this snowy night, talking quietly among themselves. Gabe formed impressions of them almost without knowing he had done so, then started weaving his way between the tables. The talk died out. Gabe's hands were empty, but he was still a vision in the buffalo-hide coat that swept to the floor. There was also a grim sense of purpose in the piercing, pale eyes that were fixed on the black-haired man sitting alone against the back wall.

Stanley Price glanced up at Gabe, alerted by the sudden silence, and a look of satisfaction gleamed in his eyes.

Gabe spun on his heel in the middle of the room, his left hand snaking inside the long coat. There was no hesitation this time. He moved like a warrior who had learned from his mistakes. He remembered the coward who was afraid of a boy with a pitchfork and knew there had to be a reason for the captain's lack of fear. Understanding and reaction came in the same instant.

Gabe kept Price in view but turned his back on a man and woman at the table next to him. They hadn't looked like killers. The other three customers were all men, and they all belonged to the captain. The two at the table by the front door were already reaching for pistols tucked in their belts while the third, sitting two feet behind Gabe's elbow, was pulling a sawed-off shotgun out from under a coat on the floor.

The killers had him nicely boxed. But Gabe had known as much when he started to turn, reaching for the cross-draw holster on his hip instead of the shoulder rig under his arm. After endless hours of practice he was quicker with his undamaged left hand.

The killers lost some of their advantage by being too slow. Maybe there had been too much waiting and not enough practice. Maybe the odds made them overconfident. The fastest of the three was just lifting his weapon when Gabe lined up his sights and squeezed the trigger. The Remington spat flame, and the older of the two men near the door staggered back, a geyser of blood spurting from a hole beneath one cold blue eye.

The younger man had pulled his revolver free, but the burly redhead next to Gabe was swinging the shotgun up and over the table. The short, ugly barrels were close enough to chop Gabe to pieces. He knew he could shoot the redhead, but then he wouldn't have enough time to swing the Remington back toward the door.

Gabe's right hand seemed to act by itself while he kept the revolver pointed toward the door. He yanked the knife from the sheath on his shoulder holster and slashed out in the same blinding motion. The blade swept through a glittering arc and sliced through the redhead's neck, about the time the kid by the door leveled his revolver.

Gabe snapped off a round just ahead of him, poorly aimed but good enough to stagger the kid. His shot flew wild. The redhead clutched his throat and started to scream, spewing bloody mist between his fingers. Stanley Price was leaping out of his chair, and the woman at the next table was screaming above the thundering roll of gunfire. It startled Gabe to see Price moving, but still he concentrated on finishing the gun hand near the door. He took careful aim, and the next two balls shredded the kid's heart.

All three killers were still falling when Gabe whirled back toward Price. What he saw made him freeze in place as tables and chinaware crashed behind him around the bodies.

Price had grabbed the screaming woman and lifted her out of the chair. She struggled in panic and terror, and Price had to use both arms to hold her body in front of his. He gripped a Navy Colt in one hand, pressed against the woman's waist, but her companion was getting to his feet.

"What the hell are you doing?" he yelled. "Let her go!"

The man couldn't have been thinking straight. He reached for Price, and the former Army captain simply turned the Colt a little, shooting into the man's body from a few inches away. The woman was face-to-face with him when his eyes bulged with the horror of what had happened.

"My husband!" she cried. She kicked and clawed to reach him, but Price held on to her as desperately as she tried to free herself. She was his only hope of staying alive. Gabe thought the captain might try to kill him from behind his shield, but the woman struggled with such a crazed ferocity that Price couldn't risk trying to hold her with one arm. She might break free and expose him to the same fate as his hired killers. The two men stared at each other, their eyes full of hatred, as Price dragged the woman toward an exit at the rear of the restaurant. He let go only long enough to open the door behind him, giving the woman a hard shove before he disappeared into the dark.

The woman's husband had settled to his knees, holding his belly with both hands. She stumbled toward him, but he toppled onto his face before she could reach him. The woman cried out in anguish and collapsed over his body. Her sobs tore at Gabe's heart, and for the first time he hesitated, plagued by doubt. His thirst for vengeance had resulted in death and heartbreak for the innocent.

Then he thought of the cruelty shining in Price's black eyes as he pulled the trigger, and he knew with even greater certainty that Price had to die. It was the only thing Gabe could offer the woman now. He started toward the back door and stopped just as suddenly, staring at it with a thoughtful frown. There was no reason to believe that the captain's trap had finished springing shut. Gabe knew the door opened onto an alley—he had walked through it that afternoon—but he didn't know what was there now.

Gabe turned and ran through the front entrance of the café, jumping over the two bodies sprawled in front of it. Outside, a rifle exploded and a bullet smacked into the doorjamb, but Gabe was already past, bounding across the boardwalk. He fired a shot to keep the sniper cautious while he was getting to the chestnut packhorse. Then he holstered the Remington and yanked Jim Bridger's old Sharps carbine out of its scabbard, earing back the big side hammer and watching a puff of white smoke that drifted from a doorway across the street. He thought he heard someone running, but the sound was swallowed by another explosion. The chestnut squealed and began to kick, twisting and falling, while the big dun reared its head and tried to pull free.

Above the squeals someone started yelling about the law. About giving up. Gabe glanced off to the right and saw a man coming along the boardwalk, staying in the deeper shadows as he ran. Light from a window glinted on a star pinned to his coat. Then there was a third shot and the deputy was slammed against a storefront window.

Gabe heard shattering glass, but he didn't watch the lawman go down. He was already turning and lifting the Sharps, seeing across the street a faint shine that might have been a rifle barrel. He put his sights on a place in the blackness just beyond the shine and squeezed off. A man stumbled out of the doorway and fell over the edge of the boardwalk. His body twitched in the snow and then lay still.

The packhorse was still thrashing in agony. Gabe put the muzzle of his Remington behind the pony's ear and winced when he pulled the trigger. The squealing and thrashing ended in a shudder, while the echoes of the blast rolled away. Gabe put the now empty revolver back on his hip.

He kept moving fast, pulling his war bag out from under the downed packhorse and leaping onto the nervous dun. His other supplies could be abandoned, but not the sacred pipe or his mother's Bible. The bag also held extra cylinders for the Remingtons, as well as powder and balls for the Sharps, but Gabe decided that the six shots left under his arm would have to be enough for the time being. He wanted to keep away from other deputies and stay close to Price.

He ran the horse to the end of the block without seeing anyone else. Nor did he see anyone in either direction along the side street, even though he'd only been delayed a minute or less. It didn't surprise him to find the snow undisturbed at the mouth of the alley.

Gabe slipped the revolver out of his shoulder rig and walked the pony into the alley. There were no lights at all here, only a soft white reflection from the snow. Crates and barrels stood out as silhouettes against the walls. Then one of the barrels changed shape, and Gabe fired.

There was a double flower of flame in the alley, and a long crack like the close sound of lightning, two shots coming almost together. The other slug hit a brick wall behind Gabe and whined off into the night, the sound mingling with a soft groan from the bushwhacker. He leaned slowly out from behind the barrel and fell on his side just as a shaft of yellow light crossed his body. Gabe jerked around, lifting his revolver and blinking against the glare. A round man in an apron was opening the back door of the café. He threw up his hands when he saw Gabe and started to back away.

"Sorry," he said.

Gabe smiled at that and jumped down off his pony. He was glad to have the light. But his smile turned grim when he glanced into the restaurant and saw the woman still collapsed over her husband's body. She was rocking back and forth and moaning while the man in the apron continued to back away.

Gabe held his gun on the open door and kneeled beside the back steps, trying to ignore the woman's moans. He saw that Price's tracks were blurred on the stairs, as if the captain had slipped in the wet snow on his way out. But Price had slowed down after he crossed the alley and turned to face the door.

Gabe could imagine him standing there with the Colt, waiting
to fire through the door as soon as it started to open. But Price
hadn't faced the door alone. The tracks of five other men
converged on his from different directions, as if the men had
come from hiding places in the alley. They had stamped their
feet and shuffled around and then decided to retreat—or make a
stand somewhere else. One of the five men had been left behind
as a rear guard. His tracks pointed back to the barrel where he
died.

Gabe had learned almost everything he needed. He hurried
on through the alley, looking for any distinctive markings
wherever the prints were clearer. He came to the other end and
peered carefully out into the street. It was empty except for the
swirling snow. Gabe scowled, knowing how hard it would be to
track his prey and watch for an ambush at the same time.

Gabe was pulling himself into the saddle when another set of
tracks caught his eye. They came off the boardwalk at the mouth
of the alley and crossed the ones he was following. He looked up
quickly, but there was still no one else in sight. He scowled
again, wanting to stay as close as possible to Price but also
wanting to understand this mystery and avoid surprises.

He worked quickly, following the new tracks back onto the
boardwalk and into a recessed storefront. Whoever had made
them had stood there for a while but only after first coming out
of the alley. Gabe frowned and kept following, still working
backward, but the tracks didn't lead very far in before they
doubled back—in much larger strides. The stranger apparently
had come running down the street and into the alley, then
stopped and crept back out.

Like a lawman coming to investigate, then finding himself
alone in a situation he didn't understand or like the looks of.

Gabe didn't like it, either. He could only hope the lawman
didn't know what he looked like. He mounted the dun and
followed all six sets of tracks up the street. The day's traffic had
churned the snow, but it was wet and the newest prints had crisp
outlines. Gabe saw the place where Price and his men had
broken into a run, either because they had seen the lawman or
heard the shooting in the alley. Then the tracks turned a couple
of corners, and Gabe pushed the dun into a lope, straining to
hear the sound of drumming hooves.

The tracks were heading straight for the same livery stable

where Gabe had bought his horses that afternoon.

There were small warehouses and work sheds on the outskirts of town, and the stable loomed beyond, with a corral in back and a few bare trees off to one side. All the outlines were obscured by thick-falling snow, but Gabe saw no movement in the corral, no lights in the stable.

That worried him. He didn't think Price and his men had had the time to get their horses and ride away. It was possible that the captain had chosen to finish the fight between them in yet another stable.

Then Gabe realized he didn't have to risk anything to find out. The weeks of city living fell away, and he was thinking like a Lakota again, thinking he could cut for sign. He would simply make a wide circle and look for fresh pony tracks leading away from the building. He veered off on a road between the trees and a long, low-slung brick warehouse on his right. He made good time at first because he could see at a glance that no one had used the road all day. The snow lay in smooth, rolling drifts that—

A gun crashed behind him and he dropped low in the saddle, sliding over on the off side out of habit and instinct. The pony danced and wheeled around, but Gabe hung on with both legs and one hand while he cocked his Remington in the other. He peered under the dun's broad neck, looking for a target, but what he saw didn't make sense.

There was a man behind one of the trees and he was holding a rifle, but Gabe couldn't see any smoke in the air around him. Gabe was still trying to understand why when he noticed that the killer was weaving on his feet, struggling to steady his rifle against the tree. Gabe stayed low against the side of the wheeling pony, looking for a clear shot until he heard the same gun crash a second time. The man behind the tree shivered, and the rifle fell out of his hands.

Gabe sat up again and trained his revolver on a slim, black-haired man who was slowly getting to his feet on the roof of the warehouse, not much higher than Gabe's head. The man was also holding a revolver but it was down at his side, and he was staring at the body sprawled in the snow beside the tree.

"Jesus Christ," said a familiar voice. "Did I really do it?"

Gabe blinked and said, "Rory?"

"Dammit, Gabe, I did. I got him. And you're still alive!"

CHAPTER
TWENTY-FOUR

Gabe cast a nervous glance toward the stable. "Keep your voice down!" he said in a harsh whisper. "Where the hell did you come from?"

"If you're worried about those men, Gabe, they're gone already."

"Gone?"

Rory jumped off the low roof of the warehouse, landing in dreamlike silence in a deep drift. Gabe felt as if his head were spinning. Then the boy came toward him with a proud and happy grin, his teeth shining whiter than the snow.

"Am I glad to see *you*," he said. "Yeah, I think they had the horses ready. They went in and galloped right back out. But I saw which road they took."

"How many?"

"Five," said Rory, nodding toward the tree. "Counting him."

Gabe nodded with satisfaction. Price and four men—now only three—just as Gabe had thought. "How long?"

"Just left, practically. I bet we could catch 'em!"

Gabe held out his arm, and Rory pulled himself up on the back of the dun. He pointed the way over Gabe's shoulder and then held on tight as the big horse broke into a run. The war bag and the Sharps bounced around on the end of their saddle strings.

"Hey," Rory yelled against the wind, "this is how you and me got started!"

"Except that I saved your life the first time. Tonight you saved mine."

The boy's laugh was high and giddy. "That's why I followed you, Gabe. I wasn't sure you took this guy serious enough."

"What about the night I left?" Gabe called back. "When you suggested we go back to your aunt's house."

Rory laughed again. "To get my money and the pistol. I just jumped onto the end of your train and bought my ticket on board."

Gabe shook his head with exasperated admiration. "You followed me all day today? Watched everything I did?"

"You never would've made a move if you knew I was here, right? Then you put on that coat and I figured it was time."

"So you ran around to the back door," said Gabe. "You wanted to cover me, but you saw something when you got into the alley. You went out again and hid in a storefront."

"You got all that from my tracks?"

"Not until right now. I thought you were a policeman."

"Don't I wish," Rory said with a laugh. "I just got into the alley when all the shooting started and someone came out the back door—"

"Price," said Gabe.

"That's what I was afraid of. I figured he was getting away, or maybe you were even dead already. Christ! Then I see movement, and suddenly there's a whole bunch of guys standing out there. I was way outnumbered, so I snuck back like you guessed."

Gabe nodded thoughtfully, feeling better after he realized that the boy was already hiding in the storefront when Price set up the ambush in the alley. Gabe didn't realize that Rory was holding his breath.

"Was I being a coward, Gabe?"

"Coward! How can you—"

"I had to make a choice between lookin' for you and tryin' to keep an eye on Price, and I didn't know if I'd really be that much help in a fight."

"Rory—"

"So I figured you'd want to know where Price was, if . . .

you know, if you made it through.'' It sounded as if the boy had already spoken the words to himself many times. "And if you didn't''—his voice hit a rough spot—"well, then I was gonna take care of Price myself someday."

"No one could have done better, Rory."

"Really?"

"You acted wisely and showed courage. You have the head and heart of a great warrior."

The boy was silent for a moment. Then he said, "There they are!"

Gabe and Rory had covered two or three miles on the open prairie, easing the dun back to an easy lope over the flat road. The snow still fell and covered the great pastures, bathing the air in a luminous blanket of light. But Gabe had eyes only for the vague moving shadow of four riders another half mile in front of them. He lashed the pony to close the distance.

"I wonder why they ran," Rory yelled.

"Good!" said Gabe, thinking of his second meeting with Price. "I only learned to ask such questions after a bitter mistake."

Rory was silent again, as if he feared that his voice would betray his pleasure.

"One of Price's men already killed a deputy," Gabe told him. "Maybe they want to avoid interference as much as I do."

"But what if it's another trap?"

"It probably is," Gabe admitted. "It makes me think of the decoy trick we used on the soldiers, making them chase us into an ambush. Here, take these."

He thrust the reins into Rory's hands and took the Remington from the holster on his hip while the big dun raced along the road. Gabe slipped the empty cylinder out of the revolver and dropped it in his war bag, then reached deep inside for a spare that was already loaded and primed. He was locking the replacement down when he felt the boy stiffen behind him.

"I think they're turning off!" he said.

Gabe and Rory were closer now, and they could see the shadow separate into individual riders, faintly visible through the falling snow. Price and his men were moving toward a larger shadow beside the road. Gabe squinted at it and saw a farm with a house on one side and a small barn on the other. He thought the barn had an odd shape, but he was concentrating on the riders. They merged with the dark outlines of the buildings and didn't reappear.

Gabe took the reins back from Rory and mused aloud, "Why would they go inside? I would much rather stay out and fight in the open." He felt the boy shaking his head against his back, against the painted Wakinyan on his coat. Then he saw muzzle flashes from the barn and halted the dun. The balls fell short and the firing quickly died out. "Seems like just the four of them," Gabe said. "But I don't understand any of this. Why here? Why this barn? Why retreat at all?"

"Maybe it's the captain's own farm," said Rory.

Gabe shrugged, holding the horse in check while he studied the barn with a perplexed frown. He saw that it was surrounded by tiers of baled hay, giving it the odd-shaped outline. "Price did talk about the livestock business," he said. "And this would be as good a place as any to keep all the men who work for him."

In the next moment Gabe's frown had disappeared. "Or the men he commands," he murmured. "They're used to forts, Rory! That's why they holed up like this. Look at those bales. Feed for the stock, maybe, but also protection against attack. What if those men are all soldiers like Captain Price?"

"I hope not!" said Rory. "I'd hate to think I'm goin' up against the U.S. Cavalry."

Gabe frowned at that, wishing the boy hadn't followed him here. It was possible that Price had lied to get the help of his men, and possible that none of them deserved to die. Yet six were already dead, as well as a bystander and a town deputy. And that was only in the space of one hour. Gabe began to think that death surrounded Price, following him wherever he went. He thought of the woman who had lost her husband in the Stockman's Café, and then he was thinking of his wife and his mother again. He saw their deaths as he had a thousand times before. But their suffering was so vivid on this night that he almost cried out in anguish. Then Rory broke into his thoughts.

"But what if it *is* a trap?" said the boy. "Could he be hoping for reinforcements from anywhere?"

"Climb down, Rory. He will not have time if he is."

"But, Gabe—"

"Climb *down*!"

Rory jumped off the horse as if he'd been knocked off by a bolt of lightning. He looked up at Gabe and was afraid to speak.

"It will be your job to watch the road," Gabe commanded. "You will warn me if anyone comes."

"Jesus!" said Rory. "Don't tell me you're goin' up there."

"Rory."

"But *alone*, Gabe? Against them odds?"

"Is this how you obey your teacher, boy?"

"I'm sorry."

"You'll watch the road?"

"Sure. Anything you say."

Gabe remembered Rory using those words in New York, rolling too easily off the tongue. "No matter what else happens," he insisted, "that is what you must do. Failure will bring dishonor."

Rory nodded and Gabe kept going, partly for the boy's sake and partly for his own. He dug in the war bag as he spoke, pulling things out and stuffing them in the pockets of his trousers.

"Tonight the spirits have shown me what must be done," he said solemnly. "There can be no more delay. It is time for Price to die, and the spirits have said it can happen in one way and one way only. If you violate your pledge, Rory Cavanaugh, then surely I will die."

The boy hesitated, giving Gabe a skeptical look. Then he stood a little straighter. "I'll be here," he vowed.

Gabe nodded, then turned his face up into the snow and the black sky. He gathered the reins in his hand and gathered in his heart something else he could not have named. Something like the concentrated power of hatred. He gave the eagle cry and pushed the dun up a shallow wash toward the barn. His long coat flared behind him on the wind, and then there was a burst of fire from inside the barn.

Gabe ignored the bullets that sang through the air around him, his face impassive while he studied the pattern of the muzzle blasts. Then he dropped out of sight on the off side and tried to see the pattern again in his mind. He decided that only a few men had fired before, hoping to lure him closer. But now Gabe thought that the four men he'd followed there had been joined by at least as many who were already at the farm.

Gabe lashed the dun harder and prayed to the spirits, knowing they had heard him when the horse didn't fall in the next flurry of rifle fire. With the third volley Gabe could feel the pony shake under the impact of at least two balls. But the proud animal kept running, and Gabe thanked its spirit for this fine sacrifice.

The big dun faltered with the fourth round from the rifles and fell on the fifth, throwing Gabe into the snow a hundred feet short of the barn. He jumped up, pulling both his Remingtons, screaming a war cry as he zigzagged into the withering wall of fire. He emptied his revolvers at any muzzle blasts he could see or remember while bullets ripped into the snow around him or tugged at the long coat. But Gabe trusted his shooting, knowing it would keep the men in the barn off-balance. He also believed he could feel the yellow Thunderbird across his shoulders. It seemed to burn against his skin, assuring him that it protected him.

The captain's voice came from inside the barn: "God damn you all to hell," he was shouting, "can't you kill one man!"

But Gabe had already crouched against the nearest corner of the building and started wrestling some of the snow-covered bales off the top of the stack against the walls, exposing dry bales underneath. With a grim look he produced a lucifer from his pocket, scratched it alive, and touched it to as many of the bales as he could reach. The cured grass flared up and Gabe crawled on, hugging his body tight to the stack. He was turning the tables on Price's men, always keeping at least a couple bales between himself and the barn. They absorbed the balls when the men tried shooting at him through the thin wooden walls.

Occasionally one of them caught sight of Gabe from the loft. He usually saw the rifle in time, poking out of a window or a chink hole, but carelessness cost him a burning graze on the side of his neck and a bullet hole through the fleshy part of his thigh.

Then someone saw a spurt of fire and the shooting gave way to a confused excitement of voices in the barn. Gabe listened to them with a bitter smile on his lips, losing some of their words in the crackling of the flames.

"We'll roast in here!" they were saying. "He wants to burn us alive!"

"No, I don't," Gabe called out, speaking for the first time. "My only quarrel is with Stanley Price. Anyone else who—"

"Don't listen!" Price yelled.

"Anyone who comes out the door will go free."

"He's lying! Get out there and kill him, or we'll all die."

"You don't have to," shouted Gabe. "The captain does. He killed my mother and my wife, and now it's his turn to—"

"No!" Price yelled back. "Don't listen. He's crazy. Get out there and kill the bastard."

The fire was getting hotter, sucking in more air and drying out the snow-covered bales on top. Then the flames began to lick up the walls and to the roof. Smoke began pouring out of the loft windows. Gabe relaxed a little, moving around toward the big swinging door on the front of the barn. He stood there and calmly punched the spent cylinders out of his Remingtons, replacing them with his last two spares.

"The fire is already on the walls and roof," he called out. "Pretty soon everything will be burning and there won't be any escape."

"If you go out," Price yelled to his men, "you damn well better go out shooting."

"That way lies death," Gabe warned. "Do you want to defend a man who escaped me by using a woman as a shield?"

"He's lying!" Price screamed. "Get out there."

"Come out in peace and you will be allowed to go in peace," called Gabe. "Six of your brothers have died already. That is enough."

For a while Gabe didn't hear anything except the roar of the fire at the height of its fury. He started to worry that his idea would fail. Then the big door swung open, and Gabe stepped to the side as seven men ran past him, bent low and racked by coughing. Their hands were empty. But then a revolver started crashing inside the barn, and the men scattered, two of them stumbling. Gabe poked one of his Remingtons into the doorway and fired all six shots into the wall of flame inside the barn, but that didn't keep the captain from trying to shoot his own men in the back.

"Deserters!" he screamed after them. "Every one of you will hang!" He kept shooting even when the men were far down by the road, near Rory, and still running hard—except for the two who had collapsed in the snow, their still bodies looking like stones in the field.

Then the shooting stopped, and Gabe looked carefully into the barn, recoiling for a moment from the heat and noise of the fire engulfing all the stored hay and the dry wood that made the walls and roof. He moved to the middle of the doorway and stared into the inferno, a revolver dangling at his side.

"Come and face me!" he shouted into the fire. "Or are you afraid because there is no woman to shield you?"

The flames roared and cracked through the barn. Beams began to crumble and fall from overhead.

"It is just as well," Gabe said tauntingly. "You will die a coward, just as you lived."

Gabe waited, watching the flames, and then he was sure that Price was dead. He was starting to turn away when he heard a scream that raised the hairs on his neck.

The figure of a man came running through the flames, a smaller body of fire that detached itself from the larger body. The burning figure charged Gabe with a pitchfork held like a lance, aimed for Gabe's belly. He stood transfixed for a moment by the vision of charring flesh that ran from the barn, letting Price come within five or six feet before he brought his revolver up.

But Gabe felt no mercy, even now. He dropped the revolver back to his side and stepped out of the way.

The burning figure tried to change direction but stumbled and fell and started to writhe in the snow. "Shoot me!" it pleaded. "Oh God, shoot me!"

Gabe heard the screams from very far away. He wondered vaguely how the words were being formed, since he no longer saw anything he could call a mouth. Or a face. Gabe stood and watched the captain burn, melting through the snow. Then he gathered two of the horses that had been left outside the barn, for the long ride he and Rory still faced that night.

Price stopped screaming when Gabe was halfway back to the road, when he could no longer smell the burning flesh and hair. There was only the cold, clean air, fresh against his face, and the endless stretch of pure snow that crunched solidly beneath his boots.

WHAT CAME AFTER

Omaha lawmen never had a satisfactory explanation for the slaughter that began in the Stockman's Café. All they ever heard about was a long-haired wild man in some kind of rawhide coat with a yellow symbol on it. But this so-called wild man seemed to have come out of nowhere—with no known motive—and then disappeared into thin air, taking with him a slim youth sporting coal-black hair and the devil's own green eyes. Only when the legend of Long Rider began to work its way back to the city in later years did the surviving witnesses insist that they had, in fact, seen the very incarnation of the legend.

The following year, 1867, was a troublesome one for emigrants on the Bozeman Road, with rumors persisting that the Lakota and Cheyenne were aided in their strategy by a reclusive light-haired Oglala. Whatever the truth of those rumors, Red Cloud adamantly refused even to discuss a treaty until the whites had abandoned their forts along the Bozeman Road.

The U.S. government capitulated completely the following year, closing the forts in the summer of 1868. Indians burned the stockades, and then Red Cloud finally came into Fort Laramie in November, touching the pen to a treaty that promised the Black Hills to the Lakota.

Crazy Horse did not join him, believing that white men could not be trusted. And when he was bayoneted by an Army corporal just nine years later, the Black Hills had already been taken from the Lakota.